Superdeaths

Superdeaths

A Novel by
Barry Blair

Right Field Press
Jonesborough, Tennessee
www.rightfieldpress.com

ISBN: 978-0-692-73773-6

Also by the Author
UNWOUND
ALL FOR A SONG

*To the memory of
my brother, Chuck
1946-2016*

CHAPTER 1

PASADENA, CALIFORNIA

There is probably not a more beautiful setting anywhere in America for a football game than the Rose Bowl, located in Pasadena, just a short drive northeast of downtown Los Angeles. Fans are able to sit in shirtsleeves in eighty degree weather, while off in the distance they have a commanding view of the snowcapped San Gabriel Mountains. It is a true bowl, with no upper decks. The grass seems greener, the sky seems bluer, more so than any other place on earth.

On Sunday, January 20, 1985, over one hundred thousand fans jammed the historic stadium to witness what was becoming the grandest of all the American sports spectacles, the Super Bowl. The game, having not yet reached the point where it will be switched into the prime time slot on Sunday night television, was set to kick off at 1:00 p.m. pacific time. The combatants were to be the New York Jets and the Washington Redskins. The Jets had stormed through the American Football Conference with only one loss and were listed as a heavy thirteen and one half point favorite out of Las Vegas by the people who do such things. Most of the money bet on the game had been going their way. Washington had made it to the big game on four straight one point victories. They didn't even qualify for the playoffs until the last week of the season when they beat their archrival, the Dallas Cowboys, who had faltered down the stretch and lost their last four games, to let the Redskins in. For those reasons, New York entered the Super Bowl as a prohibitive favorite.

As the Jets gathered to meet early on Super Bowl Sunday at 7:00 a.m. for a team breakfast, they were greeted by the stunning news that their starting quarterback, Tommy Prince, had just been taken by the team's medical staff to a Pasadena hospital to be treated for injuries he had sustained sometime in the early morning. At that point, no one knew for sure what had happened. So the main rumor, passed on by their longtime equipment manager and floating all around the room amongst the players, was that he had slipped and fallen down a flight of stairs at the hotel. They said it happened as he came down earlier that morning, around 5:00 a.m., unable to sleep, for a quick run that he hoped would take the edge off and calm him down. Supposedly, he was using the stairwell to avoid any distractions and the team's security personnel who were staked out all night in the lobby. He then somehow made his way to the room of the team doctor and awoke him. Tommy's face was badly bruised, cut, and bloodied, and he complained of soreness in his side. The most damaging thing, the doctor quickly deducted, was that he had what appeared to possibly be a broken right wrist, the hand he threw with. The doctor was also suspicious of his story as the blood on his face was somewhat dried and not fresh, and he smelled alcohol on Tommy's breath.

By the time the Jets finished breakfast and gathered for their 8:00 a.m. team meeting, the word came from the hospital that Prince had indeed broken two ribs and the wrist on his throwing hand, which was now being put in a cast. The coach addressed the team on his situation. "He will not be playing," he said.

"No way," their star defensive tackle, Hunter LeBeau, all amped up on steroids, said loudly to those sitting around him. "I ain't buying this story." He got up, pushing his way across the room to Tommy's roommate, safety Donn Moore. He grabbed him by the front of his shirt and pulled him out of his chair, a rage fueled by the juice he had been taking for years. "You know what happened," he said, then slammed him back down. "Tell us."

"I slept like a baby," Moore said defiantly, then rose back out of his chair and went for the man who easily outweighed him by over a hundred pounds. Their teammates and coaches stepped in and separated them, and things quickly calmed back down. But there was definitely an air of apprehension in the room. For a lot of these guys, they knew it would probably be their only chance to win a Super Bowl ring as the average career in the NFL lasts less than three years. And for whatever the reason, now they were going into the biggest game of their lives without their star quarterback. There was no reason to have a lot of faith in his backup, for he was a rookie who had taken eight snaps from center all season long.

The Jets coaches adjourned the team meeting for half an hour as they scrambled to redo their game plan for a young and inexperienced quarterback. At best, they wanted to keep him out of situations where he could make a crucial mistake and hopefully let their defense win the game. By the time the team buses left the hotel at 10:00 a.m. for the short trip to the stadium, the word was out on the fledging all-sports cable channel ESPN that Tommy Prince was lost for the game. It was news that was not well-received in Las Vegas. Most of the betting had been on the Jets, with their giving points to the Redskins. That outcome was considered by most to now be in serious jeopardy. Millions of dollars could very well be lost the other way.

The team would come out to warm up before the game with their rookie quarterback, who would be backed up now by one of their defensive backs, who had not played under center since college. It was, as an assistant coach told the CBS sideline reporter off the record, "a disaster waiting to happen."

But the Jets, playing conservatively, opened a 10-0 halftime lead. An interception and lengthy return by safety Johnny Rockett led to another touchdown and a 17-0 lead early in the third quarter. Then the Redskins mounted a comeback that started with a pronounced eighty-four yard touchdown drive at the end of the quarter. Another drive, with a little over four minutes to go in the game, stalled out near the goal line and brought them a field goal to cut the lead to 17-10. On the ensuing kickoff, Donn Moore took the ball at his goal line and went one hundred yards untouched for a touchdown. He crossed the goal line, looking back over his shoulder. His blockers had knocked down any Redskins that came near him. In the end zone, his teammates jumped and pounded on him while he stood there, seemingly stunned, and barely made a move. After a few moments, he politely handed the ball to an official and made his way back up the sideline. The Jets made the extra point and the score was now 24-10. The Redskins fumbled the kickoff at their own thirty-five yard line; the Jets recovered, the ball bouncing right into Moore's hands, and they ran out the clock.

Donn Moore would accept the game's Most Valuable Player Award, though he appeared stunned and apologetic in doing so. He had the look of a man who would rather be somewhere else.

The final margin of victory in Super Bowl XIX was fourteen points, which covered the thirteen and one half point spread. The night before in Las Vegas, New York, Chicago, Pittsburgh, and Detroit, an unusually large amount of money had started coming in at the last minute and had been bet on the Redskins. So much so that it got the attention of the Federal Bureau of Investigation and their people who watch these things. The people who made those bets had now lost, and they had lost a lot of money. They were not the kind of people who ever lost at anything.

On this beautiful sunbaked day in Southern California, most Americans had watched a Super Bowl that seemed no different than others that came before and those that would come after. But it was different, very different, and its outcome would affect the lives of people that were involved in many ways for years to come. It was a storm off on the far horizon.

CHAPTER 2

NORTHEAST TENNESSEE CORRECTIONAL INSTITUTE
MOUNTAIN CITY — 28 YEARS LATER

It wasn't the slight push in the back that bothered him as much as it was just a built up over time feeling of never being in control of his own life. The guard nudged him down the hallway with a hand in his back. It ate away and ate away at him until he felt he was ready to snap. God knows he wanted to snap. But he wouldn't, not now, as he knew that was a battle that could not be won. He was Tennessee inmate 9-07631. Robert Wayne Foster. Bobby Wayne, to his family and friends. He had been at Northeast now going on nine years, and there were ten years spent at the infamous Brushy Mountain before being sent here. The state sent him up twenty years for second degree homicide, and now he was down to a year to go. A suspect bar fight over a woman in his hometown of Newport led to the killing. People that were supposed to protect him and get him out of the situation backed away. They saw that he was caught, tried, and convicted as a payback. He was doing the whole time, nothing on his sentence had been cut short. Two fights that had left the other inmates in critical condition, one at Brushy and one here, had seen to that. He didn't start the fights, but he sure finished them. The one that had him sent up didn't plan to see him get out. Up to this point, he had managed to survive the attempts on his life.

The guard nudged him again in the back as they went through the door of the prison library. His shoulders stiffened. It was in a small way his response back. Some of them liked to let you know they were in control, and this guy taking him was one of them, young to the job and cocky. Bobby Wayne liked to think that once he was out of here, he would run into one of these guys, maybe in a bar one night when they had both had a few beers, and the payback would be sweet. But then again, he planned to never see anyone associated with this place ever again.

He checked in at the desk with Pops Luttrell, a lifer, now near eighty, who ran the library.

 The story on him was he had shot and killed the owner of a small convenience store back in the 1970s in a failed robbery attempt outside of Chattanooga. The guy drew down on him as he went out the door and so Pops shot him. "I had no idea he had a gun…he was an old man, some foreigner, for God's sake. Came running out of his office, waving the gun around, hollering in a language I didn't understand, then stopped and pointed it at me. So I shot him, or he would've shot me I guess. I wasn't takin' the chance…" He shook his head, remembering that fateful day. "The price I paid for the line of work I was in," he told Bobby Wayne one slow day in the library as they discussed what had gotten them both on the inside. Pops had spent more than sixty years of his life incarcerated for one thing or another. More than once he had commented that he hoped they never let him out as he had no place to go at this late stage of his life. "If they do, I'll just start robbing all over again until they catch me or kill me, whichever comes first. Next time I'm gonna rob a bank, get some federal time, try that out for a change."

Bobby Wayne could only imagine an almost eighty-year-old man trying to rob a bank. What he couldn't imagine was getting to a point where you ever wanted to stay in this place for the rest of your life. "Let's hope it never comes to that. You don't need to be robbin' no banks at your age," he answered him.

The old man just sadly looked back at him. "I figure to die in here, let them take me into Mountain City, cremate me, then bring me back and dump my ashes out back," he said another day as they worked over a stack of books. "Might as well…prison has been home to me most of my life." This Tennessee state prison was located just outside the small, remote town of Mountain City, near both the Virginia and North Carolina state lines.

There was a cart full of books and magazines that Pops had ready to go for Bobby Wayne to put back on the shelves. He always had one waiting for him whenever he came to work. As Bobby Wayne took it and rolled it around, doing his duty, another inmate came by and handed him a book. It was a guy he had seen around, but he didn't really know him or anything about him.

"You mind putting this up for me?" he asked. "I found it lying out on a table. I've tried to read some of it, but it's not my thing and I'm not sure where it goes. I'd appreciate it." Bobby Wayne took it, a copy of Truman Capote's classic, *In Cold Blood,* put it on his cart, and figured what the hell. At least it was giving him something to do. The inmate went and waited in the outer room for a guard to take him back to his cell. Bobby Wayne went about his business, putting things back where they belonged. The library was quiet, more so than usual, especially for a place that is supposed to be. It wasn't a big place. No windows except around the top, next to the ceiling some twenty feet up, that made it seem even smaller than it was. There was an area with about ten metal tables, each with eight metal chairs. After that came the shelves of books that went about twenty deep. The first few rows were law books, then everything else came behind them. Usually there were several inmates going over the law books, most of them looking and hoping for a way out, others for a way to sue for change. There were some that, for a pack of smokes, offered their services as jail house lawyers. He took the book the inmate had handed him and saw that it went near the end on the back row. He worked his way back there and another inmate stood at the end of the aisle, looking over a book. Bobby Wayne observed him as he rolled down that way, making him to be unusually nervous with his sweaty shaved head that seemed to glisten from the overhanging lights. He had tattoos on his neck and all over his arms that appeared to have been expensively done, a more and more common sight in here. Most of the younger guys now entering the system seemed to have them, lots of them. It was an obvious culture change that had taken place while he had been locked up. The con was right in front of where the book was to go, holding the book he appeared to be reading right at his chest. He figured this guy to be no more than twenty, maybe twenty-one years old at best.

"Would you excuse me while I put this book up?" Bobby Wayne said, more telling than asking. The young man didn't move. Bobby Wayne was ever on alert, knowing that he couldn't see the young man's right hand as it was under the book. As Bobby Wayne started to reach the book out to where it would go, the man came out with a shiv from under the book and thrust it towards his neck. But from training he had received many years ago, Bobby Wayne knocked the homemade knife from his hand, kicked it away with his foot, spun the young man around, and with lightning-like force, swiftly dislocated the inmate's shoulder out of its socket as he took him to the ground. With pressure exerted from his foot onto the forearm, pulling it back, then twisting it with his hand, he smashed the young man's body down hard against the floor. "Who sent you to do this?" he asked, almost in a whisper. He continued to twist the arm as he spoke.

"I...I...don't know...m...m...mister. Oh...my...God..."

"God can't help you when it comes to dealing with me, boy. Now you tell me who sent you or I'm gonna break your arm in two." He pushed down more with his foot.

"I don't know," he gasped. "Really...oh, Lord...I...don't know." His head glistened even more with sweat. He felt nauseous and started to gag, then felt like he might pass out. He wished he could.

"If you think you need to be scared of someone in here, it better be me," Bobby Wayne said softly as he pushed down even harder on the arm, all the while continuing to twist it with his hand. He knew how hard to push and when to stop. Another inmate stepped around the corner. Bobby Wayne glared at him with a look that said to mind his own business, and he stepped away and was gone.

"I...I...oh...Lord, I...don't...know. PLEASE STOP! I can't bear it..." the boy said.

"I don't care whether you can stand it or not. You expect me to believe you just came in here and tried to shiv me for no reason?" Bobby Wayne pushed down again with the foot and pulled up and twisted the hand even more. "I can make you hurt in ways you never dreamed of, boy." The foot went down harder on the arm. With the other hand he pressed down on his fingers, creating even more pain.

It was unbearable. The shoulder dislocated, and now he was pulling it out from the body as he twisted the arm and exerted even more pressure with his foot. "Somebody else sent you to do their dirty work. What kind of fool are you?" Then he let off the tension in the arm. "I've never seen you before. How long you been in here?"

It took the boy a moment to spit out a response. "A…a…ah…week. Please…don't hurt me any more…oh, please." He was relieved that Bobby Wayne had eased off on his arm and shoulder, then on his fingers, as the pain was more than he thought he could possibly stand.

But after a momentary pause, Bobby Wayne started pulling and twisting the arm while once again putting pressure on it with his foot. "You tried to kill me, boy…"

The boy screamed, then seemed to sense that giving the correct response was the only way out of this. "He said it came from outside… that's all…I…I…know." His body rocked back and forth on the floor. "The guy who gave…you…the book…he is going to pay me if I killed you." Looking into Bobby Wayne's face, he felt for a moment that what he saw was the face of the devil himself. Never in his young life, and it had been a rough one, had he seen a look like he was now staring up into. In a way it was like he was confessing his sins. "He…he…also said he would… see that I got protection from the predators in here, man…I'm new…here. I didn't know…what to do…they've been coming for me every night…"

"How much?"

The boy gagged.

"How much?"

"I don't know, man…What…do you mean…how much?" He rocked on the floor.

"How much money is he offering to pay you?" Bobby Wayne twisted harder on the arm.

"Hundred…a…hundred dollars. Go after…him, man…not me…oh my God."

"You ain't quite got the grasp on how things work around here, boy."

"I got nothing against you…I did it for the money…and for them to leave me alone…honest."

"You want to take a man's life for a hundred dollar bill? You ain't got nothing against me? You just gonna kill me?"

"Yeah…yeah…I guess so." His body quivered and shook, sweat poured off his head.

"You'll never get out of this place alive, son."

He soiled his pants.

"You've told me all I need to know, but next time you might want to get your money up front. These guys won't pay you and they won't leave you alone either." He pushed down hard on the forearm until he heard the sickening sound of a bone breaking.

"You mention my name about what happened here and I'll be back for you." Bobby Wayne let go of the arm and it fell limply to the floor. The young man laid there, his arm now pointing out in the wrong direction, and sobbed uncontrollably, his body seeming to be bouncing off the floor with each gasp. Then, he seemed to lose consciousness. Bobby Wayne stepped over him and pushed his cart back to the front of the library. He leaned on the counter and looked at the old man. "Pop, you might want to call a guard, there's a guy passed out on the last row down there. Must have slipped or something."

CHAPTER 3

JONESBOROUGH, TENNESSEE

The Jonesboro Country Club was located three miles outside of town, going south, on State Route 81. Stay straight on it and the road winds its way to Erwin, along the river and into the mountains. If you go across the Nolichucky River Bridge, turn right on what the locals call "the 107 cutoff," you wind through the valley with the river to your right and the mountains to your left and eventually wind up in Greeneville. It is beautiful country, either way you go.

Jake Bender had retired from the Nashville Police Department after thirty years of service and returned to his hometown. His mother, living alone in Jonesborough, had died exactly two months to the day before his retirement ceremony. Heart attack, her doctor believed. Jake let them put her into the ground without an autopsy. The thought of it was more than he could bear, he saw no purpose in it, and politely told the doctor no. He had seen too many of them as a homicide detective, the bodies on a metal slab all stitched back together, while he listened to the doctor drone on about the cause of death. It served no purpose with her in his mind, she was gone, no matter what the reason. She was eighty-nine when she went and had lived a good, long life.

After tying up the loose ends in Nashville, he moved back home to the family farm, which she had left him. For the next year, with the help of some old friends and neighbors, he had built six golf holes on what had once been prime tobacco land, or at least it was until the government took the subsidies away, destroying a way of life for many small farmers. Where the golden leaves had once grown, now there were two par threes, three par fours, and a par five that incorporated the large pond his late father had once used for irrigating his crops. It made for a tricky second shot if you didn't layup and try to go for the green in two. The front half of the green sloped back towards the water and if you didn't carry the shot far enough back, there was a pretty good chance the ball would start slowly rolling backwards, gaining momentum, until it went into the pond. The watery grave, stretching all across the front of the green, gave Jake a good source for used golf balls to sell in the golf shop. The locals gripped about buying back their own balls.

The shop was actually an old, well-constructed barn that he had converted to serve his purpose. It contained a counter where the golf course transactions took place. Three old round wooden tables in the middle of the floor served as both a place to eat and a home for card games that usually broke out in the late afternoon. Two large seventy-inch VIZIO televisions hung side by side on the back wall with a large old leather couch, bought at a garage sale in one of nearby Johnson City's better neighborhoods, in front of them. One TV was usually tuned to ESPN and the other to Fox News. On weekends they stayed strictly on the most important sports events of that day. *Golf, Golf Digest,* and *Sports Illustrated* magazines laid all around. A small grill and kitchen was built in the back right hand corner. Hamburgers, hot dogs, grilled cheeses, and fried bologna were the choices. An old Pabst Blue Ribbon "COLD BEER" sign hung on the wall right beside a painting you could find at most any flea market in the South of all the Republican presidents from Teddy Roosevelt to Eisenhower, Ford, Reagan, and both Bushes taking part in a spirited card game. Tennessee's and East Tennessee State's football and basketball schedules hung on the wall, and each time they played, someone religiously marked beside the game who had won or lost with a

W or an L and the score out beside it. It would remain there until the next season came around and it was replaced with a new one. Jake's dog Butch came and went as he pleased whenever someone would open the screen door. There probably isn't a small golf course anywhere in the South that doesn't have a dog hanging around, and this one was no exception. A door in the back left hand corner led to Jake's office where he ran the affairs of the golf course and also his private investigation business. Out the back was another old tobacco field that had been converted into a driving range. Three dollars for a small bucket and five for a large one. Give him ten bucks and you can hit balls all day long if you wish. The barn had been painted a bright red and the title, JONESBORO COUNTRY CLUB, was painted above the door in white letters with a blue outline. A few years back, the town, which had gone by Jonesboro for years, decided to change the spelling to Jonesborough, which some said was the original way. Jake went with the shorter version since the idea that this was really a country club was tongue in cheek to begin with. An American flag, supplied by the local VFW, hung on a pole beside the door. Every year they would come and have a ceremony, taking down the old flag and replacing it with a new one. The current flag came from the local congressman who saw that it had first been flown over the Capitol. For that, he showed up once a year to play golf for free. He offered to pay, but Jake always waved him off. The congressman normally played at the Blackthorn Club, a 'real' country club located out on the other side of Jonesborough. It was the one surrounded by large homes, several of which were said to be valued at well over one million dollars. Across the road from Jake's golf club were two mobile homes. One of them had a deck with a hot tub. Both had satellite dishes.

A smaller sign, painted on a block of wood to the right of the golf shop's front door, read:

BENDER PRIVATE INVESTIGATIONS

423-753-1212

Back inside, behind the counter was a sign for a ten dollar green fee for the first six holes, twenty dollars to play all day. A monthly membership was one hundred dollars, allowing you to play as many times as you wanted. At the bottom in bold letters the sign said:

NO CARTS ALLOWED – WE PLAY GOLF THE WAY IT WAS INTENDED TO BE PLAYED – WE WALK!

The course was short but somewhat tough. Hit the ball in the rough and you would be lucky to find it. Each hole had three sets of tees, allowing you to play 'eighteen holes' if you liked. On this morning, things were slow, and Jake sat on the couch reading the paper and occasionally looking up to watch the TV if he heard something that caught his interest. In a moment, the screen door slammed and in walked Virgil Smith. He and Jake had been friends since the first grade. They had played ball together at Jonesboro High School; football, basketball, and baseball, all flowing from one season to the other. While Virgil went to ETSU to play football, Jake was off to the Marines and Vietnam. Virgil owned a construction company, a lot of rental property, and a used car lot, most of which was in the Jonesborough area. There was some real estate in Sarasota, Florida he was also involved with. Condos, he told Jake. He had been a big help to Jake in getting the golf course built and hung around there from time to time. Every couple of weeks they would make the trek to The Cottage in Johnson City for a lunch of burgers and beers. When Jake started school at ETSU after getting out of the Marines, Virgil saw to it that he joined the Sigma Chi Fraternity, just as he had done.

"Jake, I need to see you in your office."

"We can just talk here, Virgil, there's nobody else around."

"Let's go to the office, I want to talk in private." He looked around when he said that. "Hell, somebody might walk in on us. This is serious business I'm needing to talk with you about." He looked around again as if he thought someone was going to pop out at any moment. "Investigative business I'm wanting to talk about."

Jake, up from the couch, shrugged and pointed to the office door. Virgil went in. Jake followed, sat at his desk and propped his feet up on it. He motioned to Virgil, pacing back and forth, to sit down. Virgil shut the office door, then came down hard in the chair.

"So what's up?" Jake asked.

"It's Betty. She's cheatin' on me, I know it."

"Let's see…Betty, she's wife number four, ain't that right?"

"She's the fifth one, actually. One of 'em I married twice. But what's that got to do with anything?"

"Nothing, I'm just building up a little background here." He scribbled something out on a legal pad. "I was gone for a long time, and I kind of lost count on the number of wives you've had." Jake picked up a hand exerciser and started squeezing it as they talked.

"Well, she's number five and I'm pretty sure she's cheatin' around."

"How's that?" Jake said, squeezing away and glancing over his bifocals.

"She sells real estate, you know. I seen her going into the Carnegie Hotel in Johnson City and right after that, this banker fellow she says she works with, I seen him there, too."

"And what were you doing at the Carnegie?"

"I was followin' her. I've had my suspicions. She meets him there every Wednesday afternoon at one, soon as he gets out of the Kiwanis Club meeting." He paused for a moment then asked, "So what can we do to catch her?"

"Does the whole Kiwanis Club know?"

"Come on, Jake, I'm bein' serious here."

"You sure that something is going on?"

"Four weeks in a row that I know of."

"You been following her that long?"

"Sure."

"Why?"

"Well, the first week I wasn't following her, I just kind of stumbled upon them."

"Can I ask again what you were doing at the Carnegie?"

"I'd just as soon you didn't."

"Anybody I know?"

Virgil sat there for a moment, nervously tapping his feet on the floor. "All right, if you must know, I was meeting Barbara Jean there."

"As in Barbara Jean, your second wife?"

"She was actually my third."

"The third. Sorry for my miscalculation."

"What's that got to do with what she's doing? Damn it, Jake, are you going to help me or not? This thing is driving me crazy. I can't eat, I can't sleep…"

"You got a prenup with Betty, I presume?"

"Not exactly."

"Not exactly? What does that mean?"

Virgil fidgeted in the chair. "We talked about it, but it would get her upset, so I just dropped it."

"And now you want me to catch her in the act, which I presume is going to lead you into divorce court?"

"I can't live with no woman that's cheatin' on me."

"You're cheating on her."

"That's different."

"I can see how, with your line of rational thinking, you have been married five times."

"I have a hard time telling pretty women no."

"Obviously."

"Jake, you gonna help me or not?"

Jake looked at him long and hard. "Virgil, there are two ways we can do this. Neither is very pretty. The first way, we let them check into the room at the Carnegie. Give them, say, fifteen minutes, and then we enter the room, catch them in the act, you and me, take pictures of what is transpiring, and we confront her. You will have caught her in the act red-handed." He paused for a moment. "This way can also lead to an altercation if you let it get out of control, you being in the room with him and her. As soon as we get the pictures, I push you out of the room and we leave."

"How do we get in the room?"

"I'll take care of that."

"You mean someone can come in the room on you?" He pondered on that for a moment. "And the other?"

"I find out which room it is they are using and I go in beforehand, place a camera in there that is motion-activated, and we get pictures of them in the act. This keeps you out of the equation of being present."

"Is all this legal?"

"Whether it is legal or not should be of no interest to you. If you want to catch them and have proof, this is what we will have to do. I'm gonna take a wild guess that the guy, since they are meeting in a hotel, is married?"

"Married with two small kids."

"You can bet he won't be a problem then."

Virgil sat there for a minute then said, "Jake, this is a dirty business you are in."

"Virgil, there is nothing pretty about it. Unfortunately somebody has to do it." He looked over the top of his glasses at him and shook his head as he said it, considering the source.

"Let's just do the pictures, Jake. You know, maybe when I show them to her she will quit and we can get back to our life, the way it was before."

"Yeah, well maybe you better let the Barbara Jean thing go, if that's what you truly want."

"Am I paying you to be a marriage counselor, too?"

"No, just a little friendly advice. Take it or leave it."

Virgil stood up to go. "Jake, one more thing, what do you charge for this service?"

"Normal fee is two grand if we catch her. One grand if we don't."

"Women, they cost me money no matter what I do." He shook his head. "You want the money up front?"

"I'll send you a bill as soon as you send me one for the work you did on the golf course."

"Jake, you're the best." He got up to leave.

"Hey, Virgil, one more thing before you go. I heard on the radio this morning that Bobby Wayne had disappeared at the state prison."

"Bobby Wayne." He paused. "I hadn't heard his name in a long time." He stopped for a moment as if mulling this over. "Disappeared?"

"That's what they are reporting."

"They didn't say how, did they?" Virgil asked.

"No, guy on the news said he was gone. Warden told them that as best they could tell he just disappeared. They reckon he escaped somehow. Only had a year to go. It don't make sense to me."

He looked at Jake, then paused for a moment before saying, "It don't, does it?"

Jake pondered, his thoughts going way back in time. "Nothing that boy done ever made much sense." With that said, Jake looked up and Virgil was heading out.

In a moment, Virgil stuck his head back in the door. "There's some old stubby-looking guy out in the parking lot smoking cigarettes and asking for you. Don't look like no golfer to me."

Jake got up and moved to the door and sure enough, there in the parking lot stood his old Nashville homicide partner, Ralph Bowers. He was leaning back against his car, a restored '68 Buick convertible. White paint job, white wall tires. At 5'10" and pushing over two hundred pounds, he filled out the Bermuda shorts and white t-shirt he wore. On his crew cut head were a pair of aviator sunglasses and a Nashville Sounds baseball cap. In one hand was a sixteen-ounce can of PBR, and in the other, a Marlboro.

"Looks like you're living the good life," Jake said as he came out the door.

"That I am," he replied, tipping his can of beer at Jake.

"Passing through?"

"Not exactly," Ralph answered as he dropped his cigarette and ground it out with the toe of his wing tips which were set off by a pair of calf length black socks. He pulled on the beer, reached out to shake Jake's hand, then they hugged.

"Ralph, this is a good friend of mine, Virgil Smith. Virgil, Ralph here is probably the best homicide detective in Nashville."

"Was."

"What are you talking about?"

"Not anymore, Jake. I've hung it up."

"Really?"

"Really. Two weeks ago Friday was my last day."

"I should've known about that."

"I didn't tell anybody. Got my time in, the boss ticked me off, and I told 'em I was done and walked out." Ralph hit the beer again, then shook Virgil's hand. "Any friend of Jake's is a friend of mine." His grip was somewhat overpowering to Virgil, himself a pretty stout guy.

"So what brings you up here to this neck of the woods?" Jake asked.

"I don't know…I just been sitting around the house bored and I thought I would ride up and see you." About that time, Butch came bounding in from somewhere off the golf course and about knocked Ralph over. He sat down his beer on the ground and hugged the dog around the neck, rubbing his head, all the while being licked all over the face.

"Old friends," Jake said to Virgil.

"I can see that," he replied.

"I think he's glad to see you, Ralph."

"Likewise," he replied.

"Jake, I've been meaning to ask you," Virgil said. "What the hell happened to that old dog's nose?"

"Snake bit."

"Snake bit?" Virgil replied, somewhat taken back.

"Yeah, but that's a story for another day."

"What kind of snake?"

"Timber rattler. Probably four and a half feet long, wouldn't you say, Ralph?"

"Every bit of it," he replied, still getting licked.

Virgil stared at the dog. "Damn."

"Like I said, that's a story for another day. He's a dog you don't want to mess with," Jake said with all seriousness, then started to laugh.

Virgil looked at Butch, then at Jake, and just shook his head.

"So, Jake, what do you say I stay for a few days?" Ralph asked. All the while Butch continued to lick him and his tail beat against Ralph's leg.

"How can I say no to you and the dog?" Jake replied, a big smile on his face.

CHAPTER 4

LITCHFIELD BEACH, SOUTH CAROLINA

Larry Little studied his approach shot into the eighteenth green at the River Club. One hundred forty three yards, he estimated, to the flag stick that was sitting in the right front corner of the green. If he put a good swing on his nine iron, and could put a little juice on it, he should be able to hit the ball to the front of the green and roll it near the hole. All that water to the left side of the hole he blocked out, he had never hit a shot in there yet. He quickly took care of business and his ball wound up five feet from the stick. When his turn came, he knocked the putt in, turned around to his playing partners, and said, "I believe you boys each owe me a five spot, but it's my turn to buy the drinks, so I guess we'll come out about even, like usual." They all took off their caps and held them in one hand while shaking hands with the other. It is a gentlemanly touch of etiquette that seems somehow lost on a new generation of golfers.

At 6'5" and thin as a rail, Little still cut a rather imposing figure at seventy years of age. His athletic prowess and his ability to come through in the clutch were legendary with his playing partners. He had played college baseball at the University of South Carolina and for a couple of years in the minors until an arm injury did him in. This was in the days before Tommy John surgery or he probably would have made it all the way to the majors.

From there he went into the Navy where he spent most of his four years as an intelligence officer on aircraft carriers. He got out, applied for a job with the FBI, and was hired. After two years as a field agent, he was assigned to work in the area of sports-related gambling. It was not a high profile position in the Bureau, but it was an important one. Most people with some knowledge of the inner workings of the FBI had no idea that these positions existed, you wouldn't find any mention of it on any material they put out. Professional and college basketball gambling and horse racing were where he spent most of his time over the next five years. He made his reputation at the Bureau quickly, busting a basketball gambling ring involving players from several Boston area colleges and the mob. Then they put him on the NFL, and he quickly rose to being their point man on professional football gambling. He worked out of the FBI office in Manhattan and had a very good relationship with NFL commissioner Pete Rozelle. He had one direct superior in Washington, other than the director himself. He would spend a lot of time in his career in New York and Las Vegas. By the time Little retired, he counted sixteen players that had served some type of suspension for betting on NFL games. Most of them were listed by the league as 'injuries' as the league worked to keep away from any type of bad publicity, especially when it came to gambling. Only two players were ever actually suspended by the league for gambling, both of whom were made to sit out a year. Each year, as the Super Bowl continued to get bigger and bigger, with more and more money bet on it, the fear that the games could somehow be fixed grew greater and greater. Larry Little was the point man for the FBI and the NFL to try and make sure that didn't happen, and if it did, then he had to find out who did it and how. Only one time in his career did he feel that something had taken place on the game's biggest stage. Knowing it and proving it proved to be tougher than anything he ever had to do at the Bureau.

After thirty years on the job, he retired, and he and his wife moved back to their home state of South Carolina. He was from Georgetown and she was from Sumter. They had met while students at Carolina and were married right before he left to join the Navy. Three kids and eight grandkids, all in the New York City area, were their legacy. Now they lived at North Litchfield Beach and he spent most days playing golf and cards at the River Club or the Litchfield Country Club. For a guy who had spent most of his career fighting and trying to stop illegal gambling, he laughed at the irony that he now spent most of his days taking small wagers from his golf and card partners.

After the round, he had lunch and a couple of drinks with his friends in the grill that overlooked the eighteenth hole. They talked sports and politics, and ribbed each other pretty good about their golf games. Around 2:00 p.m. they were all gone but him. On this day he was in no hurry to head home as his wife had gone on a shopping excursion to Charleston with some of her church friends.

He picked up a copy of the Myrtle Beach *Sun News* that someone had left lying around and sat back to read it. He started with the sports, then the business section, the local news, and then last, the national news. A headline on page eight caught his eye, it said "Prisoner Disappears from Prison." He glanced through the story, wondering how this would go. What really got him looking was when he saw that it was from the Northeast Tennessee Correctional Facility. Then he read the name Robert Wayne Foster. He pulled out his cell phone and did something he hadn't done in several years, he called the FBI headquarters in Washington.

"This is Larry Little and I need to speak with the director." He listened to the response on the other end. "Yes, ma'am, he knows who I am, and I'm pretty certain he will take my call." With no pun intended, he replied, "I'd bet on it."

CHAPTER 5

NORTHEAST TENNESSEE CORRECTIONAL INSTITUTE

Following the attack in the library, Bobby Wayne knew that it was time to make his move. Two weeks later, after lunch in the prison mess hall, he was led to his job in the library. He knew that even though they had tried and failed, another attempt would be forthcoming. They wouldn't stop until they killed him. A job had been paid for and it better be completed. If not, the man who had handed him the book would wind up dead and they would find someone else to carry out the mission. The first thing he did, when the rotating surveillance camera moved off of the desk area, was to slip down under the library's front counter where he took out a paper bag that Pops had waiting for him that contained a can of shaving cream, a razor, a wet towel, and a mirror. He had wet his hair when he stopped to use the rest room on his way in. Quickly covering his head with shaving cream and holding the mirror on his knees, he shaved his head, mustache, and beard. The facial hair had been grown for this very purpose, it wasn't his thing. He reached into the bag and pulled out the small wet towel and wiped down his head and face. He stuffed the shaving cream, razor, and towel back into the bag and handed it to Pops, who was standing guard at the desk. Pops tapped twice on top of the counter to let him know that the camera had rotated back off of the desk area again. Bobby Wayne then crawled on all fours to the back wall where he sat on the floor behind a filing cabinet. From the corner of the room behind the main library desk, Pops once again gave him the two tap signal that all was clear, giving him forty seconds. This time Bobby Wayne removed from the file cabinet another brown paper bag that contained a navy blue suit, white shirt, a tie, and shoes and socks. Pops had gotten them smuggled in for him and they had been stored in the cabinet waiting for the moment to move. Bobby Wayne sat in the floor in the corner, waited for the next tap, and then made the change. It was a dead spot not picked up by the camera. Also in the bag was an I.D. badge on a lanyard that identified him as Joseph A. Collins, Deputy Director of Education Services, Tennessee Department of Corrections. He stuffed his prison clothes into the bag and after the next tap, stood up and handed it to Pops, who looked at his watch that said 2:15 p.m. The prison guard staff had just changed shifts.

Pops picked up the phone and rang out, "This is Luttrel in the library. I've got Mr. Collins from the Department of Corrections in here and he says he's finished his inspection of the library. Somebody needs to come get him, says he's ready to go." He paused for a moment as he listened to the response on the other end. "I'll tell him." He looked at Bobby Wayne and winked, then said, "Mr. Collins, they are on their way." He handed Bobby Wayne three folders, all different colors, containing various papers and reports on the library. "In case somebody asks to see them."

Bobby Wayne pulled out a pair of tortoise shell glasses from the suit coat pocket, looked them over, then slipped them on. In a mirror Pops had at the desk, he looked at his clean-shaven face and head. He pushed up on the knotted tie, then twisted his neck. "I'm not used to wearing one of these." He looked at Pops and winked at him. "I can't thank you enough."

"Just be careful and have a good rest of your life. No offense, but I hope I never see you again, my friend. Not in this life." This time he smiled, then quickly looked away.

In the prison transfer office a clerical guard pulled a form for a Joseph A. Collins, Tennessee Department of Corrections, giving him permission to do a yearly inspection of the prison library. It was a perfectly forged document that had been put in the proper place by an inmate clerical trustee working in the office, lost in the confusion that took place just as all the guards switched. The new guard on duty took the paper, then handed it to an associate who set out to retrieve Mr. Collins. The guard found him waiting in the library, and he led him back to the transfer office.

"Don't believe I've seen you in here before," the guard said, making small talk as they walked.

"It's my first time here, new on the job you know."

"Well, just what is it you do?"

"I inspect the library for the state, then give a report on it to the warden and his staff."

"Not today you won't. I think he's in Nashville."

"No, no, I have to write it up. I'll come back up at the proper time, meet with the warden then to do that."

Typical prison bureaucrat, the guard thought to himself, wondering what someone had to do to get a job like his. Probably had at least a couple of college degrees. Two trips up here for a lousy report that no one would even read or care about. He was sure this guy was paid a lot more than he was making, and doing nothing to earn it.

They arrived at the transfer office, went through two sets of checkpoints, and then went on in. There Bobby Wayne was handed a brown manila envelope that had also been placed there for him. He shook out of it a wallet, cell phone, watch, pen, wedding band, belt, and a set of keys. He put on the watch and ring, and he looked inside the wallet which contained a flawlessly forged Tennessee driver's license for the nonexistent Joseph A. Collins of Murfreesboro. The cellphone was an older model that snapped open. He knew a little bit about them as he had used ones smuggled into the prison over the years to take care of business from time to time. If he made it to the outside, he would be shocked to learn of their use by the public and what all they could do. They barely existed when he went in. He flipped it open and looked at it.

"Don't use that phone in here!" the guard snapped. "You'll have to wait 'til you get outside the compound, outside the administration complex or the parking lot. Warden Jackson's rules, applies to everyone."

"No problem, I'm kind of new at this," he replied. "I can live with that."

"Looks like they need to get you a smart phone," the guard said, now being nice.

Bobby Wayne looked at the guard, at first not sure what to say. "Yeah, you're right. A smart phone is what I need." He smiled and thrust the phone in his pocket.

In a moment he was ushered through, from the prison into the lobby of the administration building.

"You have a good day, sir." The guard re-entered the prison and left him, standing alone.

Just like that, he was out and on his own. Bobby Wayne paused for a moment, not quite sure what to do. It had been almost twenty years. He quickly surmised his way to the front of the building. Ahead was his last obstacle, the guard on the main door. He had been told what to do. Just walk up, show him your badge, act like you know what you are doing, sign out, and then just go on through. That is exactly what he did.

He stepped out the front door into the sunshine and fresh air and took a deep breath. At that moment, a black Chevrolet Suburban with heavily tinted windows pulled up to the curve. He opened the passenger door, got in, and they pulled away.

"You brought me a cold beer I hope?"

"That I did, sir. It's in the back seat in the cooler."

Bobby Wayne reached back and got one, popped off the lid, and took a good slow pull. It had been a long time. "That is good, my friend. I thank you." He raised the bottle up as if to make a toast. He pulled out the cellphone, dialed in a number, and just as they hit the main highway, he hit the send button. The phone rang twice, then out of the back of the car they saw and heard the explosion from the associate warden's car. He had innocently drove it into the lot that morning after dropping his kids off at school, not knowing that a bomb had been planted under his back seat during the night. It went off with such force that Bobby Wayne and the driver saw the car summersaulting up into the air as they drove away.

"That should keep 'em busy for a while, I would think," Bobby Wayne said to the driver.

They drove down the mountain towards Hampton, the road winding around the edge of Watauga Lake. They turned off sharply at the entrance of the Lakeshore Marina and pulled up at the start of the wooden dock. Bobby Wayne jumped out of the car, walking briskly to the end that protruded some one hundred feet out into the lake, then stepped down into a fourteen foot V-hull aluminum fishing boat that was awaiting him. He nodded to the man at the back of the boat who gunned up the motor and took them on out from the boat dock towards the main part of the lake. At the same time a yellow biplane made a pass on the main channel and the man at the controls of the boat took off his hat and waved it in the air. The plane went back up the lake, made a sweeping turn, then came back and made a picture perfect landing in the middle of the main channel. The boat went out towards the plane, pulling up beside it, and Bobby Wayne got out and climbed into the back seat. Before entering the plane, the operator of the boat pulled out his Glock, screwed on a silencer, shot four holes in the floor of the boat, and then pushed it away from the plane with his foot. It quickly started filling with water and in a little over a minute it sank into the clean, cold mountain water. The plane taxied its way down the lake and then the pilot revved it up, picked up steam, and lifted it bouncingly up and off the lake, its wings momentarily dipping back and forth. And just like that they were away. No one around here thought anything about the plane as there was a nearby school in Elizabethton that trained missionary pilots to land and take off from the water in a mountainous setting before sending them off to do their duty in South America to save the lost souls. The planes came and went from the lake all the time.

As the plane circled back over the water, Bobby Wayne looked out at the beautiful lake and mountains. But in his mind, he was already scheming. He had unfinished business to take care of. He reached out and squeezed the pilot's shoulder with his hand and gave him a thumbs up. "My brother, it is good to see you again," he shouted over the roar of the engine.

The pilot looked back at him in his rearview mirror and grinned. Down below, off to their left, they could see the smoke billowing from the parking lot at the prison. The plane banked away to the east and disappeared into the sky, taking them away from Tennessee. In just a few minutes they were rising over the magnificent mountain range of the Appalachians, from Northeast Tennessee on into North Carolina. Over Grandfather Mountain and soon Mount Mitchell, the tallest of the peaks, they went. Then, turning further south, unfolding out below them were the blue and green ribbons of the mountains and ridges of the Smokies. Most of it was desolate, unforgiving wilderness. Just the kind of place that a man who knew what he was doing could hide out and be hard to find. Bobby Wayne looked out the window of the plane at what lay below him and a smile crept over his face.

CHAPTER 6

DEL RIO, TENNESSEE

The disappearance of Bobby Wayne had befuddled Jake Bender and Larry Little. They were not the only ones taken by his escape, nor would they be the most stunned by it. On the same morning, the former governor of the great state of Tennessee, 89-year-old Edward Jefferson Foster III, sat at his office desk on his farm in Cocke County and as he did first thing every morning, he picked up the *Knoxville News Sentinel*. His servant James, also 89, had left it just as he wanted it, the sports section pulled out and laying on top, beside it a glass of orange juice. James had worked for the former governor most of his life, as had his father and mother worked for Foster's parents before him. James accompanied him to Nashville and ran the staff at the Governor's Mansion on two different occasions. Some joked around the state that this was the last vestiges of slavery in the South.

The former governor loved to read about his beloved Tennessee Volunteers, especially football. Things had been a mess in Knoxville for the last few years, and he scanned the paper hoping for some good news. When he was governor and he personally controlled the university's Athletic Board, things were always in good shape, he saw to that. Foster was a known fixture on the sidelines for practices and games. He had even been known to suggest a few plays over the years. His Republican opponents wondered when he had time to run the state. As with most southern Democrats in their day, he ran the state all too well. He was elected governor at the age of thirty. Four years later, he left office much wealthier than when he had gone in. Picking his time, he ran for office a second time, some twenty years later, and again he was elected. This time the political landscape had changed, and when he left office at the end of the second term, his administration was mired in scandal.

He tried to keep his hand in play on Tennessee athletics, even after leaving office. Last year they had brought back former Tennessee and NFL quarterback Tommy Prince to be the head football coach. He would be the fourth one in six years. It was done over the former governor's strong objection to the university's president and athletic director. His clout had waned over the years and now they wanted his money but not his input. If he still had his way, he would get rid of the whole lot of them. Likewise, they would like to see him gone. Fortunately for them, with the shift of Tennessee to a Republican state, Foster was considered nothing more than a harmless old dinosaur.

As he did every day, he read through the sports section before picking up the front page. Inside, on page three, he saw it, the article about Bobby Wayne missing from the state prison. He felt lightheaded, then began to feel sick to his stomach. Slumping back in his big leather office chair, he rang the buzzer and ordered James to come and fix him a drink. In just a moment he entered the room.

"Awful early in the morning to be doing this, don't you think, Governor?"

"Just fix it, James."

"All right, if that's what you want, sir."

"It is what I want."

James poured him some bourbon on ice and Foster quickly drank it.

"Give me another one."

"You sure about that, sir?"

"Damn it, just do as I say. Another one."

James fixed it and handed it to him. "Anything else, sir?"

"That's it." He waved him away.

When James was out the door, Foster picked up the phone and dialed the county sheriff's cell phone. It was a call the sheriff was waiting on, as he had already heard the news.

"I thought you told me you were going to take care of my problem?"

"Obviously, sir, something up there must have gone wrong."

"I would say that is a vast understatement. I want round the clock surveillance on my farm and house, right away."

"I'll see to that, sir."

"You know, boy, I put you in office and I can take you right out of it."

"Yes, sir."

"You people are no match for this guy, you do know that?"

"I think we can hold our own with anyone, sir," the sheriff smugly replied.

"You're a bigger fool than I thought." He hung up the phone.

CHAPTER 7

CAPE HATTERAS, NORTH CAROLINA
ONE WEEK LATER

Donn Moore pulled out of his old beach cottage in Avon and pointed his 1967 International Scout south on Highway 12. On the front bumper was a homemade bait and ice box with his rods, rigged up and ready to go, in the plastic holders he had attached to the front. He looked at his watch, saw it was straight up at 5:00 a.m., and turned on the old AM radio to a station out of Manteo to listen to the local news and fishing report. It faded more in than out and that was fine with him. He heard what he wanted to hear. Driving slowly through the fog, brought on by a night of unseasonably warm temperatures for early February, he could barely make out what lay in front of him. Visibility was almost zero. He sure didn't want to hit a deer that might dart out on the old beach road. That happened to him one time before and it had cost him close to six hundred dollars to get the old Scout fixed. So he prodded along, sipping his coffee, until he finally reached Buxton, her lights appearing out of the hazy fog at almost the last moment. He pulled into the Red Drum Tackle Shop. It was a block building; a combination garage, convenience store, and bait shop, with gas pumps out front. It had been a fixture on the Outer Banks for many years and had long been a bastion and gathering point for those heading out to fish the surf. The white lights of the store eerily glowed through the fog with a misty halo forming around them. It was the only place open at this time in the morning.

The bell rang as Donn went through the front door. "Mornin'," he said to no one in particular. He grabbed the usual; a six pack of sixteen-ounce PBR cans, a bag of ice, and a couple of packs of peanut butter crackers and went up and put them on the counter. Two men were behind it. "Anybody been catching anything?" he asked them, the same question they would be asked hundreds of times every single day of the year. This morning, at a quarter after five, he would be the first.

"Just the usual stuff in the surf is about all I've been hearing, Mr. Moore," the younger of the two men said as he started ringing him up on the register.

The older one had shuttled off as soon as Donn came through the door and was back with two paper bags of bait waiting for him on the counter. "Got some fresh mullet today," he said.

Donn nodded in reply and paid them. He grabbed it all up and headed for the door.

"Mr. Moore, what do you think about the Jets? It looks like they got a chance to win the Super Bowl this Sunday," the young man said.

"I haven't really kept up with it."

"No kidding? I thought you'd like that, you having played for them."

"I don't follow it much anymore," he said without looking up.

"Don't catch 'em all, Donn," the old man said after him, changing the subject.

"No danger of that," he replied as he backed into the door and pushed it open with his backside. "Hope to see you boys again in the morning."

The old man waved him off. They had been doing that most every morning for the past couple of years. After he was out the door, the old man turned to the younger one, his son, and said, "Don't ask me why, but he don't like to talk about it." He shook his head. "I don't know why."

"He ran a kickoff back a hundred yards for a touchdown in the Super Bowl against the Redskins. They showed it the other night on ESPN on a show about the biggest plays in Super Bowl history. Now he don't care nothing about it? It's crazy, if you ask me."

"Nobody's asking you."

Donn had run the kickoff back for a touchdown for the Jets in their win over the Redskins. He came into the NFL as an undrafted free agent out of Virginia Tech, considered by the scouts as too small, yet by his third game was a starter. His reputation as a fierce hitter had carried over from college to the NFL. Teammates dreaded practicing against him, but when it was game time, they were glad he was on their side.

Two years after the Super Bowl, he was out of the league. The Jets coach told him when he cut him that "for some reason, son, you have flat out lost that fire to play. Maybe you can get it back with another team." That didn't happen as Donn never returned the calls of the teams that reached out to him. He returned to his hometown of Millboro Springs, Virginia and took a job teaching high school English for the next twenty-five years. When the time came to retire, he packed up and went to the Outer Banks. At his home in Virginia, when he moved out, they found boxes of unopened letters from fans sent to him over the years. Football cards, pictures, letters from former teammates trying to contact him, and offers for paid appearances, all left unopened and unanswered. He had given his Super Bowl ring to a nephew who one time asked him about it, wondering why he never wore it.

Out in the parking lot, Donn set the bags of supplies on the hood of his old Scout, pulled out a cigarette, and lit it. He inhaled, then coughed. As it dangled from his lips, he put the ice, the bait, and then the beer in his bait box on the front bumper. Finished, he leaned back against the vehicle, took a few more drags, then flicked the cigarette away, got in, and drove off. It was cold and wet, too cold for most people to be out fishing. But his threshold for fishing was fifty degrees. Any day he got up and it was above that mark, he headed on out to the ocean. This morning it was fifty degrees on the dot, but the howling wind made it seem much colder.

When he reached the entrance to the beach, he got out, locked in the front hubs on his Scout so he could engage his 4-wheel drive, then eased on out the sandy path that would take him to the ocean. The Scout rocked and rolled, pitching through the sandy ruts until he reached the beach itself. It was still dark when he stopped just back from the point. His headlights caught the clashing of the waves. It was here that the water coming up from the Gulf Stream met the water coming down from the North Atlantic and had made it a favorite spot for fishermen since they were first able to access it. On this early February morning, Donn was the first and only one out there. He poured coffee from his thermos and sipped at it. Most days of the year he made his way out here. Even when it was too cold to fish, he came and enjoyed the solitude and beauty, watching the sun come up. The wind seemed to be dying down.

At a few minutes after six he could start to see the first signs of daybreak: a yellowish, pinkish hue out to the east on the horizon. In another twenty minutes it would be high tide. He got out of the Scout and began cutting and rigging his bait. He pulled on an old pair of chest-high waders, careful to tightly pull the safety cord around his chest. When done, he slipped on a pair of woolen gloves. He kept three pairs with him and when a pair got wet, he would change them out. He moved down the fifteen yards or so it was from his Scout to the edge of the surf. For the next thirty minutes he fished the pounding waves for flounder. He caught a couple and flipped them into the plastic five gallon bucket he brought for that purpose. If they stretched across the mouth of the bucket, they were big enough to keep. He only kept enough to eat, the rest he would throw back in the ocean.

A feeling, something he could not explain, made him turn around, and when he did he saw a man standing beside his Scout. The sun was starting to make its way up now, and he could see clearly. He stood there, watching him, the man not moving, with his hands thrust in his pockets. Donn looked up and down the beach and saw no other people nor any other vehicles. It seemed odd to him, but he kept fishing, all the while keeping an occasional eye on the man. In a few minutes, the man started walking his way. Donn noticed he was dressed in blue jeans, an old Army field jacket, and a navy stocking cap pulled down around his ears.

As the man approached, he called out the same greeting as most people here would do. "Good morning. You having any luck?"

Donn looked back at him, then responded, "A couple of flounder, in the bucket there."

The man pulled out a cigarette, turned his back to the wind and lit it with a Zippo lighter, with a little trouble, then glanced into the bucket and smiled.

"Hard to light 'em in this wind," Donn said, still keeping an eye on him.

"Yeah, but I got it." The man took a deep drag then laughed. "Probably should quit 'em I guess. I'm just out walking the beach. You're the only person I've seen out here so I thought I'd stop and watch you fish. Hope you don't mind, the brave soul you are on such a chilly morning."

"As are you. You got a vehicle?" Donn asked, his curiosity getting the best of him.

"Yeah, I parked at the lighthouse parking lot and just started walking. No 4-wheel drive for me."

"That's a pretty good hike." By now he was right up next to Donn.

"Beautiful morning, but it sure is cold to be fishing," the stranger commented.

"That's why you don't see anybody else out here," Donn replied. "It's all a state of mind."

"Yeah, that makes sense." He seemed to shiver in his jacket, hands still thrust in his pockets.

"The wind, it makes it seem a little colder than it really is. It's right above fifty. That's my cutoff point. Any colder than that and I usually won't fish. I got hot coffee up there in my thermos if you want some. A cold beer, too, if you'd rather have that."

"Thanks, I might get some in a few minutes. You must love to fish is all I know."

"I guess so."

"You know, you look familiar to me. I think I know you from somewhere in my past."

"I don't think so," Donn replied.

"No? Maybe it will come to me…"

Donn flipped the bail on his rig and cast it back into the surf, landing it in a spot between two rolling waves. Just as he did, the man, having taken a look around and seen no one, slipped his way in behind Donn, pulled a military issue knife out from under his coat, and before Donn knew it, he had run the knife into his back, skillfully inserting it in a way that would take it right into his heart and destroy it. He put his other arm around Donn's neck, holding him up. The body seemed to jump. Donn made only a gurgling sound, then he slumped. The man pulled out the knife, then took it and cut the safety tie loose on Donn's waders and pushed him face first out into the surf. The next wave that crashed ashore filled his waders full of water and pulled his body down and sideways, out into the sands and surf of the Atlantic. The man washed his knife off in the surf, reinserted it into its sheath on his belt, and walked back up to the Scout. He opened the bait box, fished his hand around in there, and then came out of it with two cans of beer. He looked around and still saw no signs of anyone else. One can he stuck in his pocket; the other he opened, then leaned back against the Scout and slowly drank it. When he finished, he crunched up the can with his hand, walked back down to the edge of the water, and tossed it in the surf.

"Yeah, now I remember. Donn Moore, Mr. Super Bowl MVP." There was no signs of Donn, his body having been pulled into the ocean at high tide. The man stuck his hands back in the pockets of his coat, turned and walked on back up the beach, heading for the parking lot at the Cape Hatteras Lighthouse.

The body of Donn Moore would be found later that morning at low tide, half buried in the retreating surf, anchored down by his sand-filled waders. The sharks that plied the waters of the surf had done enough damage that the body would be sent to the state medical examiner's office in Raleigh where they would have a hard time determining the exact cause of death.

The next morning in North Litchfield Beach, South Carolina, the retired FBI agent Larry Little read about the death of the former NFL star in the newspaper. He folded the paper, laid it on the table, and then finished his cup of coffee. The paper said the cause of death was still being investigated, but Little was pretty sure Donn had been murdered, and he bet he knew why.

CHAPTER 8

ATLANTA, GEORGIA
TWO MONTHS LATER

Johnny Rockett had once been the biggest of stars. He had been born with the perfect name to go along with his stardom. A high school prodigy in McDonough, Georgia; he was recruited by every major college football program in the country. He narrowed his choices down to the biggest and best of them all: Southern Cal, Texas, Notre Dame, Alabama, Ohio State, Tennessee, and his home state Georgia Bulldogs. He took recruiting trips to each one. He heard from boosters from all of the schools and many promises were made. Cars, money, women. In the end Georgia won out as it would be easier on his mother to be able to come see him play every Saturday. She also wound up with a well-paying job working in the insurance office of a powerful Bulldog booster in McDonough. And play for the Bulldogs he did. Johnny became a three time All-SEC and two time All-America safety. The New York Jets took him in the first round of the NFL Draft with the tenth pick. He started the first NFL game he had ever been to and for three straight years he went to the Pro-Bowl.

But knee injuries, alcohol, and drugs became his enemy, and a career that many thought would end up in Canton, Ohio, at the Pro Football Hall of Fame had fizzled out by the time he was twenty-nine. A year after his appearance in the Super Bowl, the Jets unceremoniously released him mid-season due to "conduct detrimental to the team." He finished the year out with New England, who didn't offer him a contract for the next season. He went to camp the next year with the Oakland Raiders, where he would ride the bench and play only on special teams. They released him after the season ended. There were no other calls from others wanting his services. He fired his agent and hired another. The new one got him a job in the Canadian Football League with the Montreal Alouettes. After a few months, Johnny quit and came home. "Too damned cold," he told anyone that asked him.

Then came a decade-long period of alcoholism, drug abuse, and an inability to keep a job of any kind. He lost four jobs over a six year period, including a gig with ESPN. When he did show up for work, he was usually drinking. Tired of all of his lies, his wife had finally given up on him and kicked him out. Now he had three children that he no longer saw or paid any child support for. His former teammates stopped taking his calls, knowing he was just looking for a handout. At the age of forty, he had gotten just about as low as he could go. Broke, homeless, and living on the streets of Atlanta, his weight down to only one hundred forty pounds, he was arrested for dealing cocaine and wound up being sentenced to ten years in state prison. The judge, a former classmate at Georgia, cried when he handed down the sentence. But he also put Johnny in a place where he thought he could be helped, and made a phone call to former NFL player Bubba White who ran a prison ministry out of his hometown in Greenville, South Carolina. A tight end for the Kansas City Chiefs, they had gone head to head many times during their careers. Within days Bubba showed up at the prison to see him. Johnny turned him away. For three months Bubba came once, and sometimes twice, every week until Johnny finally gave in and agreed to meet with him. They had a tearful meeting that lasted for three hours, thanks to the benevolence of the warden. Johnny took the Lord into his life before it was over. Bubba put Johnny on the right track, and after being a model prisoner for the next three and a half years, he got out early. While in prison, with the help of the judge, Johnny had finished the work to obtain his degree from Georgia. He reconciled with his wife and children, and when released, she allowed him to come home on a trial basis. He never left again.

Johnny got out with a plan. He soon started his own church, renting an old run down supermarket building in McDonough. The first Sunday, he had twenty people, mostly relatives, show up. In a little over a year, he was averaging over five hundred every Sunday and a move to a bigger building quickly followed. They soon broke ground on their own building, moving into downtown Atlanta. The church in McDonough was taken over by one of his associate pastors, allowing Johnny to make the move. He paid back the favor done to him and began his own prison ministry. Soon he was traveling and speaking all over the country, but never where he couldn't be back home to preach to his own congregation on Sunday mornings.

He was hired by the NFL to counsel the young men coming out of college and into the league with a seminar to be held every June in Atlanta. There he would preach to them about the perils of fame and fortune and the pitfalls that awaited them if they were not careful. As he spoke, on the wall behind him hung two pictures; one of a strong, robust defensive back for the New York Jets, and the other a mug shot of him at the time of his life when he was the most down and out. Until he told them, the young men in the room had no idea that the pictures were of the same person. As Johnny started to speak to them, he looked around the room and could tell the ones that paid little or no attention to him. At one time, he would tell them, he had been just like them. By the time he finished, most, if not all, were listening.

On this Sunday night Johnny worked alone in his office at the church. Aware of the death of his former teammate Donn Moore, he had been following it in the news and online. For years he had wrestled with a dark secret that he knew he needed to bring out into the open. He felt that until he did, he would never find total peace in his life. The death of Donn brought the issue back into sharp focus for him. Maybe the time to do so was at hand. But if he did, he knew it would create a firestorm in the media and would destroy the life and career of someone else. It could hurt his new relationship with the NFL. If he told his story, maybe he could convince them it was what needed to be done. Maybe he could keep it from happening again to someone else. He struggled with just what to do. He looked at the note laying on his desk with the name and personal phone number of the University of Tennessee football coach Tommy Prince. His fingers tapped at the note and he debated whether to call. Finally, he built up the courage and dialed it. It went to voicemail. He hung up after leaving a message saying that he had called.

Johnny turned off the light in his office and walked down the hall in the dark until he reached the door. Setting the alarm, he stepped outside the building. He moved down the sidewalk toward his black Cadillac Escalade, pulling out his keys and cell phone, unlocked the door and slid into the driver's seat. He inserted the key into the ignition with his right hand and then hit the button to call his wife on his cell phone with his left. "Hey, baby, I'm on my way home," he said at the same time starting to turn the ignition switch. At that moment, he saw a man leaning up against the side of the church, some fifty yards away. As the ignition kicked in, an explosion ripped from underneath the Escalade, flipping it up and into the air. It violently crashed back down on its top, a massive fireball moving heavenward.

Some six miles away, Johnny's wife held a phone that had suddenly gone dead. She feared the worst each time she dialed back and continued to get no response. After several tries, she called the police and asked them to go and check the church. "I feel something is wrong," she told them. "Very wrong."

"Ma'am, we do have a call about an incident at the church," the police operator said. "We have officers on the way. Someone will be back in touch with you shortly."

She dropped the phone and fell to the floor.

The man leaning against the church pulled out a pack of cigarettes, shook one out, put it in his mouth, and lit it with a Zippo lighter. He snapped the lid closed, deeply inhaled the cigarette, slid the lighter back into his coat pocket, then turned and walked away.

Whatever the secret was that bothered Johnny, he was taking it with him to the grave.

CHAPTER 9

CARNEGIE HOTEL
JOHNSON CITY, TENNESSEE

Jake peered over his sunglasses at the girl behind the main desk. "Room 301 is already taken?"

"Yes, sir, I'm afraid so."

"That is my favorite room." He looked around as if irritated and wanting someone else to complain to. "That is why I like to stay here. Are you sure they didn't put that down as a request when I called in?"

"I'm sorry, sir, but there is no notation of that, or of you calling in for that matter."

"The girl said she would hold it for me."

"I'm sorry, sir. I don't know why she would have told you that," she said, peering into her computer screen. "It looks like we have a standing reservation for that room every Wednesday."

"I love the view of the university from there. Sentimental reasons I guess." He looked at her and smiled.

"303. I can put you in 303. It's the adjoining room." Now she smiled. "You will have pretty much the same view."

"Really?" He pondered on it for a moment then said, somewhat reluctantly, "I guess so, let's do it."

"And how will you be paying?"

"Cash, my dear."

"Do you need help with your bags?"

"No, I'm just going to go up and freshen up a bit. I'll get the bags later. I've got some paperwork to go over before my meeting," he said, showing the girl the manila envelope he held under his arm.

"Do you have a presentation to make?" the girl asked him inquisitively.

"Yes, as a matter of fact, I do."

"We have an office area if you need to do any last minute preparations."

He looked at her name badge. "Linda, is it? You, my dear, have been very helpful. If I see your boss while I'm here, I will put in a good word for you."

She blushed. "Thank you. That's what we are here for."

Jake picked up a copy of the *USA Today* off of a table and headed for the elevator. Glancing at his watch, he saw it was 11:30. If the Kiwanians were on time, he had a few minutes to spare. Once upstairs, he was pleased to see a couple of maids' carts on the hall. He went into 303 and was glad to see the girl was right, it was an adjoining room to 301. He stepped into the hall and waited for one of the maids to come out. In just a moment, she did.

"Ma'am, can you help me?" She looked at him without saying a word. "I have locked myself out of my room, I left the key on the dresser. I'm in a hurry for a meeting and don't have time to go back downstairs."

"Locked you out, si?"

She was Hispanic and he quickly picked up that her English may not be that good. So he spoke the universal language. He pulled out a roll of money and peeled off a twenty dollar bill. She looked around to make sure no one else was looking, then took it.

"What room?" she asked, continuing to glance around nervously.

"301." He tapped it with his fingers.

She looked around one more time to make sure no one was watching and then took her pass key and let him in.

"Gracias," he said as he went inside. He unlocked the adjoining door then stepped back outside where the maid stood. "Muchas gracias," he said handing her another twenty which she quickly took and stuck in her pocket before scurrying back up the hall into the room she was working on. Jake waited until she was gone then went back into his room, opened the adjoining door, and went back into 301. He looked at his watch, it was now ten minutes until noon. He sat down in the chair nearest the door and began reading his newspaper. At five minutes after, the man arrived just as scheduled. He stepped into the room briskly, but when he saw Jake he came to a sudden stop. He glanced at the door number to make sure he was in the right place. By the way Jake held the newspaper in his lap, with one hand under it, the man was quick to judge that he was possibly holding a gun.

"Just let that door go nice and easy and ease on over and sit down on the bed."

"I…I don't have much money on me, but I'll give you what I have." Nervously thinking, the man said, "Here, I've got a Rolex. I won it in a sales contest. You can have it if you'll just let me go." He held out his wrist. He imagined having to explain to his wife what he was doing in a hotel room in the middle of the day when he was robbed.

"You think this is a robbery?" Jake asked. "You just stay there on the bed 'til your girlfriend arrives." He got up, folded the newspaper, and laid it in the floor next to the chair. Moving over, he got between the man and the door.

"You don't have a gun…" the man said.

"I've got a gun, but unless you do something really stupid, Roy, I don't plan on having to use it. Your name is Roy, right? Wife Martha, little Ben and Sarah waiting for you at home when you get there this evening?" Jake pulled out a picture he had taken of them at a soccer game the day before. The attractive blond wife and two blond-headed children. He wondered what would make a guy cheat on such a beautiful woman. Roy's face was now ashen and beads of sweat were forming on his forehead.

"This is your wife and kids, taken yesterday at Optimist Park," Jake said.

"Oh my God, how do you know all of that?" he stammered.

Jake moved on over to the door and stood behind it. "It's my job. Your girlfriend will be here any minute now. I do know that, too."

Roy just looked at Jake, not really sure what to do next. "Who are you?" he got up the nerve to say.

"You see, Roy, I'm a private investigator hired by your girlfriend's husband to bring an end to this little weekly meeting you two are having." At that moment, before he could respond, there was a slight rap at the door. Jake quickly opened it and Virgil's wife Betty stepped right in. Jake grabbed her by the arm and pushed her over onto the bed next to her lover.

"Oh my God, Jake, what are you doing here?"

"What the hell do you think I'm doing here? Virgil hired me to bring an end to this thing you two have going on."

"Jake, it's not what you think...please," she pleaded. "We're meeting here over a real estate deal." Then her tone changed. "Do something, Roy! What kind of man are you?"

"He knows my wife's name, my kids' names...He has a gun, for God's sake."

"You know Virgil wanted to come with me, so I hope you appreciate the fact that I talked him into thinking that was not such a good idea."

Roy, building up his nerve, barked at her, "You told me you two were separated and he no longer cared what you did. I know his reputation... he's liable to kill you and me both! This is unbelievable."

The comment about Virgil's reputation and killing both of them settled into the back of Jake's mind for now. "Here's the deal," he said to them, pulling the manila envelope out from under his arm and shaking it in the air. "If you don't want your wife to get this little package in the mail, then this thing comes to an end right now, today. I'm keeping these pictures and if I even hear a whisper that the two of you have gotten together..."

"Pictures of what?" Roy asked.

"Pictures I took of you two here last week," Jake said.

Roy slumped back on the bed, defeated.

"Jake, has Virgil seen them?" Betty asked, then she started to cry.

Jake wasn't sure if the tears were sincere or not. "Nobody has seen them but me, and I plan to keep it that way. Six months from today, if you don't cause me to use them, I will destroy them. Got it?"

"Jake, how did you get pictures of us?" Betty asked, suddenly inquisitive, the tears gone.

"You two are a little too predictable. Same hotel, same room, same time, every week. A small camera placed right up there, hidden in the tops of the curtains." He pointed to a spot. "It works off of a timer, if you must know. So hey, this is what we have, right?" He held up the envelope and wiggled it again in front of them.

Roy quickly took inventory that Jake had a picture of his wife and kids and now pictures of him in a hotel room doing who knows what. "Yes, it's over, you don't have to worry about me," he nodded to Jake, slowly easing off of the bed and inching for the door. "She'll never hear from me again, that's a promise." He looked back at Betty as he opened the door and went out. "A promise." The door shut behind him, leaving the room in a state of silence.

Betty, now alone with Jake, again started to cry. Jake stepped into the bathroom and brought her out some tissues.

"Please, Jake, don't ever let Virgil see those pictures. Promise me that." She dabbed her eyes.

"Believe me, it's the last thing I want to do," Jake said. "Wait a few more minutes and make sure he's had time to get out of the building, then you can go."

She got up from the bed, straightened her tight-fitting dress by running her hands down the front of it, leaned over and hugged Jake, pushing her body hard against his, until he finally had to ease her away. He got the impression she was ready to move on with him, if he pushed it, probably in an attempt to get the pictures back. "Promise me you won't show Virgil those pictures. He will go crazy, Jake. You have no idea how crazy he can get. "

That was the second time he had heard that in the last few minutes.

Something told Jake she had been down this road before. "You uphold your end of the bargain, Betty, and I'll promise he'll never see them."

She eased back over, gave Jake a peck on the cheek, then he gently backed her away. She gave him a smile, turned around, and went to the door. Pausing, she looked back. "Jake, I'll do whatever you say to get those pictures."

"Bye, Betty," Jake said. With that she reluctantly eased out, shut the door, and was gone. That girl is trouble, Jake thought to himself. But that's probably what Virgil likes about her. He's always been that way about women, he never picked the good ones. Jake waited a few minutes to let her get away. He took the elevator down to the lobby, walked to the entrance, and as he stepped out of the large revolving doors, he stopped at one of the two large golden trashcans they had placed on either side of the door. From under his arm he pulled out the manila envelope, opened it and pulled out a section of *USA Today* that he had used to make it appear there was something in there, and dropped it in the can. He then tore the envelope into little pieces and dropped it in as well.

"What a way to make a living," he said to the bellman as he walked off, slipping a five spot in his hand.

CHAPTER 10

LITCHFIELD BEACH
TWO MONTHS LATER

There were now two deaths that could be associated with what had taken place at Super Bowl XIX, and Larry Little was frustrated with the response, or should he say the lack of, he was getting from his former employer, the Federal Bureau of Investigation. He had worked the case hard back in the day, had a pretty good idea of just what had transpired, and knew pretty much everyone that had been involved, including the mobsters. The problem was that no one was ever charged back then because they never could come up with enough concrete evidence to prosecute anyone. The league knew about, but never took any action against, the players. Nobody involved was willing to talk or admit to what had happened. The NFL, once they figured the story wasn't going to come out, soon became very uncooperative. They were happy to just see it go away. But Little knew what had happened and who had done it. Now, all these years later, he was sure that someone was taking them out, one by one. After reading about the jailbreak in Tennessee, he was certain he knew who that was as well. Before he retired from the Bureau, Little had made a trip to Tennessee to see Bobby Wayne and offered him a deal to get out of prison if he would cooperate. Bobby Wayne had laughed at him.

It was no coincidence that both of these guys died within two months of each other. There would be more to follow, he was sure of it, and he had a really good idea who they would be. His files were still there in Washington, all they had to do was assign someone to it and they could go through the documents, bring him in to consult, and pick up the trail from there. It was all right there in his notes. And if for some reason they had lost or destroyed them, he had his own copies. Maybe he wasn't supposed to do that, but he did. He wasn't about to leave Washington without them when he retired.

Little had talked to the associate director of the FBI, a Mr. Oliver Jones, on two separate occasions. The first time was after the death of Donn Moore, and again this week after reading about the death of Johnny Rockett. He was assured by Mr. Jones that they were looking into it, but that he had to understand that right now their main priority was the war on terror and so much of their resources and manpower were tied up on that. "We are not spending a lot of time and money to take a look at something you think might have happened many, many years ago at a Super Bowl," he smugly said.

"Even if people are dying?"

"We don't know why they are dying, it could very well just be coincidence."

"How many people have to die before we put this all together? Do you want me to give you a list of who I think is next?" Little was obviously very upset. "I'm not some cranky old retired agent fantasizing that the Bureau still could use me," Little responded angrily.

"Nobody has accused you of that."

"Yeah, well, the FBI I worked for would be all over this."

"Correct me if I'm wrong, but nothing ever came of this when you were on the case. Times have changed, sir. Priorities are much different now," he arrogantly told Little.

The director was a man he thought he knew well. Much to his dismay, though, he had been "too busy" to take Little's call and had yet to call him back nor would he. "He asked me to handle your situation," Jones said.

"He said to tell you he hopes you are enjoying your retirement, and if ever in Washington, maybe the two of you could have lunch."

"What is wrong with you people?"

"Nothing is wrong, we just don't see the urgency on this at this time."

"And how long have you worked for the Bureau, Mr. Jones? I'm not familiar with your name," Little asked him. "I've been retired for a few years now."

"About six years," Jones responded with an air of indifference, as if this was all just a waste of his time.

A political appointee, Little thought to himself. "And what is your background, may I ask?"

"I came here from the federal prosecutor's office in New York."

"Let me guess," Little said, "you're an Ivy Leaguer?"

"Well, since you asked, I was undergrad at West Virginia, on a football scholarship, which is a long way from the Ivy League."

"And law school?"

"Well, Harvard Law, so I guess in that way you could say I am an Ivy Leaguer. It's not really the same, though."

"Let me guess, you worked for the president's campaign, you guys won, and look where you landed," Little replied angrily.

Jones didn't respond.

"Six years at the Bureau…you are on a fast track, my friend. In my day it took twenty to even be considered for the job you have."

"Times have changed here in Washington, and I might add in the Bureau as well, Mr. Little. Look, I'll look into this and get back with you. Okay?" He was obviously bored with the conversation.

No question things had changed, Little thought to himself. "Yeah, well maybe the priority on this will pick up after the next death," he replied and hung up his phone. He stormed out of the house. He got in his restored 1985 BMW, fired her up, and sped away from his home at North Litchfield Beach. He turned left onto Highway 17 and then right onto the road that would take him to the golf course. Maybe a morning of golf and an afternoon of cards with his buddies would get his mind off all of this. He wound through the residential area, probably going a little faster than he should have, his adrenaline still rushing from the phone call. He had to slow down quickly by downshifting just at the entrance to the Litchfield Country Club as an old flatbed truck overloaded with mulch appeared to be broken down in the road right in front of him, blocking both lanes. He sat there for a few minutes and observed the man who had gotten out, thrown up the hood on the truck, and seemed to be working on it on the passenger side, his back to Little. The man wore old jeans, a long sleeve t-shirt, and a straw hat pulled down low on his head. The driving range for the golf course was to the right hand side of the road. On this hot June day, at just about noon with the temperature well over ninety, there was no activity there. Most people here tended to play early in the morning before the heat became so oppressive. On the left were large trees and shrubs along the roadway, buffering the entrance to the beautiful, plantation-style clubhouse.

Still agitated from dealing with the FBI on the phone, Little started blowing his car horn. The man looked up from under the hood of the truck, picked up a white towel he had laying there, and started wiping his hands on it. The way he held the towel somewhat obscured his face.

Little put down his car window and hollered to the man, "Can't you push that thing off to the side of the road?"

The man looked at Little, motioned with one hand in the air, the towel over the other, and started walking towards the BMW. He approached the driver's side of the car.

"Look, buddy, I'm running late here. Can't you get that thing off to the shoulder so I can get around?" Little asked, clearly agitated and motioning with his hands.

The man was at the window now, continuing to wipe his hands on the white towel he had draped over them. The straw hat, worn by so many people in that area who worked out in the sun for a living, was pulled down low, covering the man's forehead, and his eyes were hidden by a pair of large, dark sunglasses. He leaned over, just at the car window, and from under the towel he pulled out a Beretta with a silencer screwed onto the barrel. He stuck it into Little's chest, right at his heart, and pulled the trigger twice. The body slowly rose with the impact of each shell entering the torso. The man wiped the gun clean with the towel and let it drop into Little's lap. He slowly walked back over to the truck, slammed the hood, climbed in, started it up, and drove away.

Larry Little, always one to be vigilant, had been caught off guard. As he sat there in the seat of his BMW taking the last breaths of his life, he recognized, just for a fleeting moment, the face of the man who had put the gun to his chest and pulled the trigger.

CHAPTER 11

KNOXVILLE, TENNESSEE

Tommy Prince sat in his palatial office in the football complex at the University of Tennessee. He was in his third year of a rebuilding job, turning around the fortunes of his alma mater. The first year they went 7-6, the second year 9-4, and now he was spending the summer preparing for his third season. The two years before he arrived, Tennessee had gone 4-7 in back to back seasons, an almost unheard of run at the storied football school. Tommy had starred at quarterback for Tennessee in the mid-1970s, gone on to a ten year career in the NFL, then moved into coaching. In 2000, he landed his first head coaching position at East Tennessee State University in Johnson City. Two years later he was off to the University of Memphis, and four years after that he landed in the big time at the University of North Carolina at Chapel Hill. He took what had long been known as a "basketball school" and in his sixth year won a National Championship with a 14-0 season. Football became very relevant in Chapel Hill.

Meanwhile, in Knoxville, things were going south. When Tennessee called, Tommy came home becoming their fourth coach in the last few years. The once-proud program, one of the winningest in the history of college football, had slipped into mediocrity. Five losing seasons in seven years under three different coaches. Each time, he had interviewed for the job but had been turned away as they hired others. The first one left after two years to take another job. It was a shock to Tennessee fans who could not imagine anyone leaving for another school. The bottom line was that he was offered twice as much money, and having no real attachment to the school, he left. The next two guys quickly failed and were paid to leave. The last one's situation was not helped by the success Tommy was having in the neighboring state of North Carolina. The Tennessee fans, just as they had longed for Johnny Majors' return from Pittsburgh in the late 1970s, clamored for Tommy's return.

On this morning, he had read on the Internet all about the shooting of Larry Little down in Litchfield Beach, South Carolina. He knew Larry, having been questioned by him on several different occasions about what was perceived to have happened at Super Bowl XIX. He also knew about the deaths of his former teammates Donn Moore and Johnny Rockett. An Atlanta homicide detective had driven up to ask him about Johnny and if he had any idea why Johnny had tried to call him on the night he had died. Tommy lied and told the detective it was about Johnny coming up and doing a motivational talk with his team. "We were good friends, going back to our days with the Jets," he told him. What he didn't tell him was that they hadn't spoken since the Super Bowl. "I'm only speculating here," he said, "but I'm sure he said he wanted to come up and talk to our kids about the pitfalls they'd face in life at some point."

"And the last time you recall talking with Mr. Rockett?" the detective asked.

"You know, sometime last winter in the Atlanta airport, we ran into each other while waiting for flights." Again he lied, but he knew this would be hard to trace as he was in and out of the Atlanta airport, sometimes several times a week during the recruiting season.

"You have any idea when that was?" the detective asked.

"I have no idea. I'm through there all the time. To be honest, most nights that time of the year I don't know what town I'm in when I hit the pillow to go to sleep. Listen, surely I'm not some kind of suspect here, am I?"

BARRY BLAIR | 61

"Oh, no. We're just doing our homework. Other than his wife, who he was talking to at the time of the explosion, you were the last person he attempted to call that night."

"The wife, what does she say? Maybe he mentioned to her about trying to call me." He was hoping that wasn't the case.

"Well, we asked her, and she said she had no idea why he was trying to call you. She said she stayed out of his business dealings, said maybe his secretary might know. She said she had never heard him mention your name."

Tommy was relieved to hear that.

The detective thanked him for his time and went back to Atlanta.

Now Tommy sat in his office and pondered what to do. First Donn Moore, then Johnny Rockett, and now Larry Little. This thing was becoming more than a coincidence. He knew who was doing it and had a pretty good reason why. He also knew how he thought, probably better than anyone, and he was not the least bit surprised. If he could just talk to him, maybe he could talk some sense into him. He thought about that for a second, then just shook his head. Who was he kidding? He also knew he wouldn't be able to find him to talk with him, unless he was the one that wanted to do the talking. The next time he saw him would be of his choosing and it would probably be too late. He was sure that Bobby Wayne felt they had ruined his life and now the paybacks were coming.

He picked up the phone and called a friend at the Knoxville Police Department. "I need help," he said. "Someone has threatened my life. I need round-the-clock security, here at the office and at my home."

"Who made the threat?" the man said.

"I have no idea. It was an anonymous call." Once again, he lied.

CHAPTER 12

JONESBOROUGH

Jake walked over from his house and entered the golf shop at the Jonesboro Country Club. It was a Friday morning and the clock behind the counter was right on 8:30 as he came through the old screen door with the Rainbow Bread "Home of the Eight Hour Loaf" ad painted on it. He had found it in an antique shop in downtown Bristol and thought it would be the perfect fit for the business. The proprietor said it came from an old country store up in Shady Valley. It took just a little bit of repair work to get it ready to go. Now, it squeaked when opened and slammed shut every time someone entered or left the shop. It was just like they used to do in the country stores, and that was what he liked about it. Ralph was behind the counter with Butch laying off to the side on the floor sleeping. He opened one eye when Jake came in and his tail started wagging, but he didn't get up. Jake was needing help at the golf shop and with his private investigating business as well. Ralph was the perfect fit, and he showed up at just the right time. After two days of visiting and hanging out, Jake offered to put him to work over a six pack of beer and a sack full of tacos. The next morning Ralph went back to Nashville, then returned two days later towing a U-Haul trailer with all his earthly possessions. He rented a mobile home from Jake's uncle that was just down the road from the golf course telling Jake they would give it a go for a while and see if things worked. He said if he liked it here, he would start looking for a house to purchase. What Jake didn't know was Ralph had already sold his house in Nashville.

On this morning, he was leaning on the counter, drinking coffee, and working a crossword puzzle. As usual, he wore a golf shirt that was a little small and tight. His Marine Corps tattoos, one on each forearm, were starting to show some age. His hat was orange with a Power T logo on the front. The TVs were tuned to ESPN. "Good morning, amigo," he said to Jake without ever looking up, concentrating on his puzzle.

"Had any paying customers this morning?" Jake wondered.

"A few," he replied, again not looking up.

"You stumped yet?"

"Never."

"Well, if you are, let me know."

"Yeah, right." Ralph took a swig of coffee, then went over and poured him some more. He held the pot up to Jake, who shook his head to say no. Coffee wasn't his thing.

"I meant to ask you, Ralph, whatever happened between you and Johnny Rose's widow?"

"What do you mean what happened?" he said, not looking up.

"Last I knew, you had started dating her, right?"

Ralph grunted.

"I'm telling that right, best I remember," Jake said.

"Well, since you asked," Ralph replied, still not looking up, "it just didn't work out."

"How's that?" Jake asked. "She seemed nice enough."

"Too nice," Ralph said. "She drove me crazy, wanting to go to church every time the doors opened. Fussed about how much I drank. Sorry, but that ain't me." He waved his arm towards Jake. "Just let that go, okay?"

"Didn't mean to hit a sore spot," Jake laughed.

"Well, you did."

"Sorry. Hey, I'm gonna need you to do some surveillance work for me this afternoon."

"All right, fire away anytime. I'm ready"

"Insurance job. Guy filed a claim saying he hurt his back working on a beer truck. Wants a full time disability. I need you to follow him around for a while and see if you can get some pictures of him. A friend told me that he thinks he has a standing tee time out at Buffalo Valley, over in Unicoi, every Friday afternoon at 2:30. Apparently he goes on out to Buffalo thinking no one will see him. A few shots of him putting a tee in the ground and getting his ball out of the hole would be real helpful. A nice full back swing would be great, too. It will make the lawyers happy."

"Sounds like he's a real brain surgeon. Hey, too bad he don't come here and play. I could just go out the door and act like I'm taking pictures of the course or something."

Jake just looked at him, then walked over and looked at the crossword. "You need my help yet?"

"I don't think so."

"Banana."

Ralph's eyebrows lifted. "What?"

"Six letters, goes in front of Republic. Banana. You know, like Buffett sings, 'Down to the Banana Republic, things aren't as warm as they seem.'"

"Enough with the singing. I was just about to get it...I really don't need your help. That defeats the whole purpose. I'm exercising my brain."

"Okay, but it's Banana Republic. Check it out."

He looked up at Jake and shook his head. "Really, I can do this without your help."

"Okay. If you really want to help your brain, you might try cutting back on the bourbon, quit killing off all them brain cells."

"Nobody asked your opinion."

Just then, a man and woman came through the front door, both in dark suits.

"FBI," Ralph whispered under his breath.

Jake gave him a look.

"You tell me banana, I'm telling you FBI."

They stood at the door for a moment, looking around, trying to figure the place out. Then the woman moved towards the counter. Jake quickly noticed that she was very attractive. The man hung just a step behind.

"I'm looking for Mr. Jake Bender, please," she said.

"That would be me," Jake replied, stepping forward and extending his hand. "And you are?"

She gave him a firm hand shake then said, "Sarah Workman, FBI. This is agent Bob Donner."

Jake shook his hand, then introduced them to Ralph who just looked at Jake and smiled. "What brings the FBI out to our little neck of the woods?" Jake asked.

"We would like a few moments of your time, Mr. Bender, in private. No offense to your friend here."

"No offense taken," Ralph replied, now back on the crossword puzzle.

"Please, call me Jake," he said, then motioned them towards his office. "Would you like some coffee?" They both declined. He directed them to the two chairs in front of his desk, then after moving a couple of cardboard boxes and a golf bag, he started to shut the door. He looked out and said, "Hey, I get any calls, take a message." Ralph gave him a thumbs up without looking up from the crossword and breaking his concentration. Jake shut the door behind him.

"You sure you wouldn't like some coffee? Soft drinks?" Again, they refused. Jake grabbed a Diet Coke from his office fridge, then moved around and sat down behind the desk.

The phone rang out front. Ralph picked it up. "Jonesboro Country Club."

"Ralph, this is Virgil. I need to speak with Jake, right away."

"He's in a meeting, Virgil. Said to take a message and he'll call you back."

"Who's he meeting with?"

"Couple of FBI agents."

"FBI? Wonder what that's about?"

"Have no idea. I'll have him call you when he gets out." Ralph wanted to get back to the crossword and hung up.

"I know your ex-wife, Susanne, or should I say, the governor," Sarah said, starting the conversation in Jake's office.

"Do you now?" Jake replied, wondering if she was just being cordial or trying to insert some form of intimidation.

"Law school together at Vanderbilt. I'm pretty sure you and I have met before, in Nashville, one night in a dark bar when you were playing music, many years ago. I was jealous of Susanne, I do remember that," she said smiling.

"I thought you looked familiar," he replied, being polite. "So, Vanderbilt Law to the FBI. I should say I'm impressed."

"Do you ever speak with her? I mean, if you don't mind me asking you a personal question."

"No, not at all. We do talk and see each other occasionally. Matter of fact, I was her date to her inaugural ball back in January."

"Well, I am impressed. You're still quite the musician, too, I understand."

"I pick and sing a little bit."

"Didn't you save her life? Susanne, that is. Or something like that, there in downtown Nashville? Seems like I remember seeing that on the news."

She crossed her legs for the second time since sitting down and again Jake could not help but notice. He felt sure she was trying to tease him. She was a very good-looking woman and Jake sensed she was well aware of the effect she could have on men. "Well, I was involved, along with Ralph out there. But the guy that actually saved her life died in doing so, unfortunately."

"Yes, the judge's son. I remember now. So tragic."

"How about you, Bob? How'd you get to the FBI?" Jake asked, steering the conversation away from talking about his ex-wife.

"Naval Academy, Navy, NCIS, and then the Bureau."

"Very impressive backgrounds for the both of you, I must say. You guys sure you don't want something to drink?" he asked again. They both said no. "So what, may I ask, brings you out to the Jonesboro Country Club? Not a pleasure visit, I assume."

Sarah spoke up. "Jake, we work on cases for the Bureau that are sports related."

"Sports related? And what would that have to do with me?"

"Well, we understand you know a Bobby Wayne Foster."

This could be interesting, Jake thought to himself. "Well, I grew up with Bobby Wayne here in Jonesborough. He moved here from Newport in the seventh grade. We played sports together all through high school, but we were never what you would call real close friends."

"Why was that?" Sarah asked.

"He was a little too crazy for me. He was a hell of an athlete though. Good at everything. He beat a lot of teams around this part of the state. Come the end of the game, you got the ball in his hands. Me, I was just along for the ride in a supporting role. Competitive as hell, but he was just different...kinda liked living on the edge, I guess you would say. Hell, he went on to start for two years at Tennessee in football. Played both ways in a time that wasn't happening much anymore. Tailback on offense, safety on defense."

"When was the last time you saw or had any contact with him?" she asked.

Jake pondered on that one. "Probably about the time I got out of college, maybe early '80s. I went in the Marines out of high school then went to college when I got out. If I'm not mistaken, he was home on leave from the Army. He was an Army Ranger, I believe, and he came into a club where I was playing music one night. I mean we're going way back here, before I moved to Nashville. Had on his uniform, lots of medals and that Ranger patch as I recall. Pretty much stood out from the crowd back in that era. Like I say, he was always a little different. Didn't anybody say anything to him though, as I'm sure if they did he would have ripped their head off. He never was one to back down from a fight. No telling what he could do once he had all that Army training. Hey, from what I understand, he's been locked up for the last twenty years or so...from a bar fight might I add, until he somehow seemed to disappear a few weeks back. How did that happen, anyway? Is that what this is all about? If you are asking me if I've seen him since he escaped, well, the answer to that is no. Nor do I know anybody that has."

This time, it was Bob who spoke. "Listen, Jake, what I'm about to tell you, you must keep in strictest confidence. We are here to solicit your help. As Sarah said, we work on issues that are sports related. In this case, gambling, and now it looks like that has led to murder. More than one actually."

"I'm listening."

"Super Bowl XIX, the Rose Bowl in Pasadena. The New York Jets versus the Washington Redskins. The Jets are a heavy favorite, thirteen and a half points by the Vegas line. That's a lot of points for an NFL game, especially a Super Bowl. Bobby Wayne is fresh out of the service and is working for his uncle, Edward Jefferson Foster III, who as you know has also been the governor of Tennessee on two different occasions. It is a well-known fact in law enforcement circles that the Governor's family, behind their legitimate farming, canning, and trucking businesses, have long been involved in criminal activity such as cock fighting, stealing and chopping vehicles of all sorts, prostitution, moonshining, and of course, gambling. In later years, drugs as well. His father moved to Jonesborough at one point to run things for the family in the northeast corner of Tennessee. As such, that is what brought Bobby Wayne into your world in the seventh grade. His father operated everything up here out of their junkyard business out on the south end of the county at the foot of the mountains. Stolen and chopped cars, especially. After his father died, Bobby Wayne's older brother Carl took over. You following me up to this point?"

"I'm with you. I know Carl. I did see him a couple months back at the post office. He didn't act much like he remembered me as he didn't have much to say when I told him who I was. He was several years older than me, so maybe he probably didn't remember."

"As you well know, Bobby Wayne goes off to Tennessee to play football after he graduates from high school. His roommate?"

"Yeah, I know that. Tommy Prince."

"That's right, Tommy Prince, former NFL star, now the head football coach at the University of Tennessee. Native of Newport, Tennessee. And did you know he's the second cousin of Bobby Wayne?"

"Yeah, I knew that from our days of playing Newport. It was always a big deal for them to play against each other."

"Well, he is, and we think that while they were teammates at UT, on at least four or five occasions during their junior and senior years, they conspired to fix the outcome of games on behalf of the family business."

"Huh? How did they do that? As I recall they didn't lose too many games. If memory serves me right, wasn't his uncle the longtime chairman of the university's athletic committee? There was a big stink a few years back when the Republican politicians worked to finally relinquish him of that job. I can't imagine him being involved in throwing Tennessee football games."

"You see, they didn't actually throw any games. Here is what the FBI has long thought happened; they picked games where they had a substantial point spread and the two of them, Bobby Wayne and Prince, would see to it that they won the games, but not by as much as the spread. Say Tennessee was favored by twelve points and late in the game they led by ten and were driving to score. Bobby Wayne was the half back and Prince was the quarterback, and one of them would fumble or throw an interception late in the game to keep the margin of victory below twelve points. The governor and his men would bet this game heavily for Tennessee not to cover the spread and then pass on three grand each to the two college boys for making it happen. That's a lot of money for two boys in college back then."

"And the Super Bowl?"

"It's a known fact that a bet for one million dollars was placed by someone from Tennessee on Super Bowl XIX in Las Vegas through the sports book at the Alamo Casino on the Strip. Largest bet ever laid down on a Super Bowl game at that time. The quarterback for the Jets was Tommy Prince, but he showed up on the morning of the game with a broken wrist and did not play."

"That's right. He claimed he slipped on the stairs and fell, breaking his wrist or something like that." Jake remembered it all very well. As any Tennessee fan would be, they were excited to see Tommy Prince lead his team to a Super Bowl, yet disappointed when he showed up hurt and couldn't play.

"You are right."

"I'd say that made the governor and his boys a little nervous."

"No doubt."

"So why, after all this time, are you looking into this?" Jake asked.

Now, it was Sarah who replied. "You know that Bobby Wayne somehow escaped from prison. Right after that, two former Jets, Donn Moore and Johnny Rockett, were murdered."

"I have seen that in the papers. One on the beach, the other blown up in Atlanta."

"Okay, then last week, a retired FBI agent by the name of Larry Little was shot and killed in Litchfield Beach, South Carolina. Mr. Little was the FBI's point man for years on professional and college sports, with most of his efforts directed to gambling on NFL football. He left a very extensive file on what he always thought was an attempt to fix Super Bowl XIX. He suspected three players were involved; Moore, Rockett, and Prince. They were not to lose the game, they were to just make sure the Jets didn't cover the point spread. Though he was never able to prove it, he felt the bet of one million dollars was placed by Governor Foster, or on his behalf. He had flown to Vegas the day before the game on a private plane and it left there within an hour after the game ended. Bobby Wayne accompanied him on the trip. What followed his bet were a lot of other substantially sized bets being placed on the Redskins, taking the points. Moving the needle, they like to say, when there is a large amount of money bet on one side. It's a good sign that somebody thinks they know something. The Jets won the game 24-10. The point spread had been thirteen and a half. The governor had bet on the Redskins and took the points. He lost, and so did a lot of other people, including some powerful Mafia types. Namely, the

Scarpino family out of New York. They owned the Alamo Casino which was right next to the Hacienda. Most of the big bets on the Redskins were placed at the two casinos so as not to draw all the attention to the Alamo. About two months after the game, the governor's wife and Bobby Wayne's fiancé were killed in an auto accident between Newport and Knoxville. The car was hit head on by a tractor-trailer that never hit its brakes or slowed down. Agent Little always felt it was payback from the Scarpinos."

"So where did Bobby Wayne fit into all of this?" Jake asked.

"He was the governor's point man. Little felt that it was Bobby Wayne's idea and that he had sold his uncle on it based on what they had done on games when they were in college. They could win the game, but just not cover the point spread. The players would all still get their Super Bowl rings and nobody would be the wiser. Bobby Wayne talked Prince into the plan and he enlisted his teammates Moore and Rockett. The starting quarterback and the two starting safeties. Who better to control the outcome of the game? They were to make a hundred grand, split between them," Bob explained. "Bobby Wayne would eventually be set up and take the fall for a murder he didn't commit, all orchestrated by the governor as payback for the loss of the money and his wife. The plan was for him to be killed in prison, but he is one tough hombre. He survived and now has escaped."

"What we think is happening here, Jake," Sarah added, "is that Bobby Wayne is on a mission to pay back all the people involved, one at a time."

"Why the FBI agent?" Jake asked.

"We think because he knew the whole story. Knew everyone that was involved and that Bobby Wayne still saw him as a threat. Little had visited him in prison on occasion and had offered him the opportunity to get out if he would give him the case and agree to testify against the others. Who knows why these guys do what they do sometimes," she said. "Larry had another guy, who claimed to be at the meeting when the plan was initially discussed, and right after he met with Little, ready to talk, he disappeared from the face of the earth."

"So who else do you think is on the list? Governor Foster? Coach Prince? Anybody else?"

"We really don't know. Logic would say Foster and Prince. Maybe some old Mafia guys he dealt with, if they are even still alive. Their life spans can be pretty short. We know the coach is worried. He has asked the Knoxville police for additional security, saying he has had a threat on his life."

"Real or perceived?"

"Pretty sure it's perceived," Sarah said. "He reads the news, he sees what is coming."

"Sounds to me like this thing is going to bring the coach's life crashing down, one way or the other, if this story gets out." Jake rocked back in his chair. "Wow," he said, shaking his head. "So what is it you need me for?"

"We think that Bobby Wayne may very well be hiding and operating around here, maybe out at his brother's junkyard off Highway 107," Bob said.

"And?"

"We need your help in finding out whatever you can about him. Is he here? We don't think he would be in Newport. Here he might have his brother's protection. We are not assigned out of the FBI offices here in East Tennessee, we work out of Washington," Sarah said. "The former governor is still a very powerful man here in East Tennessee, what with all his business dealings, legal and illegal. We're not sure who is involved, probably some local law enforcement, and dare I say it, maybe even some FBI. We need someone not connected with local law enforcement to help us out. We will pay you your going rate, which is?"

"Three hundred dollars a day, plus expenses, and another two if you need the help of my associate."

"And your associate is?" she asked.

"Ralph. You met him out front when you came in."

"I know what your background is, how about his?" she questioned.

"Retired Marine gunnery sergeant in intelligence, with two tours in Nam. Retired homicide detective, Nashville, where he was my partner. One tough and trusted son of a gun."

"Sounds like he's got a pretty good resume to me," she said. Bob smiled in agreement. "We'll pay you five hundred a day plus expenses for every day you work on this for us," Sarah said. "I have a copy of Agent Little's files on this case out in the car that I'm going to leave you if you want the job. I'll be glad to go over them with you sometime at your convenience, if you'd like," she added with a subtle look and smile.

Once again Jake couldn't help but notice her legs. "I may take you up on that," he said.

Sarah and Bob stood up to leave.

"One more thing before you go," Jake said. "Who recommended me to you?"

Sarah looked at him, smiled, then said, "Why, your ex-wife, of course."

"Of course," Jake said.

CHAPTER 13

NEW YORK CITY
ONE MONTH LATER

Johnny Scarpino was ninety-three years old when he had the stroke. Now he lay in a bed on the eighth floor at Lenox Hill Hospital in Manhattan, tubes going in and out of all parts of his body. He had once been the head of the Scarpino family of Brooklyn. Starting in the late 1950s when he took control from his father, no one in all of the New York City area was more feared or more powerful. At this point in his life, he had to use whatever strength he had left in his body just to push a button to summon a nurse before he could do anything.

At one time the Scarpinos controlled everything that went on in the eastern part of Brooklyn, their territory starting at the Brooklyn Bridge and running out to Coney Island. They also owned two casinos in Las Vegas and were rumored to own parts of some offshore. They had the largest construction companies in Brooklyn and Las Vegas. They built Hoover Dam and most everything on the Vegas Strip. In the early 1960s, Castro had cost them the casino they had just built in Havana. But by the end of the 20th century and the start of the 21st, their empire had been diminished by the New York families all turning on and testifying against each other in federal court, trying to save their own skins. There was a time when this would have been unthinkable, but in the end the government began to prevail in their battle against organized crime. The dominoes, over time, slowly began to fall.

Scarpino had been brought down by federal agents who were able to charge him with failure to pay income tax on money he made in the states of New York, New Jersey, and Nevada as well as for racketeering and for mail fraud in his dealings sent back and forth from Las Vegas. He was convicted, with the help of some of his former associates, and sent off to the Federal Correctional Institution just outside of the little town of Greeleyville, South Carolina. It is, as the old saying goes, in the middle of nowhere. His sentence was for twenty years, and for a man who was about to turn eighty, it was a death sentence. After three years, which included his not being able to attend the funeral of his wife, he told the federal agents just what they had wanted to know in exchange for an agreement to let him go. In 2004 he returned home, moving into a multi-million dollar condo on the upper east side of Manhattan, leaving behind his old Brooklyn neighborhood of Bensonhurst where he had lived since his birth.

He had three children, all boys. They were all educated at Ivy League schools and two had earned law degrees from Yale, the other an MBA at Harvard. In the early 1960s, after losing several million dollars on his Cuban casino, the old man had begun to put his money into real estate in Manhattan, Nevada, the coastal areas of South Carolina, and some select offshore properties, all in his wife's name. His children had been kept away from the old family business. Scarpino had been smart enough to know that way of life was not going to last. The boys all worked for the legitimate business of Brooklyn & Manhattan Realty and Management and its many subsidiaries. In the year of 2012, they legitimately made three hundred sixty-one million dollars and paid taxes on every penny of it. The youngest son, the MBA, was considered one of the rising stars of the New York financial world.

When the FBI went after Scarpino in the early 2000s, they had come after him hard. In his deal he eventually made to get out of prison, the government agreed to leave the companies of Brooklyn & Manhattan

Realty and Management alone. The company had surely been started with mob money at first, but it soon became a self-supporting entity on its own and had grown that way over the years, all under the guidance of his wife, at least on paper, and eventually his sons.

Since getting out of prison, Scarpino had never felt his life had been in any imminent danger. He had denied any protection from the FBI early on, and over time he would come and go around his Manhattan neighborhood pretty much as he pleased until old age started setting in and slowing him down. The days of mafiosos carrying out grudges were going away more and more.

The sons had paid extra for private nurses to sit with Scarpino around the clock as he struggled to recover from the stroke. At this point the entire left side of his body was paralyzed, and the doctors were not sure if he would ever regain the use of that side again. He had recognized his sons that afternoon when they all came together to see him. He tried to converse with them, but his speech was slurred and they had a difficult time trying to make out what he was attempting to say. The boys put on a brave front for him.

The nurse that worked the midnight shift was a smoker and every hour like clockwork, he slipped off into the stairwell to sneak a cigarette. It was against hospital policy, and if he was caught again he would more than likely be fired. Already in his file were two write-ups for smoking on the job. He volunteered for the overnight shifts as he knew there were not many other employees around and the chances of him being caught were slim. It took him the first week to figure out how often the hospital guards made their rounds to each floor. At exactly 2:10 a.m. he slipped out of the room, down the hall, and into the stairwell, three doors down from where Scarpino's room was located. At the same time he was leaning back against the concrete wall and lighting his cigarette, a man, dressed as a doctor, had slipped into the unguarded room and paused beside the bed of Johnny Scarpino. At one time he was the most feared and protected man in all of New York City. The idea that anyone could get into his room would have been unthinkable. With his nurse out to smoke, he now laid helpless in the hospital room, one half of his body decimated by the stroke, and for the most part, unable to move. Scarpino had never been more vulnerable.

"Hello, Johnny, remember me?" the man said softly as he leaned over and whispered into Scarpino's ear. "It's been a while."

The old man awoke, startled, and in a moment his eyes showed that he recognized the face over his bed. His eyes widened with fear and he began to make almost guttural type sounds, his body so impaired. The man reached down and roughly pulled the pillow out from under Scarpino's head, which he let fall back. He placed the pillow over Scarpino's nose and mouth, yet he left his eyes uncovered so he could see just what was happening. The man pushed down hard with the pillow, all the while glaring into his eyes. "I was afraid you'd die before I got the chance to kill you myself," he said. "This is for my aunt and my fiancé." The right side of Scarpino's body fought back with more strength than the man figured he had, but in less than a minute he went limp. The old eyes came to a stop, didn't close and yet seemed to be staring straight ahead. For all the horror they had seen in their life, the last thing they saw was death as it came. The monitor next to the bed flat lined. The man pulled Scarpino's head up, stuffed the pillow back under it, turned around, and walked out of the room. As he quickly went around the corner, he heard footsteps, most likely that of the nurse, coming back from the stairwell and rushing to the room. Just like that the man was gone, vanishing off into the night. Nobody at the hospital had seen him come or go.

It was assumed Johnny Scarpino died of natural causes, a tired, worn out old man of ninety-three. The nurse said as much, saying he appeared to just go in his sleep. There would be no autopsy to prove otherwise, the old man having instructed his sons some months before that he didn't ever want that to happen to him.

That didn't stop his sons from being suspicious, it came second nature to them.

CHAPTER 14

Susanne arrived home to the Governor's Mansion at a little bit after nine. She had cut back on the staff there since taking over back in January, and at night there was no one in the big, old house except her. She did have workers there during the daytime; two gardeners to keep up the grounds and two maids to keep up the inside of the house. Her longtime secretary Betty had set up an office there so they could work out of the house if they needed to. In the past, the governors had drawn their domestic staff from the nearby state prisons. Susanne had done away with that program, not believing it had virtue. Now, when she hosted a special event, they used a firm to bring in extra help. At night, the house could be a large and lonely place. She went to the kitchen, poured herself a glass of wine, and fixed something to eat.

After doing what everyone thought was a great job as a two-term mayor of Nashville, Susanne threw her hat into the ring and made a run for the governorship. Only her move came with a twist. She had been a lifelong Democrat, having grown up in a Democratic family, and was elected mayor on that ticket. After being attacked and beaten in a case of domestic violence by her second husband, a big time player in state Democratic circles, she quickly divorced him and his powerful family.

What a mistake that marriage had been in the first place. She had been charmed and smitten by him at a time she and Jake had been inexplicably drifting apart. She had let her infatuation with him destroy her marriage to Jake, and after quickly marrying, she soon discovered she was one in a long list of his women. His plan was to ride with her, first to the mayor's office, then on into the Governor's Mansion, bringing with it the opportunity for more power, money, and deals throughout the state. That plan came crashing down when he assaulted her in the kitchen of their upscale Nashville home. When the time came to file papers for the governor's race, she stunned everyone when she announced that she was switching to the Republican Party. She had divorced the Democrats as well.

Her popularity had never been higher, according to the pundits. This was due to her great job as mayor and sympathy from most of the women in the state, unfortunately, due to what had happened to her at the hands of her ex-husband, the second one. Polls showed support for her could come from both parties. She left the office of mayor in December and hit the ground running for the governorship on the first of January.

She jumped into the primary, along with a longtime state senator and the lieutenant governor, who appeared to be more interested in what was happening on the national stage than at home in Tennessee. Before the primary race was over, both opponents were facing scandals of their own making. The senator was hit with sexual harassment charges brought by an ex-secretary who claimed he was the father of her child. The lieutenant governor was being questioned by the Washington Post about large amounts of funds donated from out of state into his campaign and how those funds were possibly being used personally. He stumbled badly at a press conference where the issue was raised, and from that point on the story never seemed to go away.

Susanne worked the state hard, traveling non-stop from January until the primary election in August. She visited every town in the state, every festival, and spoke wherever she was given the opportunity. She pulled out a narrow one percentage point win in the primary and moved on to face the Democratic challenger. He was a lawyer from Jackson, and this was his first run at a political office. That would prove to be no contest as she took sixty-eight percent of the vote. The Republicans were glad for the win, but they anxiously waited to see how she would govern. Susanne quickly eased those concerns as her cabinet appointments were all well-received. Quickly, she had moved from a moderate Democrat to a moderate Republican. It was a good thing in a state where the Republicans were dominating the politics, controlling both the House and the Senate. Chances are she would have never gotten elected as a Democrat. She was also lucky that the troubles surrounding her Republican primary opponents played right into her hands.

Her date to her inaugural ball had been her first husband, Jake. He even took the stage and played a set for her. A couple of weeks before, over lunch, he had asked her if she could name her top five all-time favorite songs. First he gave her his, then she did the same. What she didn't know was that he was going to play them for her at her big night at Nashville's War Memorial Auditorium. He brought down the house, and he had a hard time stopping her from hugging his neck and crying when he finished. They had a wonderful week together, attending all the festivities that went along with her attaining the state's highest office. They also, for the first time in several years, enjoyed being back in each other's company.

Now she sat in the kitchen of the Governor's Mansion, ate her dinner, drank her wine, and then picked up the phone and dialed his number. It rang several times before there was an answer.

"Hello," came the response over a lot of background noise.

"Jake, it's Susanne," she shouted into the phone. "Where in the world are you?"

"Hey, hold on a second...let me step outside." In a moment, most of the background noise disappeared. "Now can you hear me?" he asked.

"Yes, that's a lot better."

"Hey, I'm playing at The Down Home and right now I'm on break. You called at just the right time." The Down Home is a famous music venue in downtown Johnson City. It is a small and intimate place, but the list of those who have played there over the years is legendary. Jake played there a couple of times a year, going back over twenty years.

"I wish I was there to hear you."

"Yeah, that would be great. Listen, what's up? I've got to go, I'm due to go back on."

"Jake, I'm going to be in Johnson City three weeks from Wednesday for an engagement at the university. You doing anything for dinner that night?"

"Not that I know of. I don't normally plan that far out, you know."

"So we can get together? I'm staying at the Carnegie."

He thought about it for a moment, not sure what he wanted to say, then said "Sure."

"Meet me there at 7:30."

"I'll be there."

"Jake, one more thing. I know you got to go…but I love you…and I am so sorry for all I've put you through. I just had to say this…"

"Okay…listen…" He paused, wanting to say something but not sure what to say or how to say it. "I'll see you then," he said and hung up, unable to get out just what he wanted to tell her. Standing on the street outside the side door, it was starting to rain, and he looked to the dark, drizzly sky. He had no idea where this was all about to go, or for that matter where he wanted it to go. Turning slowly, shaking his head, he went back through the side door to go inside and do his last set.

CHAPTER 15

JONESBOROUGH

It was just after midnight and Ralph trudged through the woods on his way to the top of a small ridge just across from the entrance of the junkyard located off of Highway 107. Trudging along, the down pouring rain didn't make his trip any easier. He had parked Jake's old pickup close to a mile away at a campsite, then made his way down the old country road until he was around two hundred yards from the junkyard entrance. There he cut to the left and made his way around the backside of the ridge, slipping and sliding on old, wet leaves. He was struggling to reach the top where he would set up his observation point.

"I am too damned old to be doing this," Ralph said to no one in particular. "Way too old." Twice going up the ridge he had to stop and catch his breath, bending over with his hands on knees. An old football coach had once told him that was a sign of weakness. "Easy for him to say," he said out loud as he remembered it even though there was no one to listen. Once at the top, he laid out on a tarp he brought, pulled out a camera from his backpack, and focused it in so as to be ready to begin taking pictures. It was going to be a long, wet night. The forecast was for the rain to last until late in the morning. From his vantage point he was able to see all the coming and going that went on at the junkyard.

What Ralph was observing, on this his third night of surveillance, was that starting each night around 2:00 a.m., a steady stream of high-dollar late model cars were being driven into the compound, then into a very large metal warehouse building. So far, on this night, he had observed a BMW, a Mercedes, a Porsche, a Land Rover, a Corvette, and a very expensive-looking Dodge pickup truck all come in. There were even a couple of older model cars, a Chevelle and a Mustang. Through his high-powered camera lens he was able to make out the tags on cars, and they were from all over the eastern states. An hour or two later, tractor-trailers, loaded with the same cars, would start pulling out of the warehouse. Vans soon followed, he quickly surmised, with the drivers inside. They would probably be taken to the airport where they were sent out all over to steal another round of cars. Just before daylight on the first two nights, all the activity stopped. It was obvious to Ralph that what he was observing was a major stolen car operation. He had snapped pictures of all the comings and goings. If the FBI wanted to move on the junkyard and conduct a search for Bobby Wayne, they could certainly use this as a reason to go in. Out of state car tags surely meant these people were crossing state lines to conduct their illegal business. Theft through interstate commerce would bring the federal agents into play. He laid on the tarp and snapped away. At 3:30 he watched a black, late model BMW pull up to the building and park outside the main door. He kept taking pictures as he made out what he thought were three men in the car, but he was unable to get any clear photos of the occupants since they got out of the car in the rain with hats on and their coats pulled up around their faces. Nevertheless, he snapped away.

At a little after 4:00 a.m., the steady rain kept Ralph from hearing a group of men that approached him from behind until it was too late. An ax handle into his ribs was his greeting. He rolled over and tried to get to his knees when the second blow came to his jaw and he went over hard back to the ground, blacking out. When he came to, they had him up and against a tree, a rope under his arms and around his chest holding him up. Spitting out blood from the blow to his jaw, he was trying not to choke on it. He looked around and counted; as best he could make out, there were four of them. His head felt like it was about to come off and it hurt to breathe.

"Ralph. That is your name, ain't it?" The oldest one of them did the talking, shouting in the driving rain.

Ralph didn't respond which quickly brought the end of the ax handle hard into his gut.

"Boy, it might be in your best interest to talk to me," the man said as he spit at Ralph's feet from the large wad of tobacco his mouth held. "Let's try again." He took his free hand and pushed Ralph's head back hard into the tree. "Am I getting your attention, mister?"

Ralph grunted.

"You better talk to me, boy, unless you want another shot of this," he said, holding up the ax handle with his other hand.

"You know who I am," Ralph replied, gasping for air, still trying to get his breath from the blow to his stomach.

"You're right. I do know who you are, and I know what you are doing here," he replied. He was up in Ralph's face and pieces of the tobacco flew from his mouth and onto Ralph as he spoke. The smell of alcohol, the hot and sweet, yet sickening smell from someone who drank too much, permeated his senses. "You and your partner are looking for my brother, but you ain't gonna find him here. All you boys have done is screw up my car business, and now I'm gonna have to relocate it for a while. You boys be costin' me a lot of money, and I don't much like my flow of money being cut off, you know what I'm a sayin'?" His nose was touching Ralph's face and the bits of tobacco were spraying him. The smell of his breath was nauseating, a mixture of the tobacco and alcohol. The man backed up a couple of feet. "Ya'll take him on down to the bottom," he said as he spit, then wiped his chin with his jacket sleeve. "If I kill him here we gotta drag his big ass down off the ridge." He grinned at Ralph, the rain dripping off the front of his grease-stained hat. Ralph had been in some tough situations before, but he was starting to think maybe none as bad as this.

They untied him from the tree, removed his rain gear, pulled his hands behind his back, and tied them together so tight that it cut off the circulation. One of them placed a thick rope with a noose around his neck to lead him with. He pulled it tight, all the while looking at Ralph with a profound sense of anger. He also reeked badly of alcohol, so much so that it seemed to Ralph it was oozing out of his pores.

The older man said, "Let's go, big boy." He jabbed Ralph in the ribs again with the ax handle. "You don't keep up, there'll be more of that," he shouted in his ear over the sound of the heavy rain. Someone pushed him from behind and they started moving. The ground was wet and muddy and Ralph slipped and slid along. He had trouble keeping his balance with his hands behind him, and every time he went down, someone either kicked him or punched him as they picked him up. The rope tightened when they pulled on it, and its roughness was burning his skin. The faster he could move, the less tension there was on his neck, so he pushed to keep up. Twice he went down and rolled off, only to be pulled up and continuously beaten as they drug him along, his feet slipping and sliding, trying to get back under him. By the time they finally got to the bottom Ralph was soaking wet, covered in mud, horribly pummeled and bloodied, and it was all he could do to stay alert. They pushed him up against another tree, but this time they didn't bother to tie him to it as he was so weak and exhausted he couldn't move. The mean one held him up.

"You and Jake working for the FBI?" the older man asked. Ralph didn't respond. He obviously knew who they both were and what they were up to. The man turned, took a couple steps back, then came right back at him. "They tell me you were some big war hero in Vietnam. That right?" Again, Ralph didn't answer. "You know I was over there." He spit more tobacco juice on his boots. Ralph just looked at him out of his one eye that wasn't yet swollen shut. In a moment, he gathered his strength and spit in the man's face with a mouthful of blood. The old man wiped it off with his sleeve and just laughed. Then the smile went away as he took the ax handle, turned it sideways, and came down hard twice on Ralph's knee, followed by another blow to his ribs. It was the last thing Ralph remembered as he passed out.

Jake got home at about two in the morning. He had stayed at The Down Home until a little after midnight, and as he usually did after playing there, went with some friends to the Waffle House to eat and wind down. He sat down in his living room and read a couple of newspapers that had been lying around for a few days, and by 3:00 he was in bed where he had no trouble going to sleep. Three hours later, he was awakened by Butch barking at something outside. At first he told him to knock it off and go back to sleep, but Butch kept it up. Jake made his way down the hall and quickly found that his living room was lit up by bright lights from outside that shined through the front window. Getting his handgun, he opened the front door and stepped out onto the porch. It was a vehicle with its headlights on high beam, blinding Jake in a way so that he couldn't truly make out who or what it was. He shielded his eyes with one hand, holding the pistol in the other. The vehicle was parked in his front yard, the lights shining directly at the front door.

"Morning, Jake."

The voice startled him as it came from off to his left. There, sitting in his front porch swing was a man. Jake, distracted and blinded by the lights, had not seen him when he came out.

"It's been a long time," he said.

Though it had been over thirty some years, Jake quickly recognized the voice, then the face.

"I like what you done with the old home place," the man said. He held a gun in his hand. "Jake, why don't you just ease that gun of yours down to the porch and let's talk. You are somewhat outnumbered, I got two out there with guns as well." He motioned to the yard. Jake bent over and laid the gun down, then slowly stood back up. The man smiled, motioned to the vehicle, and the headlights went off. "Sit down here, Jake, let's talk. Hell, we got some catchin' up to do, you and me." Jake sat in the rocker next to the swing.

"What brings you to see me at this time of the morning?" Jake asked while trying to look and see who else was out in the yard.

"We had some good times playing ball back in the day, didn't we, Jake? You remember that Greeneville game, our senior year? You made one hell of a block, sprung me for an eighty-yard run that won the game."

"Bobby Wayne, as best I recall, you made most of that run on your own."

"Naw, you made the block on the linebacker and Virgil took out the corner and I was gone."

"I might've got in that old boy's way a little bit."

"You just bein' modest, Jake. You was always that way. You was a hell of a football player. I played with guys at Tennessee who wasn't nowhere good as you, and that's the God's honest truth. I mean it, Jake, I ain't just blowin' smoke." He sat back in the swing and gazed off. "Those were the good days, Jake," he added, "at least for me."

"Well, they were good days, but I've had some pretty good ones since then," Jake replied. As best he could make out there were two other men with guns drawn.

"Jake, you remember that gal you dated in high school, Susie?"

"Sure."

"You know she took up with me after you left Jonesborough and joined the Marines? It was that first summer I come home from Tennessee. I think she liked it that I played football at UT. I think she liked it a lot." He looked at Jake and grinned.

"Why you telling me this?" Jake asked.

"I didn't know if you ever knew that, Jake. I guess I just wanted to come clean about it," he said, staring at him, the smile now gone.

"I don't know that I knew that, but as I recall she took up with somebody else before I got out of Parris Island, that's why we never got back together."

"I think she took up with Virgil for a while as well, Jake. I bet you didn't know that."

"You're right, Bobby Wayne, I didn't know that. She'd be one of the few that Virgil ever took up with that he didn't marry. Why you bringing her up? You getting' a kick out of telling me all of this?"

"I don't know…I guess seeing you after all these years, it just reminded me of her. I wrote her from prison a time or two, but never got a response. How about you, Jake, you ever get back with her? She still around here? I tell you now…that was one good-looking girl."

"I have no idea. Last I heard of her she was married and living in Atlanta. I saw her sister in the grocery store the other day, but I managed to avoid her."

"Yeah? Her sister was a good-looking woman, too. You know, Jake, just between you and me, I used to see her as well. She liked it that I played football at Tennessee, too. Their mamma really liked me, too. She was a good looker."

"Sounds to me like you must have been a pretty popular guy after I left," Jake said. This guy has the morals of a snake, he thought to himself.

"Yeah, I guess maybe I was."

Jake didn't really care for this conversation the two of them were having, and he didn't care for the fact that Bobby Wayne had a gun and he was compromised into putting his down. The morning light was starting to make its way up and he looked around and was now able to make out the vehicle in the yard. It looked to be his old truck. He stood up. Bobby Wayne motioned with his gun for him to sit back down.

"I think that is the truck my friend Ralph was using tonight." Jake said.

"Just sit back down, Jake, we'll talk about Ralph in a minute."

"Where is he?"

"Listen, Jake, you don't need to be worried about Ralph."

"I'm thinking maybe I do."

"I'm guessing you are wanting to know the real reason I stopped by."

"I asked you a question."

"Jake, let's just say that this is a cordial visit on my behalf to ask you to stay out of my business. For old time's sake, okay?"

"I asked you is that my truck and if it is, where is Ralph?"

"Why you wanting to help the FBI look for me, Jake?"

"I want to know where Ralph is," Jake demanded.

"The FBI...come on, Jake. You ought to know you can't trust them. The Federal Government of the United States of America. They sent you to Vietnam, Jake...how'd that work out for you?" He looked at Jake and smiled. "That woman agent, what's her name? Sarah? Yeah, Sarah. She's a good looker, Jake, but from what I've been told, you can't trust her at all. She's very ambitious and wants to make her way to the top as quickly as possible and she don't care who gets in her way. You better watch out for her, Jake. Don't be lured in by her charms, my boy, if you know what I mean. And that Bob Donner, they say he has a file full of reprimands for the way he does business. I've done had one of them FBI boys cross me up, Jake, and it didn't work out too good for him." He looked down at his gun and then at Jake. "You can tell these two that if they don't back off, the same fate awaits them."

"Sounds like a threat to me."

"It's not a threat, it's a fact."

"Where's Ralph?"

"Ralph?"

"Yeah, Ralph. You know who I'm talking about. Looks to me like you boys brought my truck, which he was driving tonight, out here with you."

"Let's just say that your buddy Ralph was trespassing tonight on my brother's property and he got caught. They say he was takin' pictures up there, and I guess my brother didn't much like it. Felt like he was interfering in his business."

"And?"

Bobby Wayne stood up. "I guess if you are really wanting to know, then follow me." They stepped off the front porch, then walked through the yard to the truck. The rain had finally stopped. When they reached it, Bobby Wayne nodded to the two men with him who stood on the opposite side. One reached down and pulled back the tarp in the bed of the truck. There lay Ralph, very badly beaten, covered in mud and blood, and not moving. Jake wasn't sure if he was dead or alive.

"What the hell have you people done?" Jake exclaimed loudly.

"He's not dead, Jake, if that's what you are worried about. Like I told you, he was trespassing on my brother's land, and well, he's paid the price for it. My brother and some of his boys, when they asked him nicely to leave, they say he tried to put up a fight." He looked down into the truck. "I would say he lost that fight." He looked back up at Jake and shook his head, all the while frowning. "I told my brother I knew where you lived, so I volunteered to bring him to you."

"You're all heart," Jake replied sarcastically.

"The least I could do."

"I need to get him to a hospital," Jake said.

"Let's you and me finish our conversation first. You see, Jake, you don't need to be helping the FBI, or anybody else for that matter, look for me. I'm doin' what I've got to do. There are people who have wronged me, and all I'm doing is paying them back." He pulled out a pack of cigarettes and shook one out. "Cigarette, Jake?"

Jake looked into the back of the truck at the badly beaten Ralph and wondered how much time he had, if he was even still alive.

Bobby Wayne put the cigarette in his mouth, pulled out his Zippo lighter, struck it, then cupped his hands and lit it. "Jake, my family has a lot of business here in East Tennessee. We've been doing business here for a long, long time, and really we don't need you or anybody else pokin' around in it. You should know enough about how things work around here, the law ain't gonna mess with us. We been taking care of them for years…"

Jake was fuming but tried not to show it. "From what I can tell, you've done killed at least four people since you escaped from prison. I heard today you have added a Mafia Don to your list. Even for you, that's pretty bold."

"Yeah, well, there are more to come. Like I said, I'm just makin' some paybacks." He dropped the cigarette to the ground and stubbed it out with his boot, then stepped up close to Jake, almost pinning him back against the truck. The gun in his hand kept Jake from going at him. "You're right, Jake, I have been killing some people and I'm getting' ready to kill some more," he whispered in his ear. Then he stepped back and said, "But I like you, Jake, I always have. We go way back, you and me." He paused, his demeanor changing. "But you know something, I think you have always thought you was a little smarter than me. Going all the way back to school, I think you have always felt that way. I think that's why we was never closer friends than we were." He paused again. "You better consider what happened to your friend Ralph here tonight a warning. You stay out of my business and I got no reason to mess with you, or for that matter, that pretty little ex-wife of yours, the governor. I know you wouldn't want anything to happen to her. Didn't I see where she's gonna be up here pretty soon for a visit?" He gave Jake a hard stare and then said, "I don't care if she is the governor, I can get to her if I want. And believe me, Jake, you damn sure don't want that to happen."

At that moment, Ralph moaned from the back of the truck. At least he's still alive, Jake thought.

"You just remember what I said, Jake. You stay out of my business and we'll be fine." He motioned for his two henchmen to come and they slowly backed out of the yard, one on either side of him, eased into a black BMW that was awaiting them, and left, throwing mud and gravel all around as they roared the car to life, fishtailing it up the road.

"Sons of bitches, your day will come," Jake said aloud to himself as he watched them pull out while running to the porch to get his gun. He then quickly returned to the truck. He reached down into the back, found Ralph's wrist, and checked to see he still had a pulse. "Hang on, buddy, we're on the way." He jumped in the truck, found the keys in the ignition, fired her up, and drove Ralph towards the emergency room at the Johnson City hospital, some twenty miles away. He was hoping and praying the whole time that he was not too late.

As Jake pulled out and headed towards town, he called the number given to him by the FBI agent Sarah Workman, and was surprised when she immediately picked up.

"Jake?" she asked, obviously recognizing his number.

"Yeah, it's me. Listen, I can't say much now as I'm driving Ralph to the emergency room…"

"What's happened?"

"Well, they caught him out at the junkyard and brought him to me in the back of my truck…beat within an inch of his life…if he doesn't die on me before I get him there."

"Oh my God," she said with an air of sorrow. "Jake…"

"Listen," he said, cutting her off, "I can't really talk now and drive like I need to…so do me a favor. Call the hospital and tell 'em we're coming and why…can you do that for me?"

"Sure…"

"We're a good twenty minutes away."

"I'll call right now."

"Hey, listen…I will tell you this. Bobby Wayne…he's here."

"You see him?" she asked.

"Yeah, he's the one brought Ralph back, he and a couple of his boys."

"Okay."

"One more thing…they were in a late model BMW, Tennessee tags. He threatened you guys, he threatened the governor, if I don't back off."

"Well, it looks like you did what I asked you."

"Yeah…"

"You found out where he is. So we'll handle it from here."

"Not now, not with what they did to Ralph. Bobby Wayne better pray he don't die."

"Listen, Jake, we take it from here, that's just the way it is."

"So you used me and Ralph as bait to bring him out? Is that it?"

"No, not at all. We just needed someone with local knowledge."

"Well, you got it, so you do what you got to do, but he's not seen the last of me, whether I'm helping you or not." He hung up.

"Jake…Jake?" she said into a dead phone. I guess we'll finish this conversation at the hospital, she thought to herself as she reached into the nightstand for her phonebook.

CHAPTER 16

DEL RIO

As they had for the last ninety years or so, people came from all over the southeast for the Wednesday night cock fights in Del Rio. Edward Jefferson Foster III had at one time been a judge, a state senator, and twice been elected governor of Tennessee. He was also the owner and proprietor of The Del Rio Gentlemen's Club. It had been a part of his family for three generations, having been started by his grandfather, the first Edward Jefferson Foster, just after his return from fighting the Germans in France with the United States Army in World War I. At no time since the club began had it ever been raided by the law. Not local, not the state, and certainly not federal agents. It was long rumored that a team of two FBI agents, sent into the area by J. Edgar Hoover himself, disguised as construction workers, had tried to infiltrate the club back in the 1940s only to disappear and never be seen again. Some say that they were buried alive one night in the TVA dam that forms Douglas Lake with cement from the mixer that they worked with during the daytime poured over their bodies.

If you wanted into the club for the cock fights, your name had better be on the pass list controlled by the governor's right hand man, Oscar DeLaterra. A Cocke County sheriff's car sat parked just across the road from the entrance. A word to them and you would be hauled off to the jail on some trumped-up charge. You entered on a dirt road that took you back almost a half of a mile from the main road. Several armed men were posted all around the outside of the building.

The action started right at midnight and usually went until around sunup. Large sums of money changed hands. It was rumored that top fights could have seen as much as a three hundred thousand dollar bet. The former governor made his appearance at 3:00 a.m. He made the rounds of the building, stopping and talking and glad-handing most everyone there. This was his domain. He signaled with his hand to make bets as he moved through the crowd. This particular night was a big night for him. His prize cock, Ol' Big Red, was going in the main event, scheduled to go last, against a top bird brought in from Mexico just for the occasion. Drinks were available at two bars, one built on each end of the building and staffed by good-looking, scantily clad women. The theory, Las Vegas style, being that the more people drank, the more they bet. The difference between here and Las Vegas was that the drinks were not given away. The cigarette and cigar smoke was so thick you could cut it with a knife. No bans on that in here. You want a real Cuban cigar? They had those as well.

The cocks were held in an adjacent room off the back of the building until it was time to bring them in. Foster had a separate room for his private stock of birds next to that. At around 4:30, his man Oscar was given the sign to have his handler sent back to get Ol' Big Red prepped and ready to go. The former governor remained at his seat, joking and laughing with a couple of longtime friends as they awaited the main match. "Gentlemen," he said, "this is the best fighter I have ever had, and as you well know, we have had some good ones over the years."

"You have always had the best, sir, make no mistake about that. That's why we came up tonight from Florida. Damn it, Ed, I wouldn't miss it," the man sitting closest to him said. "I've bet a lot of my money on this ol' bird of yours."

"Me too, Ed. When you called, I was ready to go," the other one added.

At that moment, Foster saw Oscar come running out of the back room, hurrying toward him. He knew right away something must be wrong. "Excuse me, gentlemen, I'll be right back," he said, getting up and starting to make his way toward him. He had come to his attention some twenty years earlier as the liaison and leader of the migrant workers that he brought in every year to work his farms. It wasn't long until Oscar moved his family to the United States and was working for Foster full time. He met Oscar at the side wall, out of earshot of the others.

"Sir, you must come with me. We have a problem."

"What is it, Oscar?"

"Please, sir, come with me. To the back."

"Oh, all right." They started making their way through the crowd, people reaching out to Foster to shake his hand or slap him on the back. This time he obliged them, but never stopped walking. They went through the door at the back, through the room where all the others kept their birds. People were milling around, talking, drinking, and laughing. His handler stood guard at the other door where he kept his cocks, and he nervously let them in as they approached.

It was a simple cinder block room with cages around where they kept the birds they planned to fight that night, plus ones they had brought in to be sold off. In one corner was an old wooden desk and chairs where Foster sometimes conducted business. He quickly deduced the scene. Ol' Big Red lay on the concrete floor with patterns of blood spread all around, his head having been cut off. As anyone who has ever killed a barnyard chicken knows, you cut off their head, drop them to the ground, and they will run around in circles for a few moments on adrenaline until they finally give out and fall over. Foster surmised that was what had happened here. Nothing had been done to the other cocks in the room.

Oscar said, "Sir, Jose knows nothing about what has happened in here. He says he was outside the door all night and that every thirty minutes he would come in and check on them. He says that is the God's honest truth."

"Si, senor. Every thirty minutes, just like I am supposed to," Jose replied, obviously scared to death. He was in this country illegally, liked it here, and wanted no part of something that would send him back. He was paid good money for handling the former governor's birds.

Foster looked around the room at the bloody mess on the floor, his prize bird, now decapitated. Looking up and around, he noticed it, at the back of the room near the ceiling, two windows that had been put in to allow in some sunlight. One of them was open. It was just big enough for an average-sized man to be able to come through.

"Sir, the boy says no one ever came through these doors. He has guarded them the whole time…"

"Si, senor. That is right. No one. I swear to Jesus, sir. I swear to mi madre…."

Foster put out his hand to stop them from talking. He slowly circled around the room, all the while looking at the window. His old face had lost all its color, turning ashen. "I know who did this," Foster said. He paused, staring off in the distance. "And I know how he got in and out, and I know why. He left the window open to let me know."

Oscar pulled his walkie-talkie from his belt. "I will alert the men, sir."

The old man tried to take a deep breath. He waved him off with his hand. "It will do no good, I can assure you. He is long gone from here. He slipped in and slipped out."

"Are you sure, sir?" Oscar asked.

"Damn it, boy, I can tell you that even if he's not gone, none of these men here are a match for him." He looked around the room, almost wild in his comportment. "He could kill them all, every last one of them," he said, waving his arm about, "if he had wanted to."

CHAPTER 17

KNOXVILLE

Tennessee's football season was off to a pretty good start. They opened with a three touchdown victory over Wyoming at home in Neyland Stadium. The second week of the season they took on Memphis in Nashville at the Tennessee Titans stadium and came away with a relatively easy thirty point victory. Next up was their first big challenge of the year, a trip to Chicago's Soldier Field to take on Notre Dame in one of those big, nationally-televised, made-for-TV games, this one airing on ABC. Tennessee fell behind early, then rallied from thirteen points down in the fourth quarter to squeeze out a narrow one point victory. It was the first major upset by a Tommy Prince team since his return to Knoxville. For the first time in over ten years, the Vols landed back in the top ten in both the Coaches and the AP polls. Prince was starting to do what he had been brought home to do. Lying ahead, though, was a four game SEC gauntlet. Florida at home, Georgia in Athens, back home with Alabama, then a trip to Columbia to take on South Carolina. All four teams were currently ranked in the top twelve teams in the nation.

Tommy was now immersed in football, and the dealings of Bobby Wayne, though not quite gone from his mind, had been pushed to the back. On this Monday afternoon of Florida week, he was ready to have his weekly press conference and get it over with, then move on to getting his team prepared for the incoming Gators.

He met with the media on the field in the Vols indoor football complex. It started as it usually did, the coach going over a list of players who were hurt or suspended, ones that would not be expected to play that Saturday. Then he talked for a few minutes about the big win over Notre Dame and what it meant to his program. Tommy went on about the rich history and traditions of both programs, and he talked about some of the previous games that had been played between the two schools. This was not something he would normally do, but he didn't want to pass on the opportunity to bask a little in the glow of getting his program to where it could beat the likes of a Notre Dame team on a national stage. The crowd for the press conference was much larger than normal and he wanted to take advantage of it. He figured there were at least twice as many members of the media present as there were after their first game of the season. That was no doubt a good thing, he thought to himself. Looking out over the top of his reading glasses that were pushed down on his nose, he said, "Ladies and gentlemen, let's come down off our cloud from beating Notre Dame now and shift our focus to the matter at hand, that being the University of Florida Gators. Over the years, we have all seen some really good national championship caliber teams come out of Gainesville, teams coached by Steve Spurrier and Urban Meyer, guys who I think are two of the best coaches to ever work in the SEC. After spending all day Sunday watching film of this Gators team, I think that without a doubt, this Florida team could be as good as any of those teams coached by the guys I just mentioned."

The media members let out a collective groan since so far all the Gators had done was beat up on three cupcakes, one of which they trailed at halftime.

"Believe me," he responded. "This is a very, very good football team. Very athletic."

After a few more comments, Tommy opened the floor up to the media. He started on one side and worked his way around the room. He got the usual questions a coach gets about his offense, his defense, and what he planned to do differently this week. There were questions about certain players on both teams. Someone wanted to know "had you saved some things, waiting for the SEC schedule to start?"

"We did play Notre Dame last week, so…hey, I don't think we held anything back," the coach said. "We did have to come from behind to win," he added and then he paused for a moment. "But then again, maybe we did," he said, flashing a grin. He pointed at a young lady on the far right hand side of the room. As he did, he looked down at his watch which he had taken off and placed on the podium when he started. He picked it up and started sliding it onto his wrist. It was his sign to the reporters that this thing was just about over.

"Yes, sir, Laura Beth Johnson from the *Johnson City News & Neighbor,*" she politely said.

"Have you been here before?" the coach asked. This should be an easy one he thought.

"No, sir, it's my first time," she replied, looking around and smiling. She had the attention of everyone in the room.

Tommy smiled. "And what is your question?" he said, rocking back and forth on his heels while holding the podium with both hands. He didn't think things could be going any better.

"Yes, sir," she said, now appearing somewhat nervous. "Well, I was wondering if you have any comment on the recent deaths…I should say apparent murders, for they are being investigated as that, of two of your former New York Jets teammates, and, sir, if you have had any threats on your life?" The place went totally silent, as if all the life and air had been sucked out of it. The young reporter felt the look of every set of eyes in the room on her.

Tommy was obviously stunned by the question, and for what seemed a very long moment, he didn't answer.

Seizing on the silence, the reporter seemed to find more strength and went on. "Is it true you have asked the Knoxville Police Department for added security?"

Now he was tightly grabbing the podium with both hands. Remain calm, he said to himself. Then he started to answer her. "I am aware of those unfortunate deaths, but I can assure you that I know absolutely nothing about them, except what I have read in the press. And as far as I know, there is no reason I should be concerned for my own safety. I am in no way connected to these two men other than the fact they were my teammates at one time, I'm guessing now, over thirty years ago." He glared at her, then smiled. "Do you have anything else you would like to ask me?"

"You didn't answer the question about asking for extra security," she said, tilting her head somewhat to the right then smiling right back at him. The nervousness was no longer present.

"Well, yes, I have had extra security for the past few weeks and we are just being cautious. That's really all I can say."

"And the FBI agent, Larry Little, who was recently murdered in South Carolina. Had you ever had an occasion to meet and speak with him?" she boldly asked.

"I'm beginning to think I need my lawyer here," he said, a halfhearted attempt at trying to make a joke. It didn't go over as he hoped. He looked about the room and knew the cameras and microphones were all rolling and recording. Calm down and don't say anything you will later regret, he said to himself. "Sorry, that's all I have time for," he replied to the group as a whole. "My team is waiting on me." Tommy quickly turned and briskly walked out of the room.

Within a minute, all the other reporters were trying to gather around the young woman and ask her questions. The Tennessee Athletic Department Media Relations staff was trying to corner her, hoping to find out just who she was and how she got in, obviously with credentials as they hung on a lanyard around her neck.

"Get your own stories," she said, pushing her way through them all, heading for the door. They followed her all the way out to her car, surrounding her as she fumbled in her purse trying to find her keys. When she got them, she got in, shut the door as best she could, started the car, and pulled away from the curb, almost hitting a couple of them. Then she roared away, leaving her pursuers in her wake.

One keen observer noted her car had Cocke County tags. "Didn't she say she was from Johnson City?" he asked out loud to anyone that would listen. The assembled media members at the curb all remarked that they had never laid eyes on her before. Whatever her reason, she had unleashed a media storm that was not about to go away anytime soon.

Tommy made his way through the football complex and down the hallway that exited out to the team practice fields. He knew that his life had just changed and things would never be the same again. There were too many members of today's media who wouldn't let this go. He stopped for a moment at the side of the field, bent over and tried to catch his breath. He was light headed, hyperventilating, then he felt nauseous and began to throw up. He quickly gathered himself, straightened up, wiped his mouth on his sleeve, and moved on. People were watching. Damn Bobby Wayne Foster, he thought to himself. He regained his composure, moved out onto the field, blowing his whistle hard. "By God, let's go!" he shouted. He had a team to coach.

CHAPTER 18
DEL RIO

On the following morning, as the former governor sat at his desk and read his Knoxville newspaper, most of it recapping the Tommy Prince press conference from the day before, he received a phone call at exactly five minutes after eight.

"Governor Foster?"

"Speaking." He continued to glance over the paper as the conversation started.

"Yes, Governor Foster, this is Edmund, sir…" There was a pause with no response as first. "Edmund Higgins, sir, from the First Bank of the Caymans." He talked with a heavy British accent.

"Yes, go on with it, man. I hope you're not calling me at eight in the morning with some damned investment strategy."

"Sorry, sir, but no…why no, it's not that at all."

"I don't know how many times I've told you, Higgins, I'm perfectly happy with what you boys are doing with my money. And, not that it's any of your damned business, but I'm perfectly happy with how much money I have in your bank and at this time I don't have any plans to put anymore in there. I have to keep myself liquidated, as we say here in the states, spread my money around. So don't be calling me wanting to get more of my money. What kind of outfit are you guys running down there? Haven't you people heard about all the wiretapping the government is doing up here? Someone is probably listening to us right now." On that assumption he was correct, and it was the FBI.

"No, no, no, sir. That's not the reason for this phone call at all. You say you are happy with what we are doing for you, sir? Can you hold on for just a moment, sir? I'll be right back." Foster was put on hold and some feel good island music was piped in while he waited. Aggravated would be the best way to describe him.

What could this be all about? He wondered. They better come on here with a good explanation, he thought to himself.

Higgins picked back up. "Governor, you don't mind me calling you that I hope?"

"No, not at all. It is a title I certainly earned." He paused. "Go ahead man. What is it?"

"Well, Governor, I am very sorry for the delay, sir, but we are trying to figure some things out on our end." He was starting to sound somewhat nervous at this point.

"What kind of things? What is this all about? Just what do you want?" he said, losing his patience. "Is this some kind of joke?" To the best of his recollection, every time he had gone down there to meet with him, Foster had never seen the man smile, not even when he was depositing large amounts of money into his bank.

"Well, sir, I have just returned from a two week holiday in England. And, well, when I came into the bank this morning, I was told that you, sir, had wire transferred a very substantial part of your deposits with us to one of your accounts in Zurich. I was calling to see whatever we had done to make you so unhappy with our bank that you would move this money."

"This is a joke of some kind, is it not Higgins?"

"No, sir," he replied weakly. "I'm afraid it is not a joke, sir."

"First off, what kind of money are we talking about here?" the Governor asked.

"Well, sir, we were requested to transfer thirty-one million U.S. dollars it appears."

"And does it appear that you did this?" Foster quietly replied, stunned.

"Yes sir, it was done on last Thursday evening at 4:55 eastern time." There was a long pause of silence on the other end. "Governor, are you there?"

"And what if I tell you I don't have a bank account in Zurich? I've never been there in my life."

"Well, sir, it appears that you do…with an international bank that we partner with on certain matters. That is why this all went so smoothly."

"Smoothly? Just for curiosity's sake, can you give me the current balance of my account in your bank? This has to be some kind of mix up."

"Yes, sir, I can do that. I have it right here, somewhere."

Foster could hear him typing on computer keys.

"Yes, sir. It says right here, you now have a little over three thousand dollars."

"Did you say three thousand dollars? A little over? Like how much over? I don't know why I am even asking you this question."

"One dollar and seventy-three cents, sir."

"Higgins, what I would like is for you to put me on hold while you call this bank in Zurich and see if my money is still there, and you better hope, I can't say this emphatically enough, that my money is really in an account with my name on it." He stopped for a moment then continued, "And I want you to tell them that they better transfer that money right back into my account at your bank. You got that?"

"If you will hold on, sir, I will do that." After about five minutes, Higgins came back on. "It seems, sir, that there was an account that was opened last week by yourself and another man."

"That's a little hard to imagine. As I said a moment ago, I have never been to Zurich in my life."

"You know the banks in Zurich are very secretive, but since this one is somewhat tied in with us, I was able to be persuasive and garner some information from them."

Now Higgins was talking like he was doing Foster a favor, when in reality he had just had thirty-one million dollars stolen from his bank. "And just what would that be?" Foster asked, his blood pressure rising by the moment.

"Two men came into their international banking office and opened up this account on Thursday. The older one apparently passed himself off as you. Had all the pertinent information needed, sir, including your passport they say."

As he continued to listen, Foster walked over and opened the wall safe in his office.

"They had all your account numbers as well. The man said they were in a small banking-type book that the older man produced," he explained. "They opened the account there in both of their names."

Foster dug through the safe now, pulling everything out, letting it fall to the floor. The passport and his banking books, containing all his account numbers, were gone, nowhere to be found. It hit him, a sickening feeling that all his bank accounts had probably been cleaned out by now. He felt faint.

Higgins continued. "He said the younger of the two men returned by himself early Friday when the bank opened, there is a five hour time difference you know, and had had the money wired to a bank in Dubai, closed the account, and left the bank."

"Dubai? As in out in the middle of the desert Dubai?"

"Well, yes, you know it has become quite a fashionable place for people to be putting their assets in the last few years. It is a very progressive country."

"I have thirty-one million dollars taken from my account and no one there thinks to try to call me, to verify this? And you are trying to explain to me that people are putting their assets out there? My God, man, I have been robbed. YOU have been robbed, and my money has been taken to the other side of the world. What the hell are you people doing down there?"

"Well. Sir. As I said earlier, I was on holiday and my assistant – should I say my former assistant, he no longer works for us as of this morning –

he said he didn't want to disturb me while I was off. I have fired the bloke, sir. They just faxed us a picture of the two men, and it certainly appears to be you in the picture if I do say so myself. It's uncanny, really."

"This man, the one that came back, what name did he give them?" Foster collapsed back into the chair at his desk and with his free hand searched in his drawer for his nitroglycerin pills. His heart beat as if it were going to explode from his chest. He found them and forced one under his tongue. He picked up the glass of orange juice on his desk and took a swallow, then trying to sit it back down, he dropped what was left of it from his shaking hand onto the desk. The juice went everywhere. Sweat poured from his head.

"He said the second man told him that he was your nephew, a Robert Wayne Foster. He had a United States passport as well. Told the man that everyone called him Bobby Wayne and that you liked to tell everyone that he was your favorite nephew."

"You imbecile, don't you realize that these men have robbed your bank?"

"Sir?"

"I've been robbed, you've been robbed. My God, I'm ruined. YOU ARE RUINED!" He paused momentarily. "I'LL SEE TO IT, you fool." He paused and tried to collect his thoughts.

"You better call those people and demand that I get my money back right now."

"I'm afraid, sir, that is impossible. They have moved the money from one country to another and then to another. They have dealt with people who won't work with us, sir. The Arabs, well they have little use for us British. It goes back many, many years. They dislike us as much as they dislike you Americans, if not more. I'm afraid your money is, well, sir... I'm afraid it is gone."

"Gone?"

"Yes, sir, I'm afraid so. We will notify the authorities, but I don't know that there is anything they can do. It is a risk you take when you bank offshore."

"Listen here, you better get to work on getting my money back, or you'll wish you never heard my name." He slammed down the phone. "Bobby Wayne," he said out loud, though there was no one in the room to hear him.

CHAPTER 19

JONESBOROUGH

Jake caught the story on Coach Prince's press conference on television while he was watching the morning news at the Johnson City Medical Center, all while trying to read an old magazine. He was just killing time and he came out of his chair when he saw it. This is a game changer, he thought to himself. He quickly flipped over to ESPN and saw they were reporting it as well. He was waiting in Ralph's room for the nurses to bring him back from x-rays, hopefully with the good news that he could take him home.

In a moment Ralph came moving slowly back into the room, walking with the help of a cane. "Let's go, padre. We're out of this place." The nurse helping him turned and left.

"You won't believe this, some reporter has apparently asked Tommy Prince about the investigation and if he's involved in it."

"When?" Ralph replied.

"Apparently yesterday afternoon at his weekly press conference. It's a national news story now."

Ralph stood, leaning on the cane, watching the television. "This will just drive Bobby Wayne further underground, don't you think?"

"You can't get much more underground than he already is," Jake replied, keeping an eye on the television as well. "Unless he was behind it. Don't put it past him."

Ralph moved slowly over to the built-in closet, grabbed a plastic bag, and started putting his things into it. "Let's get out of here, Jake, before somebody changes their mind."

"The doc says you're good to go?"

"Somebody did."

Jake's phone rang. He looked at the number. "FBI," he told Ralph.

"Remind them to make sure they take care of my bill here. It's the least they can do," he said to Jake. It had been five days now and his face was still very badly bruised and swollen. He came in with a concussion, a fractured orbital bone, and a broken nose. He took thirty-four stitches in three different cuts. One tooth and a crown were gone from his mouth. Two ribs were cracked. His right knee was severely swollen and bruised but there had been no structural damage or broken bones there, which was surprising for the beating it had taken with the ax handle. "All I can tell you is he's one tough son of a bitch," the emergency room doctor had told Jake that night.

Jake sat down in the chair by the bed and began talking with the FBI agent at great length. The conversation went on for fifteen minutes. When he hung up, he looked at Ralph and said, "Everything here has been taken care of by the FBI so you don't have to worry about that."

"That's good, but I'll feel better when I find out that it has actually been done. You know, I've got some Cherokee in me, so trusting what someone with the government says…well, you know, I can be a little suspicious. I'm pretty sure it's in the genes."

Jake laughed as he remembered when he first met Ralph, some twenty years before in Nashville. Ralph had a bumper sticker on the back of his car with a picture of four Native American warriors with a line underneath it that read, "So you think you can trust the government? Ask an Indian." Some of their bosses, older hard line cops, didn't like it, he recalled. He also knew that Ralph didn't really care whether they liked it or not. He was retired from the Marine Corps with two tours in Vietnam under his belt, and if they didn't want him to work there he would just go on to something else. He didn't worry about what others thought. It was one of the reasons he became such a good homicide detective, and it was one of the reasons Jake liked him so much. Nothing stood in Ralph's way nor was there a question that was too tough to ask. He wasn't concerned with offending anyone to get to the truth.

Ralph looked at Jake and asked, "What else did she say? I know she wasn't calling just to see how my accommodations were being handled."

"I think, in a polite way, they are trying to say our services are no longer going to be needed," Jake replied. "She did say she wanted to meet me tonight for dinner to talk about it."

"I bet she did. I'm thinking we could get a pretty good cat fight going here between her and your ex."

"Emphasis on the 'ex,'" Jake said.

"Really? Some people might buy that, but not me. She is still comin' to town, right?"

"Next week."

"Oh yeah."

"Anyway, I told Sarah I had other plans tonight."

"Oh, you did?"

"Yeah, so now I've got to meet her in the morning at the FBI's office in Johnson City. I probably should take you and sit you down next to me so they have to look at what a beating you took on their behalf. You up for it?"

"Sure I am. I'd like a few words with them about what happened."

"That's what we'll do then," Jake replied.

"She know about the press conference?"

"Yeah, they knew all about it. There's not much they don't know."

Ralph looked puzzled. "The reporter, how did she get on it?"

"Our pretty little FBI agent says she thinks the reporter just did her homework. It was all out there on the Internet and somebody just had to put it together"

"You buying that?"

Jake pondered on the question for a moment. "No. I'm wondering if someone didn't plant her. The story blows up, and maybe it's just what ol' Bobby Wayne wants. The reporter…I'm thinking maybe she's not really a reporter. Maybe she's sent out by Bobby Wayne to start things going against Tommy Prince. Make him start to sweat a little bit. Seems like he's touched everybody that's had anything to do with this story so far."

"I'll vouch for that," Ralph replied, wincing.

"I thought you might." Jake said, looking at Ralph's badly battered face.

"Now, this story breaks out on a national scale, the FBI decides they no longer need us, and somebody's planning to break the news to you tomorrow…is that what you think?"

"Maybe, just maybe, one very ambitious FBI agent we know."

"And so just like that they can't have a couple private eyes hanging around, they're gonna pay us off and say adios?" Ralph quizzed Jake.

"I'm starting to get that impression," Jake answered. "My guess is that FBI agents will be crawling all over the place. I think they used us to find out if Bobby Wayne was hiding around here, thinking that it might lure him out. Maybe they are worried about an inside leak with their own people."

"And it worked."

"That it did."

Ralph was now clearly upset. "I got news for her. I'm going out for this guy and his brother as soon as I am up to it, whether the FBI likes it or not." He looked in the mirror over the sink next to the hospital bed and examined his face. "Yeah, they haven't heard the last of me." He turned around and looked at Jake, then shook his head. He pulled out his sunglasses and put them on. They did little to hide his wounds. Looking back at the mirror, he gingerly rubbed his chin with his hand and said, "They sure did mess up a pretty good-looking face, Jake, don't you think?" He started to laugh but the pain from the broken ribs quickly brought an end to that. He grabbed his bag off of the bed and said, "Let's split this joint. Ain't The Cottage just down the street? I'm overdue for a cold beer."

On the way to The Cottage, Jake observed that they were being followed by an unmarked police car. Black, with tinted windows, the antennas and side lights gave it away. He told Ralph what was happening. As they turned into the parking lot behind the restaurant, the cruiser pulled up and blocked them in. Out of the car came a man that Jake recognized as the Washington County Sheriff. At one time he had been fired by Jake's late uncle, at that time the sheriff, for taking kickbacks from certain undesirables in the county. Now, three election cycles later, he had returned to win the position. These type of things always tend to happen in the South. The sheriff leaned back against the door of his cruiser and waited for Jake and Ralph to get out.

"Afternoon, Jake," he said as they approached, then spit out a large wad of tobacco. "What happened to your friend Ralph, here?"

"Well, Harvey, I think you already know the answer to that question."

Nobody bothered to shake hands with each other. Ralph stood back at the corner of Jake's truck, leaning on his cane.

"Jake, I was real sorry to hear about your uncle's passing last year," the sheriff said, wiping the remnants of the tobacco on his shirt sleeve.

"I don't recall you coming around at the time," Jake replied.

"Best I recall, I was tied up on official business," he responded.

"I'm sure."

"Listen, Jake, I hate to see things like this happen in my county," he said motioning toward Ralph. He looked at Jake who didn't respond. "You do believe that, don't you?"

"I'm listening."

"You know the FBI has a reputation for muddling things up around here?" the sheriff asked.

"Your point being?" Jake replied.

"You boys need to be careful who you get in bed with around here." Then he winked.

"I appreciate your concern, Harvey, I really do. I'll take that into consideration."

"Jake, that's what I was hoping you would say." The sheriff opened his car door and climbed back inside, the tinted window slowly coming down. "Ya'll have a nice day boys, and don't drink too many beers while you're here. I would hate to see you get pulled over on your way back to Jonesborough, Jake." The electric window raised back up, the sheriff now lost behind its dark tint, as he pulled away.

"Nice fellow," Ralph said sarcastically as he slowly ambled across the parking lot.

"Ain't he, though?" Jake replied.

CHAPTER 20

After leaving The Cottage, they headed to Jake's house. Jake didn't have a beer while they were there since he figured he was fair game after the warning from the sheriff. He passed two county cruisers sitting on the side of the road on the short ride from Johnson City to Jonesborough, one of which fell in behind him and followed on his bumper until he turned into his farm. When they pulled in, a car was parked in the driveway and a middle-aged black woman sat on the steps waiting on him. Jake recognized her as he got closer. Her name was Lucille Rogers. They had gone to high school together, and her father, Roosevelt Johnson, cleaned the golf course shop twice a week for Jake.

"Oh, Jake, my daddy is sick and he's askin' for you to come see him." She was crying and obviously had been for a while.

"What's wrong?"

"I don't know, I think his heart is finally giving out on him. He said he needs to see you, he has something very important to tell you, he says. Nothing will do 'til he talks to you."

"Have you called a doctor, an ambulance?"

"No…no…he ain't going to no doctor, he says. He's never been to a doctor in his life. Says he ain't going to start now."

"Never?" Jake asked.

"No, sir. Says he came into this world without one and he plans to go out without one."

"Where is he?"

"At my house. My son, he's a nurse, he's with him."

"He ought to be able to get him to go see a doctor."

"Maybe you don't know my daddy that well, Jake."

"I've known him almost all my life."

"We don't tell him what to do, let's just leave it at that."

"Well, let's go. You lead, we'll follow." Jake climbed back into his truck and Ralph, moving slower, soon followed. "Stay here if you want," Jake said to him.

"No, I'm with you. Let's go. I'll pop a couple more of these pain pills they gave me and I'll be all right, or at least I'll think I am anyway." He washed two down with a cold beer he had gotten from the cooler in the back of Jake's truck.

"That's real smart," Jake said, watching him mix the beer and pain medication.

"Don't worry about it, partner," Ralph replied. He laid his head back against the head rest and immediately dozed off. His head bobbed up and down with the rhythm of the truck.

They went fishtailing up the country lane in pursuit of the old man's daughter who had nervously sped on out ahead of them. Jake thought about Roosevelt. He had known him since he was a child as he had helped Jake's dad harvest his tobacco every year and helped him with other small jobs around the farm. He also knew Roosevelt had worked for Bobby Wayne's dad and brother at the junkyard for many years, but at this point, he thought no more about that. Roosevelt had four daughters and no sons. When Jake was about eighteen, they were cutting tobacco one day when he told Jake that he was about the closest thing to a son he reckoned he would ever have. When Jake moved home and was starting to build the golf course, Roosevelt stopped by one day and asked if he had any small jobs that needed taken care of, just like he had done with his father. Jake was more than happy to give him something regular to do. He had to be at least ninety years old, Jake thought, at the time. Plus, Jake was happy for his company; he had always enjoyed it when Roosevelt was around.

Roosevelt lived alone in a small, two bedroom frame house just outside the town limits of Jonesborough. His wife had died some five years earlier after a long, drawn-out battle with diabetes, but he wouldn't hear anything of it when his daughters, all of whom were married and lived close by, had started in on trying to get him to move in with one of them. Jake followed Lucille into the driveway and parked his truck. He looked around at the yard that contained all sorts of scrap and junk that had been collected over the years. Chickens scurried all about and a large dog laid on the front porch. The dog had gotten up when the vehicles approached, let out a few howls, but when he recognized someone he knew, he quickly laid back down. He was on the downside of his years as well.

"I hate to say this, Ralph, but I believe this is the first time I've ever been to Roosevelt's home, even though I've known him most all my life." They got out of the truck and followed Lucille to the house.

"I hope this old hound don't go before my daddy does. He wouldn't know what to do without him," she said, pausing momentarily on the porch and petting the dog's head. "I guess that sounds kinda bad, but you know what I mean." Once inside, Jake followed her into the bedroom with Ralph just a few steps behind.

The grandson, holding vigil, rose from his chair as his mother introduced him. "He talks about you quite a bit, Mr. Bender," the man said while shaking his hand.

"Jake, that's what everybody calls me."

The old man opened his eyes and looked about. Quickly, he saw Ralph and the condition he was in. His eyes got wider. He was laying in the bed and his breathing was heavy, noticeably so. He seemed to gather his strength, looking at Jake, then said, "I need everyone outta the room, everyone but Jake. I's need to talk at him." With his left hand he made a shooing motion for everyone else to get out of the room. He paid special attention to Ralph as he went hobbling out. Roosevelt reached out and patted the seat next to the bed for Jake to sit down, who started to do as directed. "Shut that door first. What I's got to say is just between you and me."

Jake did as told, then sat down. He noticed that Roosevelt was holding a Bible with his other hand, it laying right up against him.

"Them boys did a number on Ralph."

"That they did. How you know about it?"

"I know who done it, Jake. I heard Ralph tell Virgil the other morning when I was cleaning up that you two was doin' some surveillance at the junkyard. My grandson was working at the hospital when you brought him in. He told me about it the next day. He has heard me talk about you and Ralph. I's just put two and two together."

Jake was thinking about Virgil.

The old man shuffled around in the bed and sat up. "Jake, they all hangin' over me, think I'm dying I guess." He smiled.

"You ever think about going to see a doctor?"

"Don't say that I have."

"Just a suggestion on my part."

"I'll consider it."

"I wish you would, for me," Jake said.

"Jake, you sound pretty much like all the rest of 'em around here." The old man held up the good book. "Jake, you believe in the Bible?"

"Sure, but…maybe not as much as I ought to." Jake looked at Roosevelt, who looked back at him, then he started to laugh. The laughter soon mixed with coughing, revealing a bad rumbling in his chest. It was obvious to Jake that he was in need of medical attention, whether he wanted it or not.

"They say, the older you get, the more sense it starts to make. I heard an ol' preacher say that one time." Roosevelt laid the book down on the bed. The smile and laughter was now gone. "Jake, I been reading it a lot here lately. Wouldn't hurt you to do the same. The closer you get to going to see the Lord, the more you better know."

Jake wasn't sure what to say, so he just listened.

Roosevelt laid back against the headboard of his bed and took a deep breath. Tears began to slowly stream down from his eyes. He reached out and grabbed Jake's hand. "They's something I got to tell you, Jake." The tears continued to flow, rolling down his old cheeks. "I'm an old man, don't got no idea how long I'm gonna live, ya know?" He looked hard at Jake, all the while squeezing his hand. "You and Ralph, ya'll don't need to be fooling around them ol' boys out at that junkyard, no, sir. I been around their types my whole life, and I'll tell ya...you back 'em in a corner... No, sir, they won't think nothing about it. Jake. They'll kill a man and won't think twice about it. They's bodies back in them woods behind that junkyard, Jake. They been buryin' people back in there for years. People get crossways with them boys, they just disappear. I should've told you that before ya'll started going out there." He shook his head, let go of Jake's hand, then wiped away the tears with his sleeve. "I thought I was just mindin' my own business, but I shoulda told you. Look what happened to Ralph. In a way, I see it as my fault for not warning ya." He shook his head.

"Listen, Roosevelt, me and Ralph been dealing with bad guys a long time, we know what we're getting into. Don't you think nothing more about it."

"Nobody's as bad as them boys, Jake. Hell, you know that. You growed up with the meanest one of them all."

"That I did."

Roosevelt picked the Bible up again, opened it up for a moment, and read to himself. Then he shut it, looked up at the ceiling, then at Jake. "They's something I got to tell you, Jake. They's something I got to get off my soul before I die." He began to cough, again a deep rumbling sound coming out when he did. He held out the Bible with one hand, then spoke. "I can't take this pain with me."

"Go ahead, Roosevelt. Tell me what's troubling you."

Roosevelt lay there for a minute, seeming to try and gather strength. "Listen, Jake, I done some bad things working for those people, back in the day. The governor's daddy, Foster Junior they all called him, I worked for him since I was a young boy. I seen a lot of things over the years. Wasn't nobody as mean as that man, Jake. But as bad as them people was, they was good to me. All four of my girls went to college and they all got jobs with the state when Mr. Foster was the governor, you know what I'm saying, Jake? He seen my girls got scholarships to pay for their education. I took care of my family working for them. I done a lot of things I didn't want to do, but my family was better off for it. I guess that was how I looked at it." He lay back against the headboard and once again looked up. His old brown and red eyes seemed to be searching. "Help me with this, Lord," he said. "You think you ask Jesus for forgiveness, it can all just go away?" He paused for a moment. "Naw, I ain't so sure it can, Jake. Some things that happen are just so bad." Now he shook his head.

Jake, holding his hand, squeezed it tight.

"Oh, Lord, Jake, I was there when it happened." Now the eyes were closed, and he slowly shook his head. The cough came back, still deep in his chest. When he was able to stop, he opened his eyes and once again the tears started flowing. "Jake, I was there when they killed them two men by burying them in the concrete in the dam. FBI agents, they was. They was buried alive. They had been coming to the cock fights in Del Rio, a lot of the construction men working' on the dam came. You know, Friday was payday, and the Fosters, they would get their money back from most of 'em before the night was over. But these two boys, they had been askin' a lot of questions since they got into town. Pretty soon ol' Foster Junior figured it out. They kidnapped them one Friday night, or I guess you would say early Saturday morning, as they come out of the fights. They brought 'em out to the dam where we was a-waitin' on 'em. I thought they was just gonna try and scare 'em out of town. But no, sir, I quickly figured out that wasn't the plan, not at all. They put 'em down in two big concrete forms, their hands and feet tied so they couldn't go nowhere. Then they started pouring the concrete in the boxes all around them, a little at a time. Well, you knowed when it got up above their ankles they wasn't goin' nowhere lest somebody pulled 'em out. That one, the young one, it wasn't long 'til he was crying and begging. As it went on, yeah, he broke down, saying he didn't want to die. I seen in the paper when they was reported as 'missing' that he had two little girls, about the same age as mine. That tore me up and I've had to live with it ever since then." He gazed off into the distance. "They had me there to mix the concrete, that's all. I didn't kill nobody, but I guess you could say I played a part in it. Next off they poured it around their legs. Mr. Foster Junior, he says, 'You boys tell us you with the FBI, I'm gonna let you go.'" Again Roosevelt paused, looking upward as if he was seeing it all again. "It got up to their knees, Jake, that youngest one he's really squirmin'. The older one, he's cool, he never moves, just looks straight ahead. Paper said he was a war hero, got all kinds of medals in France in the first big war with Germany. Man go through all he did in the war, then die like that. Just wasn't right."

He shook his head and took a deep breath. "Then the concrete was up to their waist, and the young one, that's when he really breaks down, tells 'em they is both with the FBI, says they's sent there by Mr. Hoover himself. He's really cryin' and carrying on, but the other man, he don't ever move, don't ever make no sound. He just stares straight ahead the whole time. I think he knows right from the start they's gonna die. The one boy, the concrete gets up about his chest, and you can tell he's starting to have a hard time breathin'. It's setting up all around them boys. He looks at Foster Junior, then starts talking to him, gasping for air. He screams out, 'I told you…I'm with the FBI…you said you'd let us go.' I seen right then, the way them Fosters looked at each other and smiled, those two was dead men. His eyes darting all around, God how I remember that. He starts cryin' now for his wife and children. The other one, he don't ever make no sound, he just keeps looking straight on. Foster Junior, he spits tobacco juice on that younger boy, in his face, then says to 'em, 'I don't think I could get you out now, boys, even if I wanted to. That concrete, it's done set up hard around your legs now. Why, we'd have to chisel you out.' He squats down, looks at them men, the concrete now up to their chins, and he says, 'Sorry, they just ain't nothing I can do. You thank ol' J. Edgar Hoover for getting you into this mess.' He motioned to keep pouring and them boys just disappeared into the dam." Roosevelt was crying now, the thoughts of what happened that night tearing at his very soul. "I couldn't stop 'em, Jake. You know that…they'd a put me in that dam right with them other two." He paused, wiping his eyes with one hand and clutching the Bible hard in the other. "What kind of men can do something like that, Jake?"

"I've seen some mean and very cruel people in my day, Roosevelt. They will do things that's hard for a man with any decency about him at all to comprehend."

"That other one, damn him, he never moved or made a sound, Jake. The whole time. He knowed they was gonna kill him and he never let on to 'em."

"That's one hell of a thing to carry around all these years, Roosevelt."

"Ain't nothing but the truth, Jake, so help me God." He held up his hand that was clutching the Bible when he said it. "All three of them Fosters was involved, yes they was. The oldest one, the old man, he leaned on his cane, laughed and said, 'I don't think we gotta worry about Hoover anymore, I can see to that. He better take this as a warning not to come down here and mess with us.' He tossed his cigar butt into the concrete, right on top of them two boys. Then, somebody pulled out a jar of moonshine and they just passed it around 'til it was all gone. Not me, though. I ain't never drank a drop since that day."

Jake looked at Roosevelt. He was laid back against the bed and looked more tired and worn out than he had just a few minutes before. He was hot and sweating. The coughing started again, more pronounced now, and Jake stepped outside the door and told the daughter to call an ambulance. She didn't argue and did as told. Jake stepped back into the room.

Roosevelt had slid back down in the bed, almost lying down. His chest heaved and his eyes opened once again and looked straight at Jake.

"Thank you, Jake. I had to tell somebody. I couldn't take it with me." His right hand clutched the Bible to his chest as he slid off to sleep.

The story about two men buried in the dam was not an urban legend after all. It was true, so very true.

CHAPTER 21

KNOXVILLE

Tennessee had rushed out to a 21-0 lead in the first half against Florida, then cruised on to a final 28-10 win in Knoxville. The following Saturday they marched into Athens and beat the Georgia Bulldogs in an old-fashioned defensive struggle by a score of 16-3. Now they had an open week before they would play the number one ranked Alabama Crimson Tide in Knoxville. The Vols had climbed to number three in the polls, and a win over Alabama could vault them to the top spot. So despite everything that was swirling around their head coach, all was good in Knoxville. The Vols were continuing to win and were back as a national power. Tommy, at this week's press conference, had dismissed the stories about him as "nothing more than jealous recruiters and rival fans, injecting speculation, trying to bring down what we are building here at the University of Tennessee." The more he said it, and the more he won, the more the fans believed it, or at least wanted to believe it. "It's us against the world," he said on this Monday afternoon. The reporter who had asked the questions a few weeks before had not been seen since. A call to the *Johnson City News & Neighbor* newspaper only confirmed that she had never been in their employment. She had disappeared as fast as she had shown up. "Obviously she was a plant," the coach said. "Shame on us for allowing her into the press conference to begin with. The university has addressed that situation and I don't foresee it ever happening again. As you guys all well know, the process for getting in here is now a little tougher. It is believed that her credentials were counterfeited."

As was his usual custom, Tommy Prince was the last one to leave the Tennessee football complex on Monday night. It was around midnight when he slipped back up to his office to pick up his coat and keys before departing for home. His security man, a Knoxville police sergeant, was waiting outside in the parking lot for him to come down. When the sergeant received a text saying "Out", he knew Tommy would be on his way. The officer sat in his car, drank coffee, and waited for the sign.

Tommy entered the office and made his way over to his desk. The door behind him slowly closed and when he heard it shut, he glanced around behind him. There, dressed all in black, stood his old friend and teammate, Bobby Wayne Foster, a gun in his hand. He motioned for Tommy to sit down.

"Over here, on this side of the desk." Bobby Wayne pointed to the two large chairs in front of the desk. "Either one, it doesn't really matter." The coach slowly slid down. "Keep your hands out front where I can see them," he said. Bobby Wayne leaned back against the front of the desk. "It's been a long time, Tommy." He looked around, waving the pistol. "You got a nice collection of hardware in here, this is a real show place."

"What do you want? Money? I'll get you money if that's it," the coach said.

"Don't insult me. I just stopped by to catch up, see how you're doing."

"I'll get you whatever you need," an agitated Tommy replied.

"I don't need your money," Bobby Wayne said. "My uncle, even though he may not know it yet, has been real generous to me since I got out. I just got back from taking care of some offshore banking business, and just between you and me, money, my old friend, is no object." He smiled. "I was looking around in here while I was waiting on you and, man, am I impressed. You've done well for yourself since the last time I saw you. Is that your Super Bowl trophy over there?" It sat as the centerpiece of an elaborate wooden display case, a spotlight shining down on it. "What do they do, give every player on the winning team their own trophy?"

"Yeah, that's exactly what they do."

"Even if you didn't play in the game? I mean, like, even with what happened to you, they still give you one?"

"Every player on the team gets one, regardless."

"I guess Donn Moore and Johnny Rockett had one as well?"

"Everybody on the roster that day got one. It's a replica of the one the team gets." The frustration of the situation and having to repeat himself was beginning to show.

"I did not know that. That's fascinating. I bet you show it to your recruits and their mammas and daddies, don't you?"

"Sure, that's what I got it in here for."

"Really? And don't you feel a little bit like a hypocrite every time you show it to them?"

Tommy paused, then answered, "No, why should I?"

"You know, this is Bobby Wayne you're talkin' to. In case you've somehow forgot, which I don't really think you have, you and I go way back. I mean, I know things about you, and you know things about me, that nobody else knows. I know what happened to you that night before the Super Bowl and how you screwed the deal up for us all." He was leaning over now, off the desk and up in the coach's face, his anger starting to show as he pushed the pistol under Tommy's chin.

"Listen, Bobby Wayne, I got a policeman assigned to me sitting outside, and if I'm not downstairs in a few minutes, he'll come looking for me."

Bobby Wayne leaned back. "Tommy, you ought to know me well enough to know that I cover all the angles. I got men downstairs, too, and if that policeman gets out of his car, it's gonna be the last thing he ever does. Ain't nobody in this big old building but you and me." He leaned back against the front of the desk and waved his pistol about as he talked. "Tommy, you know what bothers me more than anything is that while you have been on the outside enjoying all this success – I mean look around here at all these awards, a national championship, coach of the year – I never one time heard a word from you. I mean, not so much as a Christmas card. Did you just forget all about your old pal?" He paused. "You know what I think? What I truly believe with all my heart? That just like my uncle, you never thought I'd get out of prison and you'd never have to deal with me again. Is that right?"

"No, that's not right at all," Tommy replied.

"Damn it, we used to have some good times…you remember that, don't you?"

"Yeah, sure I do," he replied, not sure where this was all leading.

"I mean, we made a lot of money fixing those games in college. We made a lot of money for two ol' college boys, and all we had to do was make sure that we won but didn't cover the point spread. Turns out, it was pretty easy for us to do. And then I give you the plan for the Super Bowl, and you go out the night before and screw it all up."

The coach nodded but didn't answer. For all he knew, Bobby Wayne was taping this to ruin him that way. He was sure of one thing and that was that his old friend was going to try to bring him down.

"How'd you like that ol' gal that I slipped into your press conference as a reporter? She sure got them old boys thinkin'. I mean it was on ESPN, FOX, CBS." He stopped for a moment. "Tommy, you know the only thing that is saving you right now is that you are winning a lot of football games. Hot damn, boy, everybody loves a winner! They really like it here in Knoxville. I mean, you and me, we was a part of it at one time. Pretty much got whatever we wanted, did whatever we wanted. We were stars, boy! They'll overlook it all if you're winning." He looked at Tommy with a look that seemed to stare right through him. At that moment the coach's cell phone rang. "If that's your police friend downstairs, you just tell him that you are almost done up here and you'll be down in just a little bit." He motioned with his pistol, "You handle that, don't do anything stupid, or it's gonna be the end of the line for you and him right here, tonight. You got it?"

Tommy hit the button and answered the phone. "Yeah, everything's good here, I'll be down in just a few minutes. Just wrapping up a few things. Bye." He looked at Bobby Wayne, who smiled back at him.

"You handled that well. Let me tell you a couple things and then I gotta go. I'm not real happy about what happened at that Super Bowl, never have been, but you know that. What you did has had a disastrous effect on my life ever since then. I mean disastrous." He was up off the desk and walking about the room now, pacing, but all the time keeping Tommy in front of him. "It led to the death of my fiancé and my favorite aunt, God rest their souls." He continued to pace. "Tommy, I just can't let that go." He paused again. "That led to my not-so-favorite uncle getting me sent off to prison for what he hoped was the rest of my life. He even tried numerous times to have me killed in there. I guess that was his plan to get rid of me, to see that I didn't get out. Well, paybacks are hell, and right now his life as he knew it is crashing down all around him as we speak. If he doesn't already know it, he's in for some real surprises. Your two teammates, who couldn't uphold their end of the bargain, well, they have been taken care of. The FBI man who wouldn't let this thing go, he's taken care of as well. Mr. Scarpino, likewise. And you, my old friend, I'm just gonna say that I am gonna bring your world crashing down on you as well, you just don't know when. Just consider tonight a friendly visit and warning." He was over by the door now and he turned off the light in the office, then slid out and was gone.

Tommy sat in his chair, at first too overcome by what had just transpired to move. After a couple of minutes that seemed to him like an eternity, he got up, got his things, texted, then made his way out of the building. He knew Bobby Wayne well enough to know that if he had wanted to do anything to him tonight, it would already be done. In the parking lot, Tommy was glad to see his police sergeant was there, apparently having not been bothered and unaware of what had just transpired. "Anything been going on out here?" the coach asked him in a manner of making small talk while in reality his desire to know was much more than that.

"Haven't seen anything but a few students walking by, sir."

"Good," Tommy said. "Let's go. You follow me home and then you can go."

"Well, sir, that sounds like a plan to me. Coach, I guess you've been up there getting your game plan ready for Alabama?"

"Yeah," he said, pausing for a moment as he continued to look around. "Let's see if we can't roll the Tide this time. It's time to turn things around."

CHAPTER 22

JOHNSON CITY

The following morning, Jake and Ralph pulled into the FBI's regional office, a discreet, unmarked building sitting behind a large shopping complex and a section of farm land that was quickly being overtaken by encroaching housing and apartment developments in the northern section of Johnson City. They were let through the fenced gateway and pulled into the parking lot.

Jake looked at Ralph and remarked, "You would have no idea what this place was if somebody didn't tell you." At the front door, they were greeted by Sarah Workman and Bob Donner and ushered into a conference room. The agents offered them coffee, and a plate of sweet rolls and Danishes sat in the middle of the table. Ralph eyed them but his face and jaw were still so sore from the beating, he didn't want to endure the agony of trying to eat one. At this point he had been subsisting primarily on tomato soup. His weight was falling off due to his inability to eat solid food.

Sarah shut the door behind them, then sat down with a thick file laid in front of her.

Jake glanced down and noticed the name Foster written in pencil on one corner.

"Let me say, Ralph, they we are very sorry about what happened to you, especially since you were working on our behalf," she said, starting the conversation.

"Goes with the job," he replied and shrugged.

"Even so, we are glad to see that you seem to be on the road to recovery."

"Slowly but surely," he said, the pain showing in his expression as he tried to smile.

She smiled at him warmly.

Don't be taken in by her charms, he said to himself. Wait until all your bills are paid.

"We are taking care of all your medical expenses," Sarah said, as if she were reading his mind.

"That's what Jake tells me, and I thank you."

"Let's get down to business," she said, shifting gears, the smile gone. "Jake, there is no question that we are dealing with a man in Bobby Wayne Foster who I would compare to some of the most seasoned operatives in the world. We now know, after the fact, that in the past few days he was in Panama, then Zurich, along with another gentleman who passed himself off as his uncle. He has proceeded to wipe out all of the money his uncle had in these offshore banks and have it sent to his account in a bank in Dubai. He has at some point taken up residence in Dubai and the government there seems to have no trouble with him doing so. They have no interest in returning him to us, or even talking to us about it for that matter. In fact, he seems to have some type of connection with them from what we have been able to gather. Probably all the money. We think he has pretty much left his uncle close to financial ruin. We'll get to him in a moment."

"This has all happened since he showed up with Ralph in the back of the truck at my house?"

"Yes, he was in Panama that afternoon. Apparently went out of the Greeneville airport that morning in a private jet registered in Dubai."

"Busy boy," Jake responded.

"That he is."

"So, my curiosity wants to know, how did he get the money out of the banks?" Jake asked.

"How is he able to jet all around the world?" Ralph said.

"He and this other man, and we think we know his identity, posed as Bobby Wayne's uncle, and of course, Bobby Wayne represented himself, and they transferred all the money to a bank in Zurich. First they flew into Panama and moved the money there to Zurich. Now having a very large account at the bank there, they flew over to Zurich, and from there had the money in the Caymans wired to them. The Zurich account is set up in the name of his uncle, who then has Bobby Wayne's name added to the account as well. The next morning, Bobby Wayne comes back in by himself and moves it all to Dubai and closes the Zurich account. In total, over sixty million dollars. He also transfers a million into another account in Dubai, we think an account for his accomplice."

"You don't know this for sure?" Jake asked.

"Apparently the U.S. agents don't operate quite as freely in Dubai as they do in Zurich," she replied. "They flew out of Zurich, but we don't know where they landed, not yet anyway. We are trying to get satellite imaging on that, but that goes through the NSA boys who don't always cooperate with the FBI."

"And this accomplice? Who do you think he is?" Jake asked.

"We think he is a Terry Brooks, originally from Mohawk, Tennessee. At one time he was Bobby Wayne's cellmate at Brushy Mountain. He also did a stint in the federal system for forging documents, mainly passports. That may answer your question about their frequent flyer status. A former actor, Brooks billed himself as 'The Man of a Thousand Faces.' He went to state prison as a con man and check artist. At one time he had a website boasting that he could make himself look like anyone. About three weeks ago, he took it down. Our people were able to retrieve it. It has him on the site dressed up and disguised as probably fifty different famous people. He also recently purchased a condo in Dubai," Sarah tells them. "Paid for in cash."

"Pretty good for a guy who didn't appear to own a thing in this world as of about a month ago. He was living in the basement of his daughter's home in Greeneville and working the night shift in an all-night convenience store," Donner piped in. "He's wanted here for having left there one night with several thousand dollars of the store's money."

"And the uncle, does he know this has all come down?" Jake wondered.

"Yes, he does," Sarah replied.

"And you know this, how?"

"Let's just say that we know," she said with a smile.

"And Bobby Wayne is where?" Jake asked.

"Now that I'm afraid we do not know," Sarah replied, giving Jake a shrug, then looking at her fellow agent.

"He apparently has lots of passports from several different countries, and this is allowing him to move in and out as he pleases," Donner explained. "He doesn't ever use the same one twice, that we can tell. The last known sighting was Zurich. I'm guessing he's back in the states, probably close by, here in Tennessee."

"I'm still not understanding how they were able to move all his uncle's money?" Jake said.

Sarah folded her hands and placed them on the table. "They had his passport and they had his bank books with his account numbers and passwords. At some point, Bobby Wayne has apparently entered his uncle's home and taken them from his office safe." She sat back in her chair, crossed her arms, then added, "The uncle also thinks he slipped in one night and murdered his prizefighting cock."

"I'm enough of an East Tennessee boy to know those things bring in a lot of money," Jake said, then whistled.

"Apparently he snuck into the guarded area and cut its head off right before it was to go in a big money match," Donner said. "At The Del Rio Gentleman's Club."

Jake looked at them both over the top of his glasses. "I know where that is. Several years ago I played a gig at a club in Newport and when the show was over that's where we wound up."

"Bobby Wayne's been a busy little boy since he got out of prison," Ralph said, wincing in pain.

Sarah pulled a picture from the file showing the two men leaving the

Zurich bank and laid it on the table.

Jake looked at the picture for a moment, then asked, "And you got this?"

"The U.S. government takes pictures of a lot of people coming out of the banks that are very secretive about who they deal with." She reached into the file and produced another one of the same two men walking out of a different bank. "Panama," she said.

Ralph sat back in his chair.

"This one is of course Bobby Wayne and the other is a dead ringer for his uncle," Donner told them. "As you can see, with the right credentials, which they apparently had, they were able to pull this off."

Sarah sat back in her chair. "Speaking of the uncle, I don't guess he is going to be needing the money anyway after we go to the hospital today and get the full story of your friend Roosevelt. I talked with Washington first thing this morning and the wheels are already in motion with the Justice Department to bring charges against him for being an active participant in the murder of the two FBI agents, and they will also charge him with violating their civil rights as well. He will die a lonely old man in prison. Everyone else involved, we believe, are dead, unless Roosevelt tells us something different."

"He might have needed the money for a high-powered legal team," Jake replied.

"I guess his nephew has made sure that won't happen," she said.

"Just remember that one thing that Roosevelt said, that there were bodies buried out beyond the junkyard," Jake said. "You should be able to hold them all in jail while you do some searching."

"That is part of our plan," Sarah responded.

"Good," Jake said.

"My how the mighty are falling," said Ralph, trying to grin. "Can't happen soon enough to such a nice group of people to suit me."

"Jake, you're sure this Roosevelt will tell us the same story he told you and he'll hold up for court as well?" Donner asked.

"He says he will. But you're gonna have to guarantee to protect him and his family. He has four daughters that live in the Jonesborough area. Plus, he's an old man who at the moment has a very bad case of pneumonia."

"Everything will be taped. Also, thanks to your undercover work, we are already moving on Bobby Wayne's brother at the junkyard. We're going on him now to get him out of the way, federal charges for interstate theft, cadaver dogs to look for bodies. The tag numbers on the cars show them as all stolen. I am just thankful that each night you shot them you sent them on to me, so that when Ralph was caught, we didn't lose all the evidence. We're just so sorry that Ralph here had to pay the price for it." She reached across the table and grabbed his hand and gently squeezed it. "Jake, what do you know about Bobby Wayne's time in the Army?" Sarah asked, abruptly changing directions, letting go of Ralph's hand, the smile once again gone.

"I know that after college he had a free agent try out with the Atlanta Falcons, got cut, and the next thing I heard he was in the Army. He was supposedly in the Rangers," Jake replied.

Sarah opened his file. "You are right, he was a Ranger. This was right after Vietnam, and so he spent most of his time in Central and South America in clandestine operations where he made the rank of Captain and then Major. A little faster than most, I might add. Strangely enough, at a time the service is getting cut back, he gets promoted while others are getting knocked down in rank or pushed out. Apparently, somebody had him helping run their own little wars down there. I guess at that time the U.S. was big on trying to hold off the Communists in our own hemisphere. Unfortunately, most of his records for that time period are highly classified and sealed, including just about anything he did and why he was court-martialed out of the service after eight years."

"I had never heard that," Jake said.

"Then he returns home and goes to work for his uncle. Before too long they are trying to fix the Super Bowl," she said.

"Why's he put out of the Army?" asked Ralph.

"That is as classified as it gets, I am told by the Pentagon this morning."

"Nobody at the FBI can find out why?" Jake wondered.

"I'm not sure the president can find that out," Sarah said, smiling back at Jake.

As the meeting wound down, Jake laughed and said, "So, we're not getting fired here today? We thought you had called us in to politely tell us our services were no longer needed."

"No, not at all. Whatever gave you that idea? We are keeping you on retainer until this thing is wrapped up. It's the least we can do," she said, stuffing her papers back into the file.

"Well, that's great," Jake said. "I just told Ralph on the way over here that I bet you were going to tell us that you would be handling everything from here on out." They were out in the hallway and moving towards the front door.

They shook hands and stepped outside into a beautiful fall morning. Sarah followed them as they moved toward their truck. "Jake, on a personal note, do you think we could have that dinner tonight?" she asked in barely more than a whisper. She reached up and touched the lapel on his jacket.

"I can't tonight, I've already got plans," he said, shrugging.

"Oh yeah, your ex is going to be in Johnson City for the next couple of days, right?"

"That she is, but I believe you already knew all about that, being as how the FBI is helping with her security."

"Well, maybe some other time," she said, brushing the windblown hair out of her face.

"Yeah, maybe some other time," Jake replied with a slight smile, then he got in his truck.

They pulled out onto the road and Ralph just looked at Jake and smiled. "You're not gonna go out to dinner with that gal are you?"

"I don't know."

"You don't know?" Ralph just shook his head.

"She is a very good-looking woman," Jake replied.

"My advice to you, and I've probably told you this before, is to never get involved with a woman that carries a gun."

Jake looked at Ralph and said, "You may well have a point." Then he grinned and laughed as they drove off down the road.

CHAPTER 23

The current governor of Tennessee, Jake's ex-wife, had arrived in Johnson City a few minutes before noon to attend a luncheon at East Tennessee State University at the Student Center. There she was greeted by the university's president and his top staff as well as all of the Tennessee state representatives and senators from the eastern portion of the state. They were meeting to discuss funding initiatives for the university and to take a campus facilities tour. The next day she was to travel on to the new Birthplace of Country Music museum in Bristol and then to Kingsport to meet with the leaders of the Eastman Chemical Company, one of the state's largest employers and businesses. She had blocked off the first evening to have dinner with Jake in her suite at the Carnegie Hotel. The security for her had been increased after Jake informed the FBI that Bobby Wayne had threatened her. It was really on high alert with her visit to east Tennessee, with the Tennessee Bureau of Investigation in charge, and the FBI with a team on hand as well, looking for any sign of Bobby Wayne.

Jake was to meet her at her suite that evening at 7:00. He was a few minutes away when his cell phone began to ring. He recognized Susanne's number and answered. "Hey, how's it going? Busy day I guess."

"Oh, Jake, I am beat."

"Well, I'll be there soon. I'm just up the road," he replied.

"I'm just sitting here looking at these beautiful roses that they just brought to my room and I wanted to thank you."

Thoughts raced through Jake's mind. His stomach felt as if he had just taken a punch to it.

"You are so thoughtful, Jake, they are beauti…"

He cut her off, "Susanne, listen to me…I haven't sent you any flowers."

"I haven't opened the card yet, I just assumed they were from you."

"Don't touch the card, don't pull it out…you may think I'm crazy…but it very well may be a bomb. Where are your security people?"

"Out in the hall."

"Get out of the room now. Let me talk to them." He was just pulling into the hotel parking lot and left his truck under the main entrance with the door open and started to run in. "The keys are in the ignition," he called out to the valet.

Susanne was out in the hall and handed her phone to the head of her security detail. "It's my ex-husband, Jake."

"Yes, sir," he replied into the phone.

"Susanne says someone just delivered a dozen roses to her room. They could be a bomb, you need to get her to a secure location. Then get someone to check out the flowers. I'm in the building and will be up there in a moment. I'd say you need to evacuate her floor."

"Yes, sir. Will do."

"I'm being stopped now by your men in the lobby. Can you tell them to let me pass?"

The man called down on a wireless earpiece, talking into his sleeve, and one of the agents said to Jake, "You just follow me, sir."

"Let's take the stairs, not the elevator," Jake offered.

They went up the five flights of stairs two steps at a time. The officer called back up as they ascended and told them, "We're on our way." At the third floor, they started to meet people on their way down. They came through the door at the top of the stairs, their lungs burning for air and thighs aching. "Her suite is down here on the left," the TBI agent exhaled.

People were being shuttled to the stairways on both ends of the hall to lead them away.

They entered the governor's room. The roses sat on a coffee table in the middle of the suite. "The governor, you've got her off to a secure location?" Jake asked.

"Yes, sir. We have taken her out the back and they are to take her across the street to the university. She is going to the president's office, he is still there working, and she will be secured there until we get this situation cleared up. We have called in the bomb squad from the Johnson City police, they should be here at any minute, and we are evacuating the entire hotel, a floor at a time, as we speak."

Sirens blared from outside and Jake walked over and glanced out the room's window and saw fire trucks and police cars everywhere. Red and blue lights bounced off the brick walls of the hotel and the university buildings across the street. The bomb squad personnel entered the room. "You guys are quick," Jake said.

"We had a crew on standby, sir, out in the parking lot," a member of the squad responded.

Jake explained the situation. "I don't know if it might be a bomb or not, but we are not sure who they came from or how they got by the security to get in here. I'm thinking it might be triggered by removing the card or by a timer." They ushered everyone outside that didn't have on a bomb suit, including Jake. They loaded the vase of roses into a bomb canister, moved it out of the building and into their truck where they took it out into the county to an area where they could try to see if it truly was a bomb or not. A scanner had shown that there did not appear to be anything inside it, but they wanted to make sure.

Jake stood with the TBI and FBI agents, including Donner, in the parking lot of the hotel and watched as the bomb squad drove it away. His phone rang, an unknown caller it said, and he answered. "This is Jake, go ahead."

"Jake, Bobby Wayne here. You are sharp, my friend, getting on that bomb like that. But, hey, it's not really a bomb. I was just letting you know that I'm watching you. If I was you, I would get out of the FBI's business. Just a little word of advice from one old friend to another." The phone went dead.

Jake looked over at Donner, "Let 'em check it out, but it's no bomb."

"How you know?"

"That was Bobby Wayne, he must be around here somewhere watching us. He says it's no bomb, just a warning to me." It was at that time that Jake saw Virgil, standing down at the end of the sidewalk near the entrance to the steps of the bridge that crossed the road to the university. He was talking on a cell phone. Had he been shaken out of the hotel on another one of his rendezvous? Was it just a coincidence that he was there? Jake was starting to get a sneaking suspicion that maybe Virgil was not as much of a friend as he thought after all.

A few minutes later they got the call from the bomb squad that it wasn't a bomb. The decision was made to bring the governor back. Jake looked up and saw Sarah of the FBI approaching. "Tell your people to be on the lookout for Bobby Wayne. He called me to tell me that it wasn't really a bomb just as soon as I came out of the hotel. He had to be somewhere that he could see what was going on. He said it was a threat to me to stay out of the FBI's business. He just wanted to let me know that he is still in control of this situation."

"And?" she asked.

"And what? I'm not about to give in to his demands, if that's what you are asking. I want to know how those flowers got to the governor's room with you and the TBI supposedly watching everything."

"Well, I'm going to get to the bottom of that for you. I'd like to know as well," Sarah said.

Jake glanced back around and saw that Virgil was gone.

Ten minutes later the governor's black Suburban pulled back into the hotel entrance with a state trooper's car in front and one in back. She got out and saw Sarah talking to Jake. "Why, Sarah Workman, it's so nice to see you on this job," all the while giving her a halfhearted hug. The state troopers and TBI agents then quickly ushered Susanne into the lobby and on up to her room. Jake followed behind them.

Once she was inside the room, she ushered everyone but Jake out the door. She shut it behind her then came over and fell into his arms. "Oh, Jake, does trouble just seem to follow us everywhere?" She hugged him hard around the neck, holding on like she would never want to let go, then began sobbing. "I wish you would move back to Nashville and be with me all the time," she whispered in his ear. "I would feel so much safer."

"It looks to me like whenever I'm around, that's when these things happen to you," Jake whispered back.

"That Sarah Workman, what was she doing down there?" she asked, pushing somewhat away.

"She's FBI of course, says she's assigned to catch Bobby Wayne Foster."

"Jake, is she the one that got you involved in this?"

"Yeah, she says you recommended me to her."

"That's a bold-faced lie," she replied emphatically.

"Well, you better take that up with her," Jake responded.

"You know she's after you, don't you? I could tell by the way she was looking at you downstairs."

"Why do you say that?" Jake asked.

"Because when I started dating you back when we were in law school, she would make these comments about you, about how good-looking you were and how lucky I was to be dating someone like you."

"You can remember all of that? It must have been what, thirty some years ago?"

"Some things, Jake, you never forget."

"Apparently so," he said.

"She can't be trusted, you know. She's always had that reputation."

"Probably why she's working for the government."

She pulled him back closer. "Let's don't talk about her anymore." She kissed him.

"Okay, you got my attention," he replied. "I thought we were going to have dinner sent up?"

"I'm not hungry."

"Maybe later?" he asked.

"Jake, are you going to stay with me tonight?" She kissed him hard.

"I'm thinking about it."

She kissed him again. "Stop thinking about it," she said.

He reached over and turned off the lights.

CHAPTER 24

DEL RIO

After interviewing Roosevelt Johnson in his room at the Johnson City Medical Center and getting his deposition on video, with a lawyer Jake had gotten him present, the FBI moved quickly on Edward Jefferson Foster III and all of his operations. They had federal warrants issued for Foster's home and offices in Del Rio and Newport. They had one for the Del Rio Gentleman's Club, and one for the bank he owned in Newport. Ralph's undercover photographs led to a warrant for the junkyard operation in Washington County and for Bobby Wayne's brother, Carl. They moved in and arrested Carl at 8:00 a.m. on Wednesday. Cadaver dogs soon picked up scents in the woods out back and they were sending in teams to start searching and digging for bodies.

In Del Rio, at the exact same time, a team of FBI agents surrounded the home of the former governor, led by Sarah and Donner who were let into the home by his servant James. They first had to get by a team of Cocke County deputies who tried to stop them at the gate, but the deputies quickly saw they were greatly outnumbered, not to mention going to have to deal with the FBI. The sheriff, knowing a losing battle when he saw one, told them to back off and they retreated back into Newport. He didn't want the federal agents looking into anything more down in his area than they had to. He figured with the FBI showing up at Foster's house, the old man was done for. What he didn't know at that moment was that teams of FBI agents were swarming all over the Newport area at the same time. The phone in the sheriff's office began to ring off the hook.

At exactly five minutes past eight, James, in his white jacket, came to Foster's home office door and announced that he had guests in the foyer.

"Who is it?" Foster asked.

"They say they are with the FBI, sir. They say they got a warrant."

"A warrant?"

"Yes, sir. They holding it in their hand, kinda flashin' it around."

"Send 'em on in, James." From his desk, he pulled out a revolver and stuck it down between his left leg and the chair bottom.

Sarah and Bob entered his office, one standing to each corner of his desk. She started with, "Mr. Foster," deliberately not using the term governor, "we have in our possession a warrant for your arrest for the kidnapping and murder of FBI agents Bobby Thomas and Oliver Smith, to have taken place in January 1943 when they were buried alive in the Douglas Lake Dam in Dandridge, Tennessee. We have evidence that connects you to the murders. You are also charged with violating the civil rights of the men as well. We hope you will surrender and come with us peacefully."

Foster didn't respond.

"Do you understand the charges, sir?" she asked.

"Statute of limitations should take care of this," he replied with a tense response.

"This is a federal warrant for the kidnapping and murder of two FBI agents on TVA land, which is government property, so that doesn't apply here, sir."

"Who says such a thing? What kind of evidence after all these years?" He waved his left hand in the air. "You people are just trying to harass an old man."

"We have an eye witness, a Mr. Roosevelt Johnson, formerly of Newport and now residing in Jonesborough, who has confessed to being a participant in the crime."

"What's that got to do with me?"

"He names you as a willing participant," she said.

"Roosevelt Johnson. I was very good to that old negra," the old man said. "This is how he pays me back? Some gratitude, I tell ya." He shook his head.

"He will testify that you, your father, and grandfather were all participants in the murders. As such, that is why you are also being charged with violating the civil rights of the two agents as well. We have a federal warrant to search your home and businesses along with any other personal property you may own."

"You have awfully broad powers it seems to me," he said, staring at her.

"Before we proceed any further, I will read you your Miranda rights."

"No need in that," he said, again waving one hand in the air. "I know what my rights are. I don't need you people to tell me anything. I am a lawyer by trade and used to be a judge. Did you know that?"

"Yes, sir. But I must tell you that you have the right to call your attorney, sir, before you make any comments to us."

"Do you people know my nephew has ruined me?" he said looking at them.

"And your nephew is whom?" Sarah inquired.

"You people know damned good and well who my nephew is, don't be tryin' to jerk me around." Anger swelled in his voice.

They didn't reply.

"Bobby Wayne Foster. I know you know who I'm talkin' about."

"Yes, sir," Sarah replied.

"He thinks I had him framed for murder and sent off to prison."

"Did you, sir? Did you have him framed?" Donner asked him.

Foster didn't respond at first. Then he said in somewhat of a whisper, "Damn that boy."

"Why is that, sir?" Donner said, hoping he would start to talk.

"Can I get you a drink? God knows I need one," the old man said.

"No, sir. It's a little bit early in the morning, don't you think?" she replied.

"Well, probably not if you're in the situation I'm in." He paged James who was soon back in the room.

"Yes, sir."

"Double bourbon on the rocks, James."

He moved toward the bar in the corner, and Donner shifted his position back somewhat so as to watch him.

"Our guests here say they don't want anything this morning. How about an orange juice or tomato juice? James here can make you one hell of a virgin bloody Mary if you don't want to be drinkin' on the job. Ain't that right, James? Bring me the bottle as well."

"Yes, sir." He brought Foster his drink and sat it on his desk on a coaster with a cocktail napkin around it. Then he stepped back to the bar and retrieved the half full bottle, which he gracefully sat on the desk right behind the drink.

"Thank you, James. Last chance?" he asked while looking at the agents.

They shook their heads no once again.

"That will be all, James. You're dismissed. Shut the door on your way out."

"Let's leave it open," Sarah said, smiling at James. She wondered just what all he would be able to tell them. They would sit him down and talk to him once they had Foster cuffed and out of the house. Once he knew Foster was gone, would he open up, or would he remain loyal to the old man? James looked at Foster, who nodded that it was okay to leave the door open, and then he gracefully stepped out.

Foster picked up the drink, swirled it around for a moment, then slowly drank about half of the bourbon and sat the glass back down on his desk. "I can't begin to tell you what a help that man James has been to me over the years. We are the same age, you know. Would you have ever guessed that? He looks ten years younger than me. His daddy worked for my daddy in the same capacity, and his granddaddy worked here as well. We all go way back, you see."

Sounds like slavery, Donner thought to himself.

"Mr. Foster, I'm going to let you finish your drink, and then we are going to have to arrest you," Sarah replied.

Again he waved his left hand. "My granddaddy, he started all of this. The farm, the cannery. Then my daddy, Foster Junior – that's what everyone called him – he took it and built it into an empire. He was a wonderful man, so proud of me when I was elected governor."

"Your daddy, as we understand it, was the main person in murdering these two FBI agents," she said. "I mean, bury two men alive in the dam? There was nothing good about your daddy. I'm sorry, I don't see it."

He stiffened in the chair. "You have no idea what you're talking about. That was all Hoover's fault. He didn't need to send those men down here snoopin' around. The federal government, they always overstep their bounds, if you do allow me to say so." He picked up the glass with the bourbon and again swirled it around in front of him. "Tennessee whiskey…it's the best, you know…no matter what them bluebloods in Kentucky think." He looked hard at the liquid in the glass, then drank what was left. "It was my grandfather's idea, not my daddy's, just for your information."

He had already said more than any lawyer would ever allow him to say.

Sarah took the bottle of bourbon and moved it off the desk. She didn't want some lawyer in the trial saying they let him get liquored up so as to keep him talking. He watched her but didn't say anything.

Donner interjected. "You mentioned your nephew. What were you going to tell us about him?"

"Bobby Wayne?" Foster shook his head. "You know at one time I loved him like he was my own son." He took a sip of whatever was left on the ice by this time. "But the boy went bad." He gazed off, his thoughts somewhere else. "Just between you and me, he was never the same after he came back from the Army. They ruined him. Had him doin' all kinds of secret stuff down there in Central and South America. He was a major in the United States Army and he's down there runnin' all these covert programs, in charge of it all? How does that happen? You figure that one out for me. At one time, the only people he answered to was some general in the Pentagon and a top aide to the president in the White House. When it was supposedly discovered by some congressman on the Armed Services Committee what these people were doing, Bobby Wayne and the general were hung out to dry, their careers ended. They said they were dealing with Colombian drug dealers. The aide? He was moved from the White House to the State Department. Not so much as a slap on the wrist. The president, who I knew personally, told me that he had no idea what they were up to. He said the records were sealed for matters of national security. I didn't believe him then, I don't believe him now. Bobby Wayne and the general were both court-martialed. They did six months in Leavenworth, then were put out of the service. Their service records were sealed. A general loses his rank and pension? That's just not somethin' that happens. So you ask me about the FBI agents sent undercover to Newport, and you come in here and try to justify what Hoover was trying to do to us? I say screw the United States government! They do the same thing to their own people." He asked for some more bourbon. "Just one more drink," he said, "before you take me away for good." Sarah relented and set the bottle back on the desk. He screwed off the lid and poured half a glass full. He looked at her and said, "You know this is probably the last drink I'll ever have." He spilled a little bit, his hand shaking. "I don't usually pour my own drinks."

"So where is Bobby Wayne now?" Donner asked.

"I'd like to know the answer to that," Foster replied, again taking another sip of bourbon. "You probably know more about this than I do, but he has managed to clean out my money from all my accounts except for the Newport Bank & Trust. The only reason he didn't get that one is because I own it. In the grand scheme of things, it only carries a small amount of my total financial holdings. Most everything is, or should I say was, offshore." He paused. "You people should be concentrating on catching him. He's nothing more than a common bank robber."

She pulled out the picture from outside the bank in Zurich and showed it to him. Foster studied it for a long moment then looked up, stunned.

"Zurich," she said to him before he could ask the question. She pulled out a second picture for him.

Foster just looked at her and shook his head.

"Panama, the day before the first one," she said stoically.

"If I didn't know better, I would say I was there with him," he said, closely examining the picture.

"It certainly looks like you were," she responded.

"The Super Bowl," he said somewhat under his breath.

"What was that, sir?" Sarah asked.

"It all started downhill with me and him with the Super Bowl. Los Angeles, 1985." He rubbed his forehead. "We got greedy, and what we thought was a foolproof plan wasn't so foolproof."

"Go ahead, we're glad to listen," she said.

Foster shook his head, his thoughts going way back in time. "Biggest mistake I made was letting him talk me into betting all that money on the Super Bowl. He said it was guaranteed, no way we could lose. Again, just out and out greed. I knew better."

"Your involvement with the Scarpinos?" she asked.

"No comment on that," Foster answered.

"Do you know that Johnny Scarpino died recently in a New York City hospital? Maybe he just died or maybe somebody, most likely your nephew, slipped in and suffocated him to death? You know he's already killed three, now maybe four people, since he got out of prison? You could be next."

He shook his head. After a quiet interlude he said, "That's really all I want to say about it at this time."

"Let's keep talking, unless you want your lawyer," she said.

"I'll talk. I told you I don't need a lawyer," he said. He drummed his fingers on the desk. "Who knows what the future holds?"

She took back her pictures and started to insert them back into her file. Donner, listening to him, had relaxed and sat down in one of the chairs in front of Foster's desk. By the time he'd get to jail, he would bet Foster would have his lawyer present and waiting and he would have him stop talking. If the old man wanted to talk now, why not let him. Let him hang himself.

With his left hand, Foster picked up the glass, looked at it for a moment, and then drank what was left of the bourbon. He sat it down on the desk rather loudly, pushing it out to the left side and knocking it over intentionally. The ice tumbled out, grabbing the agents' attentions. "You know, I have no intention of ever spending a day of my life in jail." With his right hand, he pulled out the pistol from under his left leg, inserted it into his mouth pointing upward, and pulled the trigger. The back of his head exploded all over the wall behind him.

The FBI agents, caught completely off guard, could only look at each other stunned. They would have a hard time explaining to their superiors just how they let this happen.

"He just saved the taxpayers a bunch of money," Donner said, getting up and starting to walk out of the room. "I'll go call this in."

CHAPTER 25

JONESBOROUGH

The phone rang three times before Jake picked it up. He looked at his watch and it was within a few minutes of midnight, and he was on his fourth drink of Wild Turkey on ice.

"Hey, it's your favorite FBI agent."

"I thought I might be hearing from you."

"You did?"

"Sure, you guys are all over the news. I thought you might call…. intuition I guess."

"That's not always a good thing in this job, being in the news I mean. Usually, being anonymous is best." She liked it that he thought she might call.

"I saw some clips from your press conference a little while ago," Jake replied.

"How'd we do?"

"I didn't see the whole thing, but hey, it looked to me like you hit the gold mine of crime in all of East Tennessee."

"Yeah?"

"Well, you solved the age-old story that has floated around here forever about men being buried in the Douglas Lake dam."

"Yeah, I guess that does end that urban legend, thanks to your help."

"A joint effort, let's say," Jake said. "In a way, justice has been served. I don't know that it would've happened in a courtroom. The high priced lawyers would have been like sharks."

"Yeah, I just wish that I hadn't witnessed it," she said.

"I understand," he replied. "I've been there."

"Jake, it is so hard to even imagine people being that…well…I'm not even sure what word to use to describe what they did. Bury two men alive? You can see things in this line of work that are really just beyond description, you know what I mean?"

"Oh yeah," he said. "You just can't let it bother you. Block it out."

"I just need a good stiff drink to try and help me forget all of this, for tonight anyway."

"Hey," Jake said, "you just ended the reign of probably the most corrupt politician in the history of the state of Tennessee."

"Well, let's say he took care of himself" she said.

"I'm betting Bobby Wayne would've got to him somehow before he ever went to trial."

"I guess that's one way to look at it," she demurred. "He got us to let our guard down, and then…"

"Sorry, I guess I really shouldn't be so callous about it," Jake responded. "Seeing someone shoot them self is nothing to make light of, and he took the coward's way out. The whole story is very sad, and has been for a long, long time. Those FBI agents had children that are now older than I am. I hope it will bring a little closure to their lives. I mean, at least now they know what happened to their fathers, and they know where they are buried."

"You know, I hadn't really thought about that, but it is so true. The youngest agent, his wife is still alive. They say she never remarried."

"If only we had Bobby Wayne reeled in," Jake said. "Did the old man shed any light on that situation?"

"No, not really. You should have seen his face when I showed him the pictures from the banks," she remarked.

"I guarantee you there are a lot of nervous people tonight all over the state of Tennessee, knowing that you guys moved on all his businesses, including some high-ranking political and law enforcement types," said Jake. "I'm sure they are worried their names will show up some place in his records. I say a lot of them are glad he killed himself and hope it will keep them from being exposed."

"He did say that everything between him and Bobby Wayne went bad after he returned from the Army," she said.

"Yeah…"

"And he mentioned the Super Bowl," she interjected.

"Everything keeps going back to the Super Bowl. Only problem is, everybody involved seems to be dead now, except for Bobby Wayne and the state of Tennessee's favorite coach, Tommy Prince. Neither one of them are going to be talkin' to us, I wouldn't think. I'm sure Prince is afraid the hammer will drop on him next. He'll never talk…I mean, if he does, he'll be giving up everything. He'll take his chances with Bobby Wayne, hoping for the best." Jake paused for a moment. "I just don't see how it's gonna end good for him, not that it should."

"He's hunkered down, Jake, hoping it will all just go away, and it is Alabama week you know."

"If Bobby Wayne wants to make a big splash, what better time to do it? That's what I'm thinkin'," Jake said.

"That's true, you can bet when Coach Prince knows what all happened yesterday, he should become very nervous, that is if he's not already," Sarah said. "I think you are right, Jake, everybody else that knew what went on have been pretty much eliminated, except for him."

"That's the way I'm seeing it."

"Jake, where do we go from here?"

"Sarah, let me ask you something."

"Sure."

"You ever hear the name Virgil Smith mentioned in any of this?"

"I don't believe so," she replied. "Who is he?"

"He's an old friend of mine, at least I think he is. Like Bobby Wayne, we go back to our days of playing ball in high school. Plus, he's been around since I moved back to Jonesborough."

"And?"

"Well, it's just a hunch, but somehow, everywhere I go, either he or his name keeps turning up." Jake waited for a long moment. "That's all. I just wondered if you had heard the name."

"No," she replied, "but I'll run his name in the FBI computer, something could show up."

"Yeah, that's worth a try, you never know," Jake said. "I appreciate it."

"I can call right now and get that started."

"The FBI, you guys never sleep," he said.

"We have been known to stay after it all night in pursuit of something we want."

Jake laughed, not sure where she was going with that. "I would appreciate your checking it out for me, but it's probably nothing. I hope it's nothing at all, just a hunch I have." He had quickly learned long ago to follow his hunches.

"Jake…" she said, then he interrupted.

"Where are you?" he asked.

"I just left the office in Johnson City."

"Yeah?"

"Jake," she started again, then paused. "Would you care if I came by? I mean if you're not already busy?" She thought she sounded as nervous as a school girl. "I really need someone to talk with that understands what I've been through today. I mean, I really need help in clearing my head. If I go home, well, I know I won't be able to sleep."

He didn't respond right away.

"I mean if it's a bad time, or if I'm imposing…"

"No, it's not a bad time," he softly said. Again he paused. Too much alcohol was winning this battle.

She wondered just what he was thinking.

"Yeah, the light outside is on and the front door is open. I'll be in the kitchen. What about I fix us something to eat? You like eggs?"

"Yeah, I love eggs. Scrambled," she said before he could ask.

"A little bacon and eggs and some tequila. That will have you feeling better in no time. I've been told I'm quite the cook, you know. Especially breakfast. I'll see you in a few minutes."

"OK, great, I'm on my way…"

Jake hung up. The Super Bowl, he thought to himself. Everything keeps going back to the Super Bowl.

CHAPTER 26

On Thursday morning at 6:00 a.m., Jake awoke and reached over to find an empty bed. He was okay with that. To him it had been nothing more than a physical encounter and that was the way he wanted it. He sat up, somewhat hungover with his head pounding, and dragged himself out of bed and made his way down the hallway to the kitchen to get something to drink. Sitting at his kitchen table reading the morning paper was none other than Bobby Wayne. Butch, having not made a sound, lay on the kitchen floor. When he saw Jake, his tail started to wag back and forth slowly, as if he knew he had done something very wrong.

"Morning, Jake," Bobby Wayne said, looking over the top of the paper.

"That's one hell of a watch dog I got," Jake said and the dog's tail stopped.

"Dogs like me Jake, what can I say? Actually, it goes back to something I was taught in the Army. I can do it to any dog, no matter how big or mean they are."

"What are you doing here?" Jake saw he had a handgun, what looked to be a Glock, lying on the table in front of him. He stood there with only the boxers he had on. The gun he normally carried was on the dresser in his bedroom, and he had one more in the living room in a hidden spot.

Neither one were of any use to him at this point.

"Hope you don't mind I helped myself to some coffee," Bobby Wayne said, holding up the cup. He had laid down the paper. "That gal that left here a little while ago, she left the pot going."

"You mesmerize her, too?"

"No, I waited 'til she left before I came in."

Jake just stared at him, then asked, "So how long you been watching my house?"

"That I won't tell," he smugly replied.

"And how did you get in?"

"The back door. There are not too many locks I can't pick. These old farm houses are a piece of cake."

"That's good to know," Jake said. "I guess I need some deadbolts. For years, people around here didn't even bother to lock their doors."

"I was just reading about my uncle," Bobby Wayne said, glancing at the front of the paper. "Looks like he shot himself, but with that FBI bunch, you never know. And my brother, he's in jail, it says, no chance for bail at this point. You know, I told him a long time ago that gettin' rid of bodies on his own property was not such a good idea."

Jake didn't respond, he just looked at him and shrugged.

"Sit down, Jake. Let's talk, you and me."

"Let me go back and put on some clothes."

"No, I think you're good just like you are." Bobby Wayne motioned for him to sit.

Jake pulled out the chair across the table from him, sat down, and scooted it up as close to the table as he could get.

Bobby Wayne sipped on his coffee. "That gal, she makes a pretty mean cup of coffee, Jake."

Again, he didn't respond.

"Tell me if I'm wrong, but that was the FBI agent, wasn't it?"

Jake just stared at him.

"I know who she is, Jake. Not that it's any of my business who you sleep with, but you know what they say, you really shouldn't mix business and pleasure." He gave him a glance and a sly smile, then took out a pack of cigarettes, pulled one out, and stuck it in his mouth. "You don't mind if I smoke, do you?" He lit it before he gave Jake a chance to answer.

"How long have you been here?" Jake asked.

Bobby Wayne closed his old Zippo lighter, snapping it shut, then said, "I'm always around, Jake. I'm good at that kind of thing, you know?" He looked around the room. "You got an ashtray?"

"No, most of my guests refrain themselves from smoking," Jake responded, obviously unamused by his guest.

Bobby Wayne got up and retrieved another coffee mug. "I guess this will have to do." He took the gun with him, then put it back when he sat back down. "You still playing music, Jake?"

"Yeah, when I can."

"Just curious. I hope you don't mind me asking, but why would a guy that can play like you ever leave Nashville?"

"On days like today, I'm wondering that myself," Jake retorted.

"That's a good one, Jake," Bobby Wayne responded, seemingly amused with himself.

"You shouldn't make a man sit here half-naked like this," Jake said.

"Let me guess, you want to go to the bedroom and get some clothes, and in the process I'll bet you would come back with your gun as well." He tapped the Glock with his finger and said, "I think we are good just like we are."

Jake was acting annoyed, but in reality, he wanted to turn this into an information gathering opportunity if he could. The problem was that he hoped this thing would not end badly. Bobby Wayne had the gun, Jake didn't. Information would be no good if he wasn't around to use it.

"So, Jake, how long has this thing with the FBI agent been going on?"

Jake drummed his fingers of his right hand on the kitchen table. "What business is it of yours who I see?"

"Why don't you get your hand off of the table?" Bobby Wayne seemed quickly annoyed.

"Does that make you nervous?"

"I just don't want you tryin' anything stupid. I'm the one in charge here."

"You like that, don't you?"

"Let's just say that I learned a long time ago that it's always best to control whatever situation you are in." He took a long drag on the cigarette, then flicked the ashes in the cup. "So, Jake, does your ex-wife know about you and this FBI gal?"

"I don't see where that's any business of yours."

"Well, you and the governor seemed so chummy the other night at the Carnegie."

"You created a nice little fire storm there," Jake replied.

"It was all just a joke. I just wanted to let you people know that I can strike anywhere, anytime."

"Excuse me if I wasn't laughing."

"I was impressed, Jake, that you picked up on the flowers. I mean, her own security people didn't think to check that. My delivery man waltzed right in and out." He tapped the cigarette on the top of his improvised ashtray and looked hard at Jake. "Relax, it wasn't a bomb, only made to look like one." He sipped his coffee. "I had no reason to hurt the governor, she's a very beautiful woman, Jake. If I was you, I'd get back with her." He held up his coffee mug and tipped it to Jake. "I'd leave this FBI gal alone." He leaned over the table. "Just between you and me, I'm not real sure you can trust her." He sat the mug down. "Just an observation on my part," he said, then smiled.

"I'm glad to know you are so concerned about my welfare," Jake shot back.

"Think nothing of it." Bobby Wayne paused for a second, stubbed out his cigarette, then continued. "I guess, in a way, the FBI did me a favor." He pointed at the headline in the paper that lay there. "He was a gutless old bastard, it doesn't surprise me that he killed himself when they came for him. That just takes one more off my list." He stopped for a moment. "I really would have liked to be the one that killed him, though. They did deprive me of that privilege. You know he got me sent to prison on a framed-up murder charge?" He stopped, lit another cigarette, and Jake could sense the rage building. "I was at that bar that night, but I didn't kill anybody. They found this guy's body in the dumpster out back. Had two witnesses say I killed him in a fight over a girl and tossed him in there. How stupid is that? You think that sounds like how I operate Jake? Arrested in Newport, tried in Newport, convicted in Newport. He controlled the judge and the jury. Everybody there would be scared to cross him." Anger continued to well up inside of him. "Several times he tried to have someone kill me in prison, at Brushy Mountain and at Mountain City, the last time right before I walked out. Have I told you, Jake that I was able to just walk out of that prison?" He deeply inhaled the cigarette he had just lit. "I was starting to get the impression that he didn't really want me to get out, so I arranged it to just leave," he said and then laughed hard. Just as quickly, he turned dead serious, the laughter gone. "Despite what they say, Jake, sometimes blood ain't thicker than water." He took a drag, then tapped his ashes into the mug, then stubbed out the cigarette.

The look on his face was pure evil, Jake thought. He wondered just how he had gotten to be the way he was. "Everybody has relatives they don't get along with," he responded.

"Yeah, I guess so."

"Who else is on your list?" Jake quickly asked.

"Wouldn't you like to know." He pulled out another cigarette.

"Tommy Prince, I would bet." Jake said.

Bobby Wayne lit the cigarette, then snapped the Zippo shut once again, seeming to take delight in it, showing off something he had been doing for years. Taking a long drag, he then started to blow out smoke rings. He looked hard at Jake. "Tommy's all that's left on the list. I'm saving the best for last," then he smiled. "Disappointed, Jake, you're not on the list? You probably should be, but you're not. We go way back, Jake, you and me." He leaned over and said, "I mean, your blocking is probably what got me that football scholarship to UT." He flicked ashes into the mug then laughed. "That and a little influence from my uncle."

"That worked out okay for you, I mean you were good enough to start down there. People around here were proud of you. I mean, it's a big deal to play for Tennessee."

"Yeah, it was a big deal at the time," Bobby Wayne replied.

Jake changed directions. "The FBI said your uncle said this all has to do with the Super Bowl. Just what happened at the Super Bowl?" Since they were talking, Jake was hoping to get the story.

"The Super Bowl. Yeah, it all went bad at Super Bowl XIX, at the Rose Bowl in Pasadena, Cal-if-or-na-yay."

"So, tell me about it."

"How much time you got, Jake?"

"Well, seeing as how I'm sitting here at my kitchen table in my underwear, and you've got the only gun in the room, I'd say I've got all the time in the world."

"Good point. You know, you always had a great sense of humor, Jake, going way back."

"You start, I'm wanting to hear this tale," Jake said.

Bobby Wayne leaned back in the chair. "Well, I got home from the Army just about the time Tommy's team was starting to make its run into the playoffs."

"What about you and the Army?"

Bobby Wayne's look was now almost unnerving. "The Army? Let's just say they put me in a program where we worked with some very bad guys who were able to take care of some things for the United States government in a certain part of the world. Only problem was, there were people who didn't want us to be involved with these people, and when it came out what was happening, we, the soldiers, got hung out to dry. The politicians scattered like quail. The careers of some very good patriots were ruined by some people in the White House who didn't have the guts to do the right thing. That's all I'm gonna say about that right now. That's another tale for another day," he said, obviously very upset and annoyed. He snuffed out his cigarette in the mug, then quickly pulled out another one and lit it, again snapping the lighter shut in a way that seemed to give him pleasure.

Jake was glad to hear that he might be around for another day.

Bobby Wayne quickly shifted gears. "The Super Bowl, you asked me? It all goes back to our days at Tennessee. Jake, we had some good teams in Knoxville when Tommy and I played there. Lots of games we were heavy favorites. I mean the lines were like fourteen to twenty-one points. What we did was, me and Tommy, we devised a plan where we would do games that we didn't cover the spread, but we never lost the game. You know what I'm saying, Jake? We never threw any games, we just controlled the outcomes of them. If we were favored by the bookies at fourteen points, we just made sure we didn't win by more than that. By our junior season, Tommy was the quarterback and I was the starting tailback. I mean, all it usually took was a fumble or an interception by one of us late in the game, if needed, to see that it happened. We didn't lose the games, so what harm was done in that?"

"Nothing I guess, unless you were the guy that lost a bet on a game that wasn't on the up and up."

"Yeah, well they didn't know that, so the way I see it, no harm was done. For everybody that wins a bet, there is somebody that loses one. It all washed out the same to me. That's the chance they took."

Jake just looked at him, trying to understand his logic. "Any of your other teammates in on it, or did they know about it?"

"Oh no, it was just me and Tommy. My uncle put up and bet all the money, and we got a cut of it. He never told anyone else about it. It was pretty much a foolproof plan as long as the three of us kept it to ourselves, and that's what we all swore to do. I guess us, and my uncle's bookie. Usually six grand a game was what he gave us and we split it. That's a lot of money for two college boys back in the '70s."

"I'd say. How much did he bet on the games?"

"I have no idea. We never discussed it. I'm sure he would've let me know if we had lost one."

"How many games?"

"We did it twice our junior year. The Auburn and Mississippi State games. Our senior year, we did it on Georgia Tech, Florida, and Duke.

Then we did the Sugar Bowl against Arkansas. We won every game, but never covered the point spread. You couldn't do it every game, the point spread had to fall into the right range, the fourteen to twenty-one points I mentioned, for it to work and for us to make sure we won the game as well. Otherwise it was too big of a risk. I mean, when we played Alabama and Georgia and LSU, the spread was maybe three points, one way or another. That was too close to take a risk on. I mean those were tough games that could go either way. No way could you control the outcome."

"Did you ever have one that maybe got a little close?" Jake asked him, intrigued that Bobby Wayne was talking and telling him just what he wanted to know.

"Only the Sugar Bowl was a little too close," he answered, grinding out another cigarette in the mug. "I had to fumble late in the game and then they had to take it in and score to get inside the spread. They ran it in from the one on the last play of the game to cut the lead to 30-21. I was in on defense, I played both ways, and I made sure I got blocked on the play. They ran right over me. The spread was fourteen, we won by nine. There is a picture of me and Tommy hugging and laughing as we ran off the field that was in all the newspapers. Little did everybody know why. Somebody told me they got a copy of it hangin' in the museum in the football complex. We were happy that we won, but we were happier that Arkansas scored at the end, believe me."

"Your uncle was the longtime chairman of the UT Athletics Committee. How did you get him to go along with it?"

"The only thing my uncle liked better than Tennessee football was making money and feeling like he was in control of things..... everything to him is about who has the power."

Jake just shook his head. "So you get out of the Army and you come home, and as the Jets get closer to the Super Bowl, you're thinking what?"

"I call up Tommy and say I think we can do the same thing we did in college and make ourselves a lot of money if the point spread is right."

"And he says?"

"He's all for it and he thinks he's got a couple guys on the team that'll go along with him on it."

"Let me guess, Rockett and Moore?"

"You got it, Jake. So I go talk to my uncle about it and I tell him that if the Jets get to the Super Bowl and the point spread comes out right, Tommy and I think we can do this in a big time way. I tell my uncle we should bet a million dollars on the game. It would be the largest bet made on the Super Bowl in Las Vegas at that time." He sat up in his chair and smirked.

"A million?"

"Oh, yeah. You see I've come out of the Army with a large sum of money, so my uncle and I go in as partners on this."

"And how do you come out of the Army with a lot of money?"

Bobby Wayne sat back for a moment, took out and lit another cigarette, exhaled the smoke, then said, "I was involved in some operations, like I said before, and I'll just go ahead and tell you where, in Central and South America. I was given access to a lot of untraceable cash, and let's just say I didn't always use it where I was supposed to. I skimmed off close to a half million dollars and nobody ever knew the difference. I had it in a bank in the Cayman Islands. But like I said earlier, that's another tale for another day. Hey, you might tell your FBI girlfriend about this for all I know."

"She's not my girlfriend."

"Oh yeah? Really?" He laughed, then coughed from all the cigarettes.

"Let's get back to the Super Bowl," Jake said.

"Ok. So my uncle is all in if the Jets get to the Super Bowl against the right opponent, and at this time it looks like they will as they will be heavily favored no matter who they have to play. They are just beatin' everyone to death at this point. All the prognosticators are saying they may be one of the greatest teams in the history of the NFL. They roll on through the playoffs, basically unchallenged, and into Pasadena to take on the Redskins, who were a .500 team at the midpoint in the season. The 'Skins win a lot of close games down the stretch, the Cowboys fold up at the end, they continue to win close games in the playoffs, and then they slip into the Super Bowl. The line out of Vegas opens at thirteen and a half points. That Sunday night I confirm everything with Tommy. He has his two teammates who are going along with the plan, and you were right, it was Rockett and Moore. They are the starting safeties for the Jets, and of course we have Tommy Prince, the starting quarterback. Who better to control what's going on? They are the ones that can let something happen if you need the score to tighten up. Prince is to be paid fifty thousand dollars and the other two get twenty-five grand each. They all see it as an opportunity to make what they think is easy money. So it will cost us a hundred thousand to get this done. Prince wanted more, but hey, it's not his money that's on the line. He's not about to walk away from fifty big ones, believe me, I know that better than anyone. What is in it for me and my uncle? Well, we are going to go to Las Vegas and make the first ever one million dollar wager on the Super Bowl. We're taking the Redskins and the points."

"This is where the Scarpinos come in?" Jake interjected.

"Well, we got to lay the bet off somewhere."

"And?"

"The sports book at the Alamo Casino agrees to take the bet. You have heard the name Wilfred Henry, haven't you?"

"Wilfred Henry, sure, wasn't he a senator from New York or New Jersey, right?"

"The Honorable Wilfred Henry, the esteemed longtime congressman, and later the senator, from New Jersey. Big Democrat who rose to power tied to FDR. Forty years he was in Washington. At this point he's retired and living on a very large ranch in Nevada, just outside of Las Vegas. The former chairman of the House Ways and Means Committee, which just so happened to appropriate the money to build Hoover Dam and later the TVA dams in Tennessee. You starting to follow where I'm coming from on this?"

"I believe so, but keep going," Jake said, wishing he had a recorder.

"It seems the former senator, on paper anyway, is the owner of the gambling license for the Alamo Casino. The president and general manager of this thriving Las Vegas casino is one Wilfred Henry, Jr., the son of the senator. As we now speak, his grandson, Wilfred III, is on the record as the man in charge."

"You say the senator is the owner on paper? That means the real owners of the casino are?"

"The Scarpino family."

"And the connection between the Scarpinos and the Henrys and the Fosters is?"

"The Scarpinos' construction companies were one of the main contractors on the Hoover Dam in the 1930s and also the TVA dams built in Tennessee starting in the 1940s. Thanks to, of course, at that time Congressman Wilfred Henry. As I said earlier, he was the House Ways and Means chairman. The most powerful man in Washington when it comes to money." Bobby Wayne paused to inhale deeply on his cigarette. "The main supplier for concrete in the building of all the TVA dams in East Tennessee? It's Foster Concrete of Newport, thanks to a deal with Scarpino Construction, who just happened to be the main contractor on those jobs. Foster Concrete? Started by the first Edward Jefferson Foster and still in business today. They all make a lot of money building these dams, including the congressman. Let's just say that the fix was in when the bids came in to do the work on the dams. That's the connection. Who called off J. Edgar Hoover when his two agents disappeared in Tennessee? Congressman Wilfred Henry. If you control the money in Washington, well, you control everything. You see what I'm saying? He tells Hoover to back off and let it go, according to my uncle."

"This is one hell of a story," Jake said.

"Hang on, I'm just getting started. It is arranged for us to make the bet at the casino. Of course, as soon as our bet goes down, then there will be a lot of other large bets made by, shall we say, acquaintances of the Scarpinos. My uncle and I fly to Las Vegas with a million dollars in cash on a private plane on Saturday, the eve of the big game, and we make the wager that night. Everything, and I mean everything, is at our disposal. We each have our own private suite and several beautiful young women are all around to take care of all of our needs for the weekend. In my bedroom, on the foot of my bed when I walk in, was ten thousand dollars in chips for me to play on that night. We have a private dinner with Henry and his son and Johnny Scarpino and his guys on the top floor of the casino overlooking all of Las Vegas. It is a breathtaking view, and it was all very intoxicating to say the least. Everyone is happy about the amount of money we are all about to make on Sunday. At one point, Johnny Scarpino pulls me aside, puts his arm around me, and asks, 'You're sure this plan is foolproof?' I tell him I've never been so sure about something in my life. He then squeezed me very tight and said, 'For your sake, son, I hope so.' I'll never forget that."

"Is that how you really felt?" Jake asked.

"Oh, yeah." He stubbed out another cigarette and looked hard at Jake. "The only problem was that at the same time this was happening, our star quarterback, Mr. Tommy Prince, on the night before the biggest game of his life, has slipped out of the Jets' hotel and made his way to a party out in the Hollywood Hills." Bobby Wayne leaned forward, his eyes drawn tight as he told Jake the story. "You see, there is this ol' gal from Knoxville, a former Miss Tennessee that we knew at UT. Stunning, I mean stunning, but not very smart. Best looking girl I've ever seen in my life, Jake, bar none. She's in Hollywood trying to make it as an actress. Earlier in the week, she leaves Tommy a message at the Jets' hotel to call her. He does and she invites him to this party." He starts to shake his head. "Like I said before, the night before the biggest game of his life and he slips out to go cattin' around. I mean, hell, I shouldn't have been surprised. He was always chasin' some skirt. That's just him." He paused, stuck the gun in the band of his pants and got up and got some more coffee. He held the pot up to Jake and he shook his head no. He put it back and sat down, the gun again placed in front of him on the table.

"So what happens next?" Jake asked.

"He has too much to drink and then goes home with this gal. She was living with some big-shot movie producer, but the ol' boy had flown up to Pebble Beach for a weekend of golf with his buddies. What she didn't know was that the weather up there had started to turn bad on Saturday night and was supposed to be worse on Sunday. So that evening, over dinner and drinks in The Lodge at Pebble Beach, he and his friends decide to fly home and go to the Super Bowl instead. He arrives back home at around three in the morning, comes in and finds our star quarterback in bed with his girl. The guy takes one of his golf clubs and starts beatin' the hell out of Tommy. The broken wrist, the broken ribs, the gash and bruises on the side of his head? They come from the ol' boys nine iron, not some early morning fall down the steps at the hotel. At some point, the guy turns his attention to the girl and goes after her. Tommy grabs his clothes and gets out of the house. A real gentleman, this one. Somehow he walks to a place he can call a cab and gets back to the hotel and sneaks back in. A short while later he stages his famous fall down the steps."

"How do you know all of this?" Jake probed.

"The girl, hey, I knew her, too. Apparently she couldn't act a lick, so after her Hollywood hero gets tired of her and throws her out of the house, she eventually comes back home to Knoxville. She needed a shoulder to cry on and I let her use mine for a while."

"You're one heck of a guy," Jake smugly replied.

"She didn't seem to mind."

"She still around?"

"Last I heard of her, she was workin' the cosmetic counter at Belk in West Town Mall. That was many years ago. You go to prison, Jake, you lose touch with a lot of people." Again he paused. "Most everybody, when I think about it." He shrugged.

"She didn't quite make it to the silver screen," Jake surmised.

"No, she did not. She wound up a long way from stardom in Hollywood."

"The team, the Jets, they bought Tommy's story?"

"Apparently not. It seems the team doctor and the doctors at the hospital were all a little skeptical. It was no coincidence that they traded him to New Orleans in the off-season. At that time they are the worst franchise in the NFL. He goes from the Super Bowl Champions to the Saints, the old first to worst move."

"The game?"

"Without him, the plan doesn't go off like it's supposed to. His backup plays well in his absence, and Rockett and Moore, without his guidance, they don't do what they are supposed to. Rockett gets two interceptions in the game, which he should have just dropped and nobody would've questioned. Then there was Moore, who also got an interception in the first half. After the Redskins score late in the fourth quarter and have cut the Jets' lead inside the point spread, he takes the kickoff, stumbles his way around waiting on someone to hit him, and they don't. He then cuts outside, and his teammates, who have no clue at what is happening, have set up a perfect wall and he somehow reluctantly runs it all the way back for a touchdown. The Redskins fumble the ball back to them and he recovers it. Can you believe that? What's he thinkin'? I'm thinkin' he has no idea what kind of people we are involved with here. The game ends, a seventeen point Jets victory. They have won and covered the point spread. Moore is named the MVP. An interception, a kickoff return for a touchdown, and a fumble recovery. All the money that has been laid off on the Redskins is lost. We are sitting in a room in Vegas with all these Mafia people, watching all this unfold, and I'm thinking to myself we will soon be dead men buried in the Las Vegas desert."

"Then what happened?" Jake asked.

"My uncle gives me the nod, we get up and quickly exit the room, go downstairs and get a cab, and head for the airport. In a matter of minutes we are on the plane flying back to Tennessee."

"So they just let you go?"

He lit another cigarette. "I think that because of his position as governor of Tennessee, they didn't kill us right then and there." Smoke seems to glide off of his cigarette and wind its way up into the air, around his head. His forehead is sweaty. "It's the only reason I can think of that they didn't stop us. Hell, I worried all the way back that something would go wrong with the plane, that it would blow up or something." He sat back and seemed to be looking off into the past. "They would," he slowly said, "come for us later."

"How's that?" Jake asked.

"Oh, it didn't take 'em long. My favorite aunt, the governor's wife, she was my mother's sister, did you know that? Well, her and my fiancé, one Saturday about a month later, they drove from Newport to Knoxville on a shopping trip. On their way back, a tractor-trailer, just outside of Newport, it crosses over into their lane and hits them head on and kills them both. The engine is pushed all the way into the front seat, they have to cut them out of the car." He pauses, "I met her in Florida while in the Army, she was from Tampa." To Jake's surprise, Bobby Wayne's eyes appeared to mist up. Just as fast he regained his composure. "She had been the best thing to ever happen in my life. I guess the only time I was ever in love."

"Maybe it was just an accident," Jake said.

Bobby Wayne looked at Jake, seeming to stare right through him, his thoughts back in that painful past. Then, just as quickly, he started to laugh and slowly shook his head. "No, it was no accident. The guy walked away without hardly a scratch. There were no skid marks on the road, the truck never slowed down. It was over loaded and had just come out of one of my uncle's plants. It happened in broad daylight. They take him to the jail in Newport to question him, and he asks to go to the bathroom, and before they know it, he walks right out a side door that was somehow left unlocked. Somebody is waiting outside to pick him up, and he is never heard from again. A deputy on the sidewalk witnesses him leaving in a car with New Jersey plates. His driver's license turns out to be a forgery. The driver that was supposed to take the load? Someone called him at home that morning and told him it had been cancelled, to go ahead and take a couple days off." Again he paused and stubbed out another half-smoked cigarette. "No, Jake, it was no accident."

"What happened to the three players? Did anybody go after them?" Jake asked.

"Oh, yeah. Something happened to each one of them within the next few months. Rockett had a sister he was very close to, that was a couple of years older than him. They found her dead in a flophouse in Atlanta from an overdose of heroin, the needle still stuck in her arm. Problem was, nobody ever knew of her to use drugs or to frequent that part of town."

Jake sat across the table and listened.

"Moore? He had a grandmother that helped raise him, his mother had died young and the father was an alcoholic who came and went. The grandmother died in a house fire about two weeks after Rockett's sister. Arson investigator said it was caused by a candle in her kitchen. Problem there was that no one had ever known her to burn any candles in her house. Didn't like to have them around. Why? She was petrified of fire."

"And Prince?" What about him, Jake wanted to know.

"Well, ol' Tommy had just moved to his new hometown of New Orleans. He soon meets up with a pretty little gal, as he always did, and goes out with her a couple of times. She invites him to her home to meet her parents in an affluent part of New Orleans and, smelling money, he agrees to go. When he arrives, the only people there are three of Scarpino's boys who let him in, the girl nowhere to be seen. They proceed to beat him severely, including re-breaking his right wrist and busting up his ribs once more. His nose and jaw are broken. As he lays prone on the floor, bleeding and gasping for air, choking on his own blood, one of them leans down and whispers into his ear, 'Mr. Scarpino says to tell you that you are getting off lucky this time.' For good measure, on the way out, they torch his prized possession: his fully restored 1962 Porsche that sits in the driveway. When the firemen and police arrive a few minutes later, he has a hard time explaining to them just what he is doing on the entranceway floor in the house of New Orleans's mayor, who is away with his wife on a junket to Paris. Fortunate for him, the Saints are able to clean the situation up and keep it out of the press and him out of jail. The girl, obviously a plant, was never seen again. Due to the injuries from the beating, it is October before he can again try to play football. The second breaking of the wrist pretty much ends his professional football career. He can no longer grip a football like he could before."

"So his price was they ruined his career..." Jake just shook his head at the tale he was listening to.

"That they did, but he starts a new one as a coach, and I guess by all accounts he's been pretty good at it. Only problem for him has been that my uncle, while he was still in control of the Tennessee athletics committee, he twice kept him from getting the Tennessee job. Finally the school gets him off the committee and out of the way, and Tommy gets his dream job. His only problem now is me. I'm planning to wreck it for him. Then my work will be done."

"No bigger week to do it than this week, the Alabama game," Jake said.

"Jake, I didn't say when. On Saturday morning I plan to be out for a walk."

"A walk, yeah. So you're not gonna tell me?"

"I'm not gonna lay it out for you. But it is going to happen, at some point and time, he's the last name on my list. All these people that have screwed up my life, they are having to pay for it."

"Then you're off to Dubai," Jake said with a smile.

"How do you know about that?"

"I'm tight with the FBI, remember?"

"I'd say, at this point, you're a little more than tight. Just remember my advice about trustin' her. If you ask me, you're crazy not to get back with your ex." He holds his hands up in the air in front of him. "Just a little friendly advice, that's all."

"You're a great one to be giving advice."

He looks at Jake and shrugs.

"What's the attraction to Dubai?"

"I'm takin' my Uncle's money, in retaliation for him ruining my life, and I have found a safe haven to spend the rest of my years. They have some very beautiful women there, Jake, especially if you have a lot of money. It seems to make me more attractive to them, if you know what I mean." He looked at Jake and grinned. "Also, I've been assured by my friends in their government that the U.S. government can't mess with me there."

"Sounds good, I guess, using your logic," Jake replied. He stopped for a moment then asked, "Why don't you just leave now? I mean, why risk it all on trying to get even with Prince? Why keep pressing your luck with the FBI? Sooner or later they will catch you."

"I don't think so, not if you plan everything out as you should. That is what I do, Jake. I'm very meticulous, as you should well know."

"Sometimes, things can just go wrong, no matter how well you plan," Jake told him.

"Don't try and sell me short, Jake. Don't think you can get in my head. I'm too well-trained for that. I mean, I was trained by the best that this country has to offer, and I'm not talkin' about no FBI. I mean people you don't want to know about. People that the government doesn't want you to know about or the fact that they even exist, still to this day."

His eyes appeared almost red hot to Jake, trancelike, and for a moment, Jake didn't doubt what he was telling him. Or at least, he didn't doubt that Bobby Wayne didn't believe with all his heart and mind what he was telling him.

"Jake, I need a cigarette." He shook his pack that was now empty.

"The way you smoke, you better hope they have some good oncologists over there."

He smiled. "Every man has his vices."

Jake pondered. "So why have you come here and broke into my house this morning to tell me all of this?"

"Well, Jake, you are involved, ya know." He looked again in his pack for another cigarette, but they were all gone. He balled the pack up and dropped it onto the table. "I don't guess you would have any cigarettes around the house, would you?"

"No."

He winced. "Well, I guess I'm gonna have to go. You got any duct tape?"

"Duct tape?"

"I can't just turn around and walk away, you know that."

Jake pointed at a bottom drawer beside the kitchen sink. "There's a roll in there."

Bobby Wayne got up and again stuck the gun into the front of his pants. He found the roll of tape and secured Jake to the chair, pulling his arms behind him and taping them, then wrapping the tape a couple of times around his torso. "That ought to hold you until I can get away.

Surely you can work your way out of this in a few minutes." He headed for the back door.

Jake hollered out, "Hey, before you go, what's Virgil got to do with all of this?"

He stopped in his tracks and turned around. "Who said he did, Jake?"

"I don't know, just a hunch."

"Don't you be worryin' none about Virgil."

"Yeah?" Jake asked.

"Jake, it's been real." Once again he shrugged, then turned, and just like that he was gone.

CHAPTER 27

KNOXVILLE

It was Friday morning of Alabama week. Their meeting started at 7:15 on the dot. The president of the University of Tennessee, Dr. Horatio Brown III, sat at his desk in his palatial office and stared at the two men sitting across from him. The president before him, who had been fired for – amongst other things – his extravagant spending habits, had spared no expense on the room; his loss had been Brown's gain. Andy Drum was Tennessee's athletic director. He was in his third year on the job, and his claim to fame, up to this point, was the hiring of Tommy Prince as the head football coach. That had happened after being on the job all of one month. The three coaches before Prince had all failed miserably to one degree or another. At this moment, Prince appeared to be a great hire, at least on the field. The following day at 3:30, #2 Tennessee would be playing host to #1 Alabama in the biggest college football game of the year. A nationwide Saturday morning television audience with ESPN's Gameday, and all that it brought to the campus, followed by the game on the nationwide CBS-TV telecast, was a dream come true for the Vols. The only problem was the Tommy Prince Super Bowl story was lingering out there, and it didn't seem to want to go away. The third person in the room was Mark Gammons, a long-serving professor of the law school and also the university's head legal counsel. He was also a former Tennessee football player and longtime supporter of the program. He did not really come to the table with an impartial view on what was happening. As for that matter, neither did the other two, both of which had jobs that were measured to a large degree on the success of the university's football program. Whether that was fair or not, that was how things were. They were meeting to discuss what to do, or not to do, about Tommy Prince. Sitting in the outside waiting room, and fuming, was Tommy's agent, who had been denied access to the meeting.

"Tell me again just what he said," Dr. Brown asked Drum.

"I met with him alone in his office yesterday afternoon," he started. "He assures me that he had no connection whatsoever with his two former teammates who have been murdered, and he has no idea how this story got started, or why for that matter. He says that he thinks the girl that came to the press conference was a plant, maybe from another school, to try and make us look bad and hurt us in recruiting."

"And you believe that?"

"Yes, sir, I do," Drum replied, sitting up straight in his chair as he responded, trying to give the president the impression of his self-confidence.

"It just seems so bizarre to me that another institution would stoop so low. What do you think, Mark?"

"Well, sir. I see two things here. One, the credibility of the coach. I have not seen anything since he has been here to think that we should not give him the benefit of the doubt and take him at his word."

"And the second?" Dr. Brown quickly asked.

"I know that we think that another university would never stoop so low as to send someone into one of our press conferences like that. But there is no doubt, sir, that the boosters of a program, and I mean some rogue booster, much like the Alabama man that poisoned the trees at Toomer's Corner in Auburn, well...I could see something like that happening here. I mean, I'm sure there are people that are not happy with us once again becoming a national power in football, and they would like to do something to stop us. So many of these fans that profess their allegiance to some of these universities...why, the only place on campus they have probably ever been is to the football stadium. I see that as a major problem for all schools of our size. To them it is all about the school winning, at whatever the cost. I know that everything now revolves around the money, more so than ever, but we are letting people in the door for functions that have nothing whatsoever to do with this great school, other than the hope we can get their money. I'll bet, sir, that most of the people invited to your box tomorrow for the game, they have never attended a class at this great university."

"Get off your soap box, Mark. My guests tomorrow include the governor, for God's sake, and several key members of the state legislature. And you. You are right, though. It is all about the money and the horse is out of the barn, as my daddy used to say," Dr. Brown said. "But we all know that to be successful, we better play the game, and I mean all of us, no pun intended."

"While we are talking, sir, can I ask you if you have any plans, or have you given thought to honor Governor Foster in any way? He did an awful lot for this university and especially its athletic department over the years." Gammons had been friends with the old man since his playing days, when Foster slipped him one hundred dollar bills after a big game. Both Tommy Prince and Bobby Wayne Foster had been teammates of his. He was a senior, and team captain, when they were sophomores.

"No. My God, the man went behind my back and tried to have me fired by the board when we were finally able to wrestle control of the athletic committee away from him," Dr. Brown said. "No way, Mark, will I honor that crooked old politician, unless I'm made to. I can't believe you even asked me that, or brought it up for that matter. You know full well how I felt about him and you know how hard I worked to get him out of the way."

Gammons knew that most of the hard work was done by the governor at that time, a Republican who purged as many Democrats out of their offices and appointments as he could. He was also responsible for Brown getting his job. He quickly figured out that he better let this issue go. There was no question that he had designs on the president's office for himself one day. He had played a minor part in the Foster situation, trying to keep him in charge of the committee, but he quickly sensed it was not going well and backed off. The president did not detect any involvement on his part or he would be back teaching full time at the law school. He wished now that he had not asked the president about Foster. It was definitely a mistake on his part.

The athletic director chimed back in. "Sir, I have no reason to doubt Coach Prince at this point. He has never done anything since I hired him to make me think he would lie to me."

"Well, and I want you to keep this in this room, the Knoxville police say that the FBI thinks there may be something there. I just don't know, they sure haven't come and talked to me," Dr. Brown remarked. "Not yet, anyway."

Gammons then jumped back in and responded. "If I may, sir, I just think that from a strictly legal standpoint, at this time there is not any credible evidence that has been brought to our attention that could lead us to suspend or fire Coach Prince. I mean, if we were to suspend him now, before the biggest game of the year, and then nothing comes of this, well, let me just say I think we would all be ruined in this town. We'll all be looking for new jobs." He looked around the room as he said that. "If it does come out that he has had some kind of involvement, then we take an appropriate response at that time and we go from there. If he has to be suspended or fired, if the evidence ever gets to the point that it is that great against him, then so be it." His response was just what he thought the president wanted to hear. In reality, he was excited about what was happening with the football program, and he did not want anything to mess that up.

"All we have is speculation, sir," Drum interjected. He was going to stick up for his man at this point. "If we win the game tomorrow, it will stop an eight game losing streak to Alabama and we should be the number one team in college football. That's what he was brought here to do, and he, along with his coaches and players, they are getting it done."

The president was privately beginning to have his doubts about Prince. There had always been something about him that he did not like, but he could never really put his finger on it. An uneasy alliance between a university president and his football coach was not that unusual. They usually existed in a space that made things work for the both of them. In most cases the coach was the highest paid employee on campus, but that also led to a higher salary for the president as well. The presidents knew and recognized that as a way of life at a big time football school. They were certainly making a lot more money now than they used to. The success of the coach always made the president's job much easier. Dr. Brown looked at the two men seated across from him and said, "As of right now, I see no reason for us to take any kind of action against Coach Prince. I'm sure that is what the two of you wanted to hear, isn't it?" They stood up, shook hands all around, then hastily retreated back to their respective lairs. Gammons and Drum got the decision they wanted. Dr. Brown, not totally sure he had done the right thing, just hoped it wouldn't all blow up on them.

He ushered in Prince's agent for a quick chat to assure him that he had the full support of his administration and that everything was fine.

CHAPTER 28

JONESBOROUGH

It was around 7:45 when Ralph saw the black BMW with tinted windows pull out from behind Jake's farm house, come up by the golf shop, and quickly fire itself down the gravel road that took it back to the highway. He had been out front of the shop reloading a soft drink machine. It was not a vehicle he was familiar with. He went back inside and tried Jake's home number, then his cell. Jake didn't answer either one. At that point he grabbed his gun, stuck it in the back waistband of his pants, picked up his cane, and started moving as fast as he could toward Jake's house. He was still somewhat slowed down from the beating he had taken at the junkyard. The front door was unlocked, he called out Jake's name, got no response, so he took out his gun and moved on into the house. As he got near the kitchen door, he heard a racket and with his gun drawn, he slowly moved into that room. There was Jake, standing up, somewhat bent over and hopping around the kitchen with a chair taped to his bottom. He was flailing back and forth about the room, trying to work his hands loose. His eyes went wide when he saw Ralph and he told him to get him loose.

Ralph moved over and with great delight jerked the duct tape off of his hands.

"Good God, man, did you have to do that so hard?" Jake exclaimed.

"You been robbed?" Ralph asked.

"Not hardly," he said glaring back at him.

"You get caught playing some kind of kinky game?" Ralph asked, grinning. He pulled out a pocket knife and finished cutting him loose.

"No." Jake was pulling off the duct tape.

"I mean, taped to a chair in your underwear? What am I missing here?"

"Very funny. Our buddy Bobby Wayne has been here for a little visit and he taped me to the chair so he could get away."

"Black BMW?"

"How would I know?"

"Well, that's what came out from behind your house just a few minutes ago. Late model black BMW. Tinted windows, so I couldn't see who was in it."

"He was in here in the kitchen when I got up this morning and he laid it all out for me. Told me what went on with the Super Bowl. Pretty much the same story the FBI tells, with a little more detail added to it. Then he taped me up and left."

"At least he didn't kill you."

"Yeah, he told me I wasn't on his list."

"That's good to know. Did he say who was?"

"Tommy Prince, and then he says he's done." Jake heard his cell phone ring and went to the bedroom to get it. "Hello?"

"Jake, it's Sarah."

"Well, listen, you left too soon this morning. I got up not long after you and found Bobby Wayne sitting in my kitchen drinking the coffee that you made. He says he watched you go."

At first she wasn't sure what to say, so there were a few moments of silence. "Jake, that man is so scary, I can't describe it…"

"He seems to always be one step ahead of everybody else."

"Are you okay? He didn't hurt you?"

"No."

"I'm glad to hear that."

"Thanks."

"Jake, the reason I called…I ran Virgil's name in the FBI computer."

"And?"

"It seems Virgil does, but then again doesn't have a record."

"What are you saying?" Jake responded.

"It seems he was busted down in Florida back in the early 1980s for flying in drugs from Colombia. That's Colombia in South America we are talking about, not South Carolina."

"You sure it's him? I've never heard him mention flying."

"It's him all right. Same social, listed his address as Jonesborough, Tennessee."

"Early '80s? About the same time that Bobby Wayne was down there in the Army?"

"The dates overlap."

"That's interesting."

"That's what I thought," she replied.

"What are you saying, that he does but doesn't have a record?"

"He was busted by the DEA at a small airstrip in the Keys where he had stopped to refuel. Caught with a whole planeload of cocaine. Spent a night in jail in Miami, not able to make a pretty substantial bond, then the next day the charges are dropped, just like that, and he walks. There is so much of the records redacted that there is more blacked out than what there is to read. You can't make heads or tails of it."

"Anybody know how the charges got dropped?"

"Well, I was able to get the name of the arresting officer off of the report. I know him, he is now one of the head guys at the DEA. I worked with him one time on a case. So when I see his name on there this morning, I called him in Washington, and he calls me right back. Says he remembers the case like it was yesterday. He says that the story they got was that a congressman from Tennessee, that covered the area that contained a little town called Newport, he had enough pull to get the charges dropped. Can you believe this? A congressman gets the charges dropped? Must have had something on somebody. He says it all just went away and they were told not to worry about it or to pursue it any further."

"A plane full of cocaine and it all just goes away?"

"Apparently the plane just went away as well."

"Why's that?" Jake asked.

"He said that before it was ever unloaded, the Army shows up with orders to take the plane. They got in it and flew it off while they were lining up getting it unloaded, right there in plain daylight in the Keys. It was one of those planes that was gutted so that there was only room for the pilot and the drugs. The guy at the DEA says his boss told him to let the Army take it, orders from above, and to just act like it never happened. Consider it an issue with national security implications," he was told. "He said the Tennessee congressman was also the ranking Republican of the House Armed Services Committee."

"Unbelievable. The Army takes the plane and the drugs away from the DEA?"

"That's what he said."

"How many millions of dollars are we talking about?"

"I wouldn't know where to start," answered Sarah.

"This thing just gets more bizarre by the minute," Jake said.

"Somebody had high friends in high places."

"So this all has to do with Virgil and Bobby Wayne and something he was doing while in the Army. Sounds like they were bringing in drugs from Colombia to Newport, probably for his uncle. Virgil gets pinched, the uncle calls in a political favor from his congressman, who is involved as well, and then nobody gets rolled over on," Jake said. "I mean it's hard to believe stuff like this can even happen."

"Unfortunately, it happens more than you can ever imagine, Jake. If you got money and connections in this country, you can get out of a lot of things. You didn't really hear that from me, but it's true," she said. "It looks to me that your hunch about Virgil is right."

"He told me one time that he owned a bunch of condos in Sarasota, Florida. I thought that was a little odd. I wondered to myself, how does a guy that comes from very little wind up with a bunch of property in an expensive place like Sarasota? I'd say that's what he did with what he was haulin' in off the drugs. I bet if you research it, he bought that property down there in the early '80s. It still blows my mind that he is a pilot, and apparently a pretty good one at that. I mean, it's a long haul from Colombia to the Keys. I would think you really have to know what you're doing to do that."

"Jake, we are going to be in Knoxville tomorrow, trying to help establish a presence, and to be around in case something goes down."

"In my visit with Bobby Wayne this morning, he tells me that there is only one name left on his list and that's Tommy Prince. He says when that is taken care of, we'll never see him again," Jake told her.

"You're welcome to join us tomorrow."

"To be perfectly honest with you, I'm going to be there as the guest of my ex-wife, sitting in the President's box.

"Lucky her."

"Listen, you can call me if you think something is going to go down and you need me."

"Somehow, I feel like I've been used," she said.

"Yeah, well that works both ways."

"Do me a favor, will you, Jake?"

"Sure."

"If I don't get the chance to see you tomorrow, will you tell Susanne I said hello? Tell her we must get together sometime and catch up."

"I think I'll stay out of that," Jake responded. He heard her laugh as she hung up. Deep down, he knew getting involved with her, for whatever his reason, and as good as the night had been, was a mistake that he hoped didn't come back at some point in his life to haunt him.

CHAPTER 29

They were back at the golf shop and Ralph, leaning on the counter and drinking coffee, was hard at work on his morning crossword puzzle.

"Has Virgil been in here this week?" Jake asked him.

Ralph pondered on that thought for a moment. "No, come to think of it, I don't believe he has."

Jake tried Virgil on his cell phone, got his voice mail, and hung up. "I'll be back in just a little bit," he said to Ralph as he quickly headed out the door.

"Hey, where you going?" Ralph shouted after him, but Jake was already out in the parking lot, and he didn't get a response.

Virgil lived in The Ridges, the country club community on the far side of Jonesborough, in a million dollar home. Jake knew the value of the house because Virgil had told him on more than one occasion how much his house had cost to build. It was a far cry from the mobile home he had grown up in. "Only in America," he liked to tell Jake. Problem was, Jake now was beginning to believe that the 'self-made business man' success story Virgil liked to portray was not what it was cracked up to be. Drug money somehow seemed to be in play, and more than likely it came from an alliance with Bobby Wayne. Jake now hoped to catch Virgil with a surprise visit. The drive would take about twenty minutes.

At exactly 10:00 a.m., Jake quietly pulled into the driveway. The doors on his three-car garage were all open, and he could see that Virgil's Dodge Ram pickup truck and BMW sedan were both parked inside. Jake pulled out his Glock, checked it and holstered it. He got out of his truck and slipped on his navy blazer, concealing the gun. He pitched his Ray-Bans onto the seat, squinting hard as the sunlight of the beautiful fall morning hurt his eyes. Then he walked up the front steps and rang the bell. In a moment, Betty answered the door.

"Morning, Jake, what brings you out?" she asked rather suspiciously in her tight-fitting sweater that left little to the imagination.

"I'm needing to talk to Virgil," he replied with a smile. "I was hoping he was home."

"And here I was hoping you had come to see me," she responded somewhat devilishly before opening the door all the way and letting him in. "Can I take your coat?"

"No, I'm good."

"Well, how about a drink? I fix a mean Bloody Mary," she offered.

"It's a little early in the morning for me, but thanks anyway."

"Why, Jake, it's never too early in the morning at my house!" she said laughingly. "Not for you and me."

There was not a question she was the flirtatious type, Jake thought. "Sorry, but I came to see Virgil."

"He's around here somewhere," said Betty. "Let me go get him for you." About that time, Virgil entered the room.

"Jake, I thought I heard your voice out here." He strode across the room and shook his hand. He was dressed as if he were heading out to the golf course. "What brings you out on this beautiful morning?"

"Couple of things I need to ask you in private, that is if you don't mind."

"Let's step back into my office." He tried to give Betty the sign to get lost without Jake seeing him. She didn't seem too happy about it. "We can talk back here in private." He looked at his watch. "I'm supposed to tee off in thirty minutes. Some Chinese investors in town looking for someone to build some apartments for them near the university."

"I'll try not to make you late."

He ushered Jake into his well-appointed office with its dark paneling, leather chairs, and couch. A flat screen TV hung over the fireplace. A large wooden desk sat in the back of the room. It was bigger, Jake believed, than any he had ever seen, its top cluttered with papers. There was even a pool table and a bar off to one side. Jake noticed, and thought it somewhat odd, that the room was void of any type of personal touch. Virgil had three children, one from his first wife and two by the second, and even a few grandkids, but not a picture of any of them were to be found. But then again, he probably had not won any father of the year awards. There was nothing to suggest he had any hobbies. There were some books on shelves along the walls, but they looked to Jake like they had been put there by an interior decorator and had never been touched.

"Pull up a seat," he said, pointing at the couch. Jake sat down on one end, Virgil on the other. Jake sank back into the leather. "Very nice," he remarked.

"Thanks, this is where I come to get away from Betty," he laughed, "and also to do a little work." He pulled out a cigarette, struck a match, and lit it. "I'd offer you one, Jake, but I know you don't smoke. I do have some cigars, Cuban actually, if you would like one. The best in the world, my friend."

He was tempted at that offer but said, "Perhaps some other time."

"To what do I owe this visit?"

"You know, Virgil, I keep having this hunch, and it just won't go away." He was now leaning somewhat forward. "I mean, I can't get this thing off of my mind, so here goes." He paused for a moment, cleared his throat, looked at Virgil, and began. "Ralph and I have been working this case on Bobby Wayne for the FBI, and I know that you have overheard us talking about it, am I right?"

"Yeah, I guess so," he said, then tapped his cigarette twice in an ashtray. "But what's that got to do with me?"

"I don't know, that's what I'm tryin' to figure out. You have known me most of my life, right?"

"Yeah."

"You know that I always speak my mind, I don't have a filter."

"For sure."

"Well, somebody tipped the boys off at the junkyard about our surveillance. I mean, they had to, otherwise nobody would've ever known we were there."

Virgil just looked at Jake.

"You following me on this?" Jake asked.

"Not yet."

"Virgil, this is you and me talkin' here."

"Come on, you don't think that was me, do ya? My God, I wouldn't do that."

"As far as Ralph and I can figure, you were the only other person who knew we were goin' out there. You overheard me and Ralph talking about it, did you not?"

"That's crazy, Jake." The cigarette dangled from his lips, smoke curling around his head.

"Is it?"

Virgil pulled it away from his mouth and again double tapped it on the ashtray. "You're crazy if you think I did that. My God…"

"Those guys almost killed Ralph."

"Ralph's my friend, come on, Jake. How about the FBI? They knew about it. Right?"

"They were paying us to be there."

"Yeah, but maybe someone else with the Bureau knew about it and tipped them off. Maybe a local FBI agent that knew about it."

"How do you know the ones we are dealing with are not from the local FBI office?" Jake quietly asked him.

"I don't, that was just a guess on my part, that's all."

Another strike against him, Jake thought. "I'll tell you one thing, I pity the man who did it if Ralph ever finds out who it was." He shifted his weight on the couch, pausing for effect. "I was his partner in Nashville all those years," then he stopped again as he stared hard at Virgil. "I've seen firsthand down in Nashville just what he can do." Again he paused. "You do know that he was in charge of interrogating captured VCs when he was in 'Nam with the Marines, don't you? I believe I told you about that. There's a reason they gave him that job, you follow me?"

Virgil nervously put out his cigarette in the ashtray.

"Do you have any idea of what he did over there? I mean, I've heard that he did some crazy stuff to get them guys to talk. One time they took two VCs up in a helicopter, you following me on this? He tied a rope to an ankle on both of them, and as they went up he has his interpreter ask them questions. They won't say anything. He kicked one guy out of the chopper and he's hanging below them on the rope by his ankle. They went up several hundred feet in the air, and he keeps asking the other one questions, but he still doesn't respond. So Virgil reached down with his knife and cut the rope and lets him fall to his death. At that point, the other guy started talking to his interpreter and wouldn't shut up, telling them what they wanted to know. I didn't hear that story from him...no, he'd never talk about it. But I've heard it from guys he was there with. Some of them ol' Marines, they would come to Nashville to see him from time to time. There was a reverence for him from the guys he served with. They come to town, get drunk, and they all wanted to tell me about what he had done over there. They said, to a man, that he would always interrogate the VC they brought in, and he would find out what it was they needed to know. Always. They say nobody had any problems with what he did or how he did it because he saved a lot of guys' lives. Think about who you're dealin' with here. I don't think you know Ralph as well as you think you do. If you did rat him out, you better hope he never finds out it was you."

"Come on, Jake, it wasn't me. You know me better than that."

"Do I?" Again Jake paused. "Let me ask you this, Virgil. What were you doing the other night at the Carnegie when we had the bomb threat? My ex-wife, we thought for sure that was a bomb in her room. Do you know how scared she was? Did you just happen to be there that night? I saw you out in the parking lot and I know you saw me. Just a coincidence?"

"Yeah, it was a coincidence." He lowered his voice. "I was there with somebody else when the alarm went off, we had to get out. I went one way, she went the other. Simple as that. I'm whispering because I don't want Betty to hear me. You can understand that, can't you?"

"What room?"

"What?"

"What room were you in?"

"I don't know...three something."

"I can check that out, Virgil, I got close with the girls at the front desk when I worked that case for you on Betty. I'm gonna confirm it with them this afternoon."

"I paid in cash and gave 'em a fake name." He pulled out another cigarette. "They won't tell you anything, it's against their policy...an unwritten rule."

"What name?"

"Come on, Jake, this is ridiculous." He lit the cigarette, but his hand shook when he struck the match and Jake noticed.

"Virgil, I can make them talk if I need to."

"Yeah?"

From his coat, Jake pulled out his gun and laid it on the couch beside his leg, his hand on top of it. "Let's change the subject for a moment."

"You're starting to sound just like a lawyer if I didn't know better."

"Some people aren't always what they appear to be, Virgil. You follow my drift?"

"No, not really."

"Let's move right along then," Jake said.

"Sounds good to me." His eyes were on the gun. "Why you pullin' out a gun on me?"

"How long you been flying?" Jake had his full attention now.

"What are you talking about?" he replied.

"I want to know how long you've been a licensed pilot. Flying airplanes

BARRY BLAIR | 197

all over the place. Mexico, Panama, even down to Colombia I've been told."

He stubbed out the cigarette he just lit. "This is crazy."

"Is it?"

"I'm not a pilot. I don't know how to fly a plane."

"Really?" Jake reached into his coat pocket and pulled out a piece of folded-up paper. "You know what I've got here?"

"I have no idea," he said, looking at it suspiciously, yet he knew what it was.

Jake unfolded it. "I got a copy of it right here, your FAA certification. I mean, I got it from the FBI. We are dealing with the FBI, you know. Come on now. Do you think there is anything these people can't find? According to them, you been a licensed pilot since 1980." He turned the paper around where Virgil could see it. "Just how hard do you think it is for the FBI to come up with this for me?" He snapped his fingers. "Not very hard at all."

"Where are you going with all of this, Jake?"

"Tell me about you and Bobby Wayne."

"Tell you what?"

"Start with the part about smuggling drugs into the United States?"

"You are crazy, I don't know what you are talking about."

"How about you start with you getting arrested by the DEA at an airstrip down in the Keys with a planeload of cocaine back in the '80s?"

"I don't know what you are talking about." He appeared more nervous by the minute.

"Islamorada, I believe they said."

"This is insane."

Jake reached back into his pocket and pulled out another sheet of paper. He opened it and turned it around so Virgil could see it. "Seems this one is a copy of your mug shot and…"

"There is no record of me being arrested down there," he interrupted.

Jake laughed. "Just because you boys were able to get your charges dropped with the help of your congressman, that doesn't mean that all the paper work went away. That old boy that arrested you back in the day, he's now one of the head wheels at the DEA, and he was never real happy about what happened down there. It seems that someone with the Army made off with the plane and the drugs. I guess, at the time, you guys made him look a little foolish."

"So what do you want with me, Jake?"

"I want to know what the connection is between you and Bobby Wayne." He picked up the gun from the couch and cradled it in his hand. "The FBI is going to nail you, Virgil, and when they do, when they prove that everything you've got came from hauling and selling drugs, they'll take it all. Everything. They will connect every deal you've ever made in your life to drug money. This fine home, your construction company, the condos down in Florida, your cars, whatever else you own. They will take it all and auction it off while you are sitting in some federal prison somewhere. Your best bet is to give yourself up and strike a deal with them."

He pulled out another cigarette and lit it. "I can't do that, Jake. You don't know what kind of person you're dealing with in Bobby Wayne. The man has no conscience. You cross him and he will kill you. I give him up, or try to, he will kill me as sure as I'm sitting here."

Jake saw the fear in his eyes when he said that.

"You give him up, they'll bring him in, and you'll be protected. Maybe the witness protection program, you can go somewhere and start a new life. Sure would beat goin' to prison, I would think."

"I don't think he can be caught, Jake, to be real honest with you."

"What's the connection, Virgil?"

"What do you mean?"

"There has to be some kind of connection between you and him, what is it? I mean, whatever made you get involved with him?"

"I'm not really what you would call involved with him."

"Don't lie to me, Virgil, never again." Jake rolled the pistol over in his hand.

He looked at Jake for a long moment, took a drag on the cigarette, then again tapped it twice on the ashtray. "What you don't know, Jake...oh geez, I hate to tell you this, I don't know how to tell you this." He stopped and took a deep breath. "You and me go way back, Jake, you know that."

Jake just stared at him. At this point, none of that mattered to him. They were past that.

"What I'm gonna tell you is not something I'm proud of Jake, and I hope you can understand that. Damn, this is hard." He looked around the room then said, "I need a drink."

"You just stay where you are and keep talking."

"Jake, me and Bobby Wayne ..... we are related. It's blood, Jake, it's all about the blood." He had spit it out.

"What are you talking about?" He had Jake mystified as he had known his parents when they were growing up.

"He's my brother, Jake."

"What? How can that be?"

"Well, actually he's my half-brother. His daddy had an affair with my mother. She told me the summer after we all graduated from high school. My parents, well the man I'd always thought was my daddy, and my mother, they had just got divorced. You'd done gone off to the service about that time. She said she thought I needed to know. I think she figured it best I heard it from her before somebody else told me, like Bobby Wayne, or my dad, I guess."

"You know this for sure?"

"My momma said she was a hundred percent sure. I mean, why would she make something like that up? She said she felt it was the right thing to do. Anyway, at some point right after that, one night when we'd both had too much to drink, I tell Bobby Wayne about it. He said he knew, that he had known about it for a long time."

"And?"

"Well, nothing happened right away. He went off to UT to play football. I was in and out of ETSU over the next few years, partying, just havin' a good time. At some point I decided to start a construction company, and at first I had some success. Then the economy crashes, interest rates are out the roof and nobody can afford to build anything. I'm losin' my shirt.

About that time, he's now in the Army, home on leave, and we have a few too many beers one night and he tells me he is stationed down in South America somewhere, working, he says, on some top secret stuff for the CIA. I tell him how I'm broke and I don't know what to do next. He tells me to come down to Florida and he knows some guys who can teach me to fly and help me get my pilot's license. He says if I do, he can get me all the work I want as a pilot flying things in and out of South and Central America for him. I ask him what kind of things, and he says it's for the government and it's all top secret, he can't tell me. You just fly the stuff where they tell you to and don't ask any questions. I ask if it's dangerous and he says not at all. I got nothin' to lose, so I tell him to count me in. Next thing I know, I'm in Tampa with some pretty shady characters who teach me how to fly and quickly get me certified. Soon I'm flying stuff back and forth from different points in Florida and Texas to South America, Central America, and Mexico. Sometimes I had to fly into some pretty remote places. I learned to fly all kinds of different planes. Sometimes I'd even fly stuff up to Newport for him."

"You're never knew what you were carrying?"

"I guess at first I was pretty naïve. But he was paying me a lot of money, I mean a whole lot of money, and so I never asked questions. He said it was for the government, so I figured who was going to stop and check us? At least that's what I thought until that day I was arrested in Islamorada."

"But you walked out the next day?" Jake asked.

"Some high-dollar lawyer showed up the next morning and said it was all a mistake, the charges had been dropped, and I was free to go."

"The plane?"

"It supposedly left the air strip near Islamorada about the same time I did. That's all I know about that."

"The Army came and got it. Did you know that?"

"I did not, and that is the truth."

"Keep going," Jake said.

"It wasn't too long after Islamorada that he was court-martialed, sent to Leavenworth, then after less than a year he was discharged. Honorably,

I might add, believe it or not. Seems some upset DEA guys talked to some congressman who threatened to blow the whistle on whatever it was they were doing. It went all the way to the White House I was told, and pretty soon, just like that, it was all over. I'd made enough money to buy a building of condos on the beach in Sarasota and to bankroll my construction company and get it rolling again. My money was in a bank down in the Caymans. But I tell you, Jake, that arrest scared the hell out of me."

Betty tapped at the door and stuck her head in the room. "Sorry to interrupt, but they just called from the golf shop and said your guests were waiting on you." She looked at Jake and smiled, then eased back out the door.

He arose from his end of the couch. "Sorry, Jake, I got to go," he said. "You're not going to arrest me are you?"

"Don't guess I can, I'm just a private investigator, you know. I will take you in to the FBI if you want to turn yourself in. I'm guessing that it would help your case."

"I can't do that, Jake. They would want me to roll over on him, and if I did, I'd be a dead man walking. Hell, you know that."

"You do what you got to do," Jake said, slipping his gun back into its holster.

"Sorry, Jake, it's the way it's got to be."

"I think you are probably doomed either way."

"Yeah, well, I gotta run. Betty can show you out."

Jake just shook his head.

Virgil, almost out the door, turned back around. "Jake, I never did answer your question."

"Yeah?" he replied.

"Guns and cocaine." He paused for a moment. "I took guns down and brought cocaine back." He turned, stepped out the door, and was gone.

CHAPTER 30

On Friday night, Jake and Ralph sat in the Adirondack chairs on Jake's back deck where they had grilled out steaks and now were enjoying the evening. Butch was stretched out between them, having been given a good portion of both of their steaks. They smoked cigars and Jake enjoyed a cold PBR and Ralph, trying once again to quit drinking, was nursing a Diet Coke.

"I guess that just goes to show you that you better be careful what you say and to whom," Ralph said. "I had no idea that Virgil couldn't be trusted. It's my own fault really."

"Well, I'd be lying if I didn't say I was starting to have my doubts about him for the last few weeks," Jake replied. "That's why I took off out of the golf shop like I did this morning, I was hoping I could catch him at home and get him to talk. The FBI had given me the low down on his arrest down in the Keys."

"He wouldn't go in, huh?"

"No, he's more scared of Bobby Wayne than he is us or the FBI," Jake said. "I've also thought that maybe he's in way too deep, maybe a lot more so than he let on. I mean, you get right down to it, pretty much everything in his life is a lie. You know what I mean? Maybe he was never the good ol' friend to me that he tried to portray." Jake shook his head. "I just don't know, he's really tryin' to live two lives. My guess is that if we ever get the chance to take Bobby Wayne down, and he's there, he'll probably go right down with him. I told him this morning that whichever way he chooses to go, it could end badly for him, but much more so if he sticks with him. I said, 'Give yourself up and I'll take you in.' I think he knows somethin' about the local FBI office that makes him a little nervous. He says he will take his chances with Bobby Wayne. So be it, I say. He's making the choice."

Ralph swigged his soft drink and yearned for something much harder. For him, the craving never seemed to go away. Every day he didn't drink was hard. He woke up in the morning craving a drink and when he went to bed at night, the feeling was the same. It's not something you can explain to people who don't face the same fight. "I hope he don't come back around me no more, I don't know what I'd do, Jake, if I saw him."

Jake sat down his beer and picked up his laptop. "Somethin' here I want to show you, Ralph." He opened it up and turned the screen where Ralph could see it as well. "I contacted NFL Films in Philadelphia and asked them what kind of footage they had on the Super Bowl and if I could see it. Some very nice woman there, extremely helpful, downloaded for me the television broadcast of the game, minus the commercials. Pat Summerall and John Madden doing the game. It was fun just listening to them. The lady also says she has all additional footage shot by their guys if I need to see more than what this shows. So, anyway, when I got home today I've got it, and I watch it, and I've found something very interesting. You watch this and tell me what you see."

"Sure thing," Ralph replied.

Jake searched around to the part he wanted, started it, and it's the kickoff return by Donn Moore. Moore catches the ball right at the goal line and starts up the field. "Now watch this closely," Jake said to Ralph. "He starts out just like you think he would, busting it up to about the twenty yard line. But then watch what happens. He slows down, almost to a stop, seems to pause, not sure which way to go, then he slowly shifts out toward the left sideline. The whole time I think he's lookin' around, waiting for someone to tackle him, but nobody comes. It's crazy, his teammates have blocked everyone that is near him. It's like the perfect play."

"Yeah, how often do you see that kind of execution?" Ralph said.

"So he drifts out to the sideline and sure enough, they've got a wall set up and he's just goin' down through there, waiting for someone to break through and hit him, but it never happens. It's crazy when you know what's going on. He's running and as he gets near midfield, the wall is still there and he just seems to pick up steam, and as he gets down near the twenty, he's looking back over his shoulder, and like I say, if you know what is going on, you know he is looking for someone to tackle him, but they never do. Everybody makes their blocks and he just kind of waltzes into the end zone, and he walks over and hands the ball to the official. He turns around and his teammates are pounding on him, but watch him, he shows no sign of being excited. He just starts slowly jogging back, heading for the bench, and he's got his head down. Now here is where it starts to get interesting. He's on the sideline, at about the thirty yard line, when the camera cuts back to him. Look who's there to greet him, Johnny Rockett and Tommy Prince. Prince has returned from the hospital and you see his right forearm and wrist are in a cast, he's on crutches. The two of them are beating on him and jumping around him. Pat Summerall says, 'Look there, John, even Tommy Prince is joining in the celebration.' Then Madden says, as only he can, 'He's so excited, he's jumping up and down and hitting him with his cast! I don't think I've ever seen anything like this before.' Then his other teammates start gathering round and Rockett and Prince fade back away."

"That's interesting," said Ralph.

"Ok, now I'm going to back it up, turn down the sound, and play it for you again. Only this time, watch it as if you know Rockett and Prince are mad at him." Jake started the sideline scene again, and Ralph saw just what Jake saw.

"Yeah, if you know they are upset, your view of the whole thing changes. I'll be damned."

"I think they jump him on the sideline and ask him what he was doing. It's perception. It's all in how you look at it. Tommy Prince has at some point returned from the hospital to the bench and he's upset that things are not going as planned. It's as simple as that. Madden thinks they are happy that he scored, but the reality of the situation is that they are mad at him. When other players come over to him, they back off and move away."

At that moment, coming from around the corner of the house, Jake saw her. Sarah Workman dropping in unexpectedly. We don't need this to start, he thought to himself.

"What are you guys up to?" she greeted, strolling up to the deck. "I've tried your cell, Jake, but got no answer. I tried the golf shop and the boy up there said you guys were down here grilling out. Hope you don't think I'm intruding."

He patted his pants pockets. "I think my phone is lying on my dresser back in the bedroom, I must've left it there when I came home and changed clothes. Sorry about that," Jake replied, shrugging.

Ralph stood up and pointed at his chair. "Hey, we're always glad to see a good-looking woman like you stop in. Take my seat."

"What a gentleman you are," she said as she sat down. "I was in Jonesborough at the courthouse to drop some things off, and I thought I would drive on out and maybe catch you here. I hope you don't mind." She looked at Jake and smiled.

That's a lie, he thought to himself. Why would an FBI agent, here from Washington to work a case, be dropping things off at the county courthouse? "You're more than welcome," he said. "Can I get you a beer? That's all I've got except for a soft drink."

"Thank you, Jake, I believe I will."

"Bottle or glass?" he asked as he got up and stepped toward the kitchen.

"Bottle is fine," she answered.

Trying to be one of the boys, Jake thought.

First he stepped back to the bedroom and retrieved his phone. He checked and saw he had no missed calls as he came back up the hall. That's interesting, he thought. Then he got her a beer from the kitchen.

He came back to the porch, handed the beer to her, and then sat back down. He went into the story about meeting with Virgil. Then he told her about the tape from NFL Films and showed it to her, just as he did with Ralph. She quickly picked up on what Jake was talking about. He told her about trying to get Virgil to come in and that he wouldn't. "As far as I'm concerned, he's on his own."

"He should have," she said. She took out a cigarette from her purse and lit it.

"I had no idea you smoked," Jake said.

"I like to have one every now and then," she replied.

"Well, whatever happens to Virgil, let's just say I gave him his chance to let me bring him in. There is no more I can do for him. He wants to cast his lot with Bobby Wayne, then so be it."

For the next thirty minutes they all sat out on the deck and made small talk.

Jake's phone rang and he pulled it out of his pocket. "Hello?" It was his ex-wife. She had called to go over their plans for Saturday. "I'm sitting here with Ralph and your old friend Sarah Workman."

Sarah and Ralph couldn't hear what the response was, but she certainly picked up on Jake looking at her as he listened to what Susanne had to say.

"Okay, I'll meet you at the stadium at two. In front of the statue of General Neyland, right?" Again he paused to listen. "Yeah, we'll watch the Vol Walk and then go on in. I'm looking forward to it. It should be a fun day." He paused. "The Marriott? That's where you are staying?." Again a pause. "Okay, bye."

Ralph stood up. "Jake, I'm out of here. Don't worry about things at the golf course this weekend, I've got it all under control. Miss Workman, I hope you have a lovely weekend."

"Why thank you, Ralph. You are so sweet."

He grabbed his cane, hobbled through the house, and was gone.

Sarah looked at Jake. "Sounds to me like you've got big plans for the weekend."

"Yeah, maybe."

She stood up, as did Jake. "That doesn't leave a whole lot of room for me, does it?"

"I guess not," Jake replied. This could get complicated, he thought.

She moved closer to Jake, and with the fingers of her left hand, she slowly ran them up and down the placket of his shirt, her eyes locking on his. "Somehow, I get the feeling that I've been used."

"I think that works both ways," he responded.

"Well, we are big boys and girls," she said.

"That we are," replied Jake.

"Maybe," she said, then paused momentarily, "I'll run into you and the governor tomorrow in Knoxville. If I do, I'll tell her what a big help you have been to me on this case." Her hand now pressed against his chest, and she gently pushed away, then turned to leave. He watched her go, started to call her back, then didn't. Standing on the deck, he slowly drank his beer and watched the sun sink down behind the distant ridge. In a moment the bottle was empty, he shook it to make sure, then sat it down. He went inside and for the next two hours played his guitar. Butch laid on the rug in front of him and slept, as dogs do.

CHAPTER 31

KNOXVILLE

It was game day in Knoxville. The biggest one in many years. The number one ranked team, Alabama, versus the number two ranked team, Tennessee. Everyone who cared about college football would be tuned in for this one.

Jake left Jonesborough at a quarter before noon and by 1:30 p.m. he was in the parking lot right across from the stadium, thanks to a parking pass secured for him by the governor. He was a few minutes early so he sat in his truck and listened to the pregame buildup on the Vol Radio Network. It was a beautiful fall day and he watched as fans streamed all around the stadium, dressed in orange and crimson. Their procession in was almost river-like. It was quite a colorful sight, Jake thought to himself. A festival of two states. They mingled all around, and fans from both schools talked and chatted with each other, feeling each other out, and dispensing information on their teams to one another. Somebody knew somebody who was close to somebody who shared top secret information on the game. In some cases, they invited the opposition to join them for their tailgates.

At 1:45, the Tennessee fans started lining the streets leading to the stadium so that they could get a glimpse of the Tennessee team as they marched down the hill on Peyton Manning Pass, heading straight into the statue of General Neyland. There the team would turn left onto Philip Fulmer Way, then go a little further down, and take a right and head on into the stadium. Alabama fans also joined in, wanting to size up the opposition. Invariably you would overhear one say to another, "They don't look near as big as our boys." Usually the comment was made boastfully, just loud enough that they were sure some Tennessee fans would hear it as well.

The tradition of the Vol Walk was started by former Tennessee coach Johnny Majors, and the first official walk took place with the Alabama game in 1990. Up until that time, the players walked from the athletic dorm to the stadium on their own and in no organized fashion. Today, with the walk scheduled to start at two, the team buses would pull up at the top of the hill and let the players off. Now players stay off campus at a hotel on the night before the game. The first man off and down the hill would be the head coach; in this case, Tommy Prince. As the procession starts to move, the fans step into the street and close in around the players, leaving just enough room for them to proceed. They take pictures and reach out to touch or exchange a high five with those lucky enough to be in the procession.

Jake got out of his truck and started walking to the Neyland statue, located in the stadium at the intersection of the Manning and Fulmer streets. There he was to meet Susanne and her entourage of staffers and security. On the drive down that morning from Jonesborough, the thought that Bobby Wayne told him that he would be "going for a walk" on Saturday stuck in his head. Could this be what he meant? As crazy as it might seem, Jake thought, surely he wouldn't try anything at the stadium. There were too many people, well over one hundred thousand, for him to try and pull off anything here. You could hardly turn around without bumping into someone. But then again, chaos could prove to be his friend in just such a situation. Jake's thoughts on the matter wrestled back and forth. Coach Prince was surrounded by his security detail on the walk into the stadium. The campus police, Tennessee state troopers, and the

Knoxville police, would be all around him. How in tune they would be in the midst of such a crowd, well, that Jake didn't know. He also knew that the FBI and TBI were lurking nearby as well. As far as he knew, a coach in this position had never had to worry about something happening to him. Sarah had told him that they would be there. He knew he would feel better if he decided to wear his gun. When it came time to enter the stadium, leading up to the game, if the governor's security staff could not get clearance for him to bring it in, he would take it and put it back in his truck. So he threw on his navy sports coat to cover it up. He weaved his way through the crowd and headed for the statue. He got there before Susanne, but a couple of her security people were already there, sizing up the situation, and told him she would be there in a matter of minutes. Scalpers walked around with tickets in their hands. Those in need of tickets were there, too, patrolling the sidewalks with fingers up in the air, signifying how many they were looking for.

Two Knoxville motorcycle policemen made their way down the hill, signifying to the crowd the start of the Vols' procession. Everywhere you looked, the fans seemed to be at least ten or more deep on the sidewalks, and they were starting to push out into the street, trying to get closer, hoping to touch the coaches and players as they would come by. The motorcycles leaned into the turn as they made the corner. Behind them came the cheerleaders, jumping up and down as they marched along. Part of the Tennessee band was across the street blaring away on "Rocky Top." The crowd was roaring. At that point Jake saw his first glimpse of Tommy Prince. He was coming down the hill, resplendent in his navy suit and the customary orange tie, with sunglasses keeping him from making eye contact with anyone. A briefcase swung from one hand, no doubt carrying the plans on how the Vols would beat Alabama. In front of him on foot was a Tennessee state trooper, and on one side was a Knoxville police officer, and on the other side was someone from the campus police force. Another trooper followed right behind him. Tommy worked the crowd, slapping outstretched hands as he proceeded along. Fans tried to push out into the street as far as they could to take selfies, the officers gently pushing them back, trying to keep order and making room. Fathers held up their small sons so they could see, hoping that one day their boy would be one to be making this walk. Mothers held hands with their daughters that they had outfitted in miniature cheerleading outfits. The team, large young men, many black, some white, trudged along briskly. They wore shirts and ties, and a few wore jackets. Most had on some type of ear phones, listening to music as they walked. Many were large, some not so much so. Coaches and staff were interspersed amongst the players. The fans pointed out to the ones they recognized.

It all happened so quickly at the point where Tommy made the turn at the corner. From behind him, on the opposite side of the street, someone had lit a string of firecrackers and tossed them right behind the trailing state trooper. The staccato burst of sound drew everyone's attention and all of the officers seemed to turn around at once. One of them pushed Tommy forward with his arm from behind, but as he did, it happened. A man in a trench coat, seizing the moment in all of the confusion, stepped off the curb, his gloved right hand went into the stomach of Tommy Prince, who seemed to jerk backwards, then fell over, hitting the pavement. The weapon used, a revolver with a screwed-on silencer, was dropped into the street and then kicked by the coach's sprawling foot, sending it spinning away on the pavement. The shooter kept moving and pushed his way into the stunned crowd on the opposite side. A few people in, he dropped out of the trench coat. Underneath that, he had on an orange jacket, just like most everyone else in the crowd. As he continued to push through, he pulled off his hat and a wig he had been wearing and dropped it behind as well.

What he didn't know was that Jake, by sheer coincidence, had been on the opposite side of the street and had seen the whole thing go down. His trained eyes quickly realized what had happened and he set off in pursuit, pushing through the stunned crowd trying to follow the assailant. Pandemonium was beginning to reign as word spread through the mass of people that something had happened. Jake had seen the man come out of his coat and drop the hat and wig. The man, after losing the disguises, glanced backwards and picked up that someone was in pursuit of him. The pace quickened and soon they both were running hard, bumping into and pushing away unsuspecting fans as they went by. One collision had caused Jake to somewhat stumble and lose a little ground.

The shooter went down under the south end of the stadium and cut to where the Alabama team buses had just pulled in to unload. At that point, he turned around again and looked back and saw that Jake was no more than twenty yards behind him. It also afforded Jake the opportunity to see the face of who he was pursuing, and it was of no surprise to him that it was Bobby Wayne. Jake was moving on adrenaline, pushing hard to keep up. As best as he could tell, he was the only one pursuing him. Pandemonium and confusion had taken over back at the sight of the shooting, and that was where all other action was centered. The coach lay in the street bleeding profusely from the stomach as medical personnel pushed through the crowd so they could try to help.

Bobby Wayne came off the steps at the bottom of the stadium, around the parking garage, then cut over and through the gap between the old university buildings that came next. Jake was in pursuit, keeping up, but not gaining ground. Bobby Wayne darted across Neyland Drive, slipping through the backed up ball game traffic. As he hit the far side of the road next to the river, he looked back once again and saw Jake had just reached the road. Now he had to dodge through the traffic as horns blared from the drivers who encountered him. It was at that point, just as he got across the road, that Jake saw it. A yellow biplane with floats swung down over the Tennessee River on a go around from the west and then came back around again and made a bouncy landing on the river. Boats carrying fans on the river to the game scrambled to get out of the way. A small V-hulled aluminum boat swung to the dock and picked up Bobby Wayne, who jumped in and tumbled over. His hard landing almost brought the boat awash, and as soon as he hit, the operator gunned it hard and pulled away, the boat's front end lifting hard out of the water. For a moment Jake thought the boat might capsize. As they pulled away, the man operating the boat handed Bobby Wayne a gun as he rolled over and looked back to the bank. He took aim back at Jake but never pulled the trigger as they raced across the river.

Jake jumped down on the dock, and now waving his gun, commandeered a pontoon boat full of Tennessee fans that had just docked for the ballgame. "Who's driving this boat?" he shouted.

A man, around seventy and dressed all in orange and white, raised his hand. "It's mine," he yelled back.

"Well," Jake said, waving his gun, "get everyone off the boat, I'm taking it. FBI business."

"You can't just take my boat like that!" the man, who'd had a few drinks too many, said.

"Listen, bud, if we can stop those guys right there trying to get away on that airplane, you'll be the biggest hero in Knoxville," explained Jake.

"All right then, but it's my boat, and I'm driving," the man shot back. "Everybody get off!" he hollered, waving his arms. They all did as he said. A woman, who appeared to be with him, had started to object, but he moved her on off.

"Your wife?" Jake asked.

"Just a friend," the old man said as he winked.

"You're risking your life here," said Jake.

"What's life without a little adventure?" He threw the boat in reverse and backed away from the dock, then spun it around and took off at full throttle. "Hang on!" he shouted.

"There could be shooting at us as we get closer," Jake yelled at him.

"What are you after them for?" he shouted back.

"He just shot Coach Prince, amongst other things."

"We heard something on the radio," he said. "They weren't saying what had happened."

"Yeah, the guy in the boat there, he did it."

The man reached under the steering wheel and came out with a handgun that Jake was sure was a .44 Magnum. "Let's go get 'em!" he shouted out, waving it about.

Jake just shook his head. Out on the river, the V-hull approached the plane, pulled around to the far side, and Bobby Wayne and the other man climbed in through the passenger side cargo door, the last one kicking the boat away. As soon as they were inside, the plane moved down the river to the east, then turned and headed back down the river to the west. At that moment a state police helicopter came low down the river from that direction. The pilot swung the plane around in the river and went back to the east. It bounced on the water as it started to pick up steam. The only problem was that there were bridges ahead and a limited amount of room for a takeoff, unlike back down the river to the west.

"You just drive this boat as hard as you can right at the front of the plane, get me as close as you can," Jake shouted. "And let me do the shooting," Jake shouted. "You just drive the boat. If we need your gun, I'll tell ya!"

"You got it!" the man shouted back. The boat made time and angled in on the plane, and as they did, Jake recognized the pilot. The plane continued to pick up momentum, and just as they were getting close it started to lift off of the water.

Jake had his gun in both hands, and he took aim as best as he could on the choppy water, trying to fire into the cockpit, hoping to hit the pilot. The plane bounced a time or two, then lifted completely off of the water. Jake had emptied one clip from his Glock, he dropped it out and inserted another, and kept firing. The plane was now about ten feet off of the water, and then twenty when it seemed to start going back down. Its wing dipped from side to side. It was obvious that something was wrong. It was quickly approaching the old railroad bridge. It would have to either get up quickly to go over it or stay down close to the water to get underneath it, through one of its arches. To go under would take an experienced and confident pilot. Jake did not think they had room to get up and quickly surmised that they would have to go under or crash into the bridge. He continued to fire.

"To the bridge!" Jake shouted at the old man while also pointing to it with his gun. "Follow them!"

The plane slid under the first bridge, but the Henley Street Bridge, with its large concrete stanchions, loomed right behind it. Again, there was not enough room to get the plane up and they would have to pass underneath it as well. The plane seemed to momentarily level off just off of the water, and Jake thought it would pass underneath the structure before possibly again making its ascent into the sky, and they would get away. But as it got to the second bridge, the plane veered somewhat up and to the right, clipping one of the bridge's arched stanchions. Its right wing sheared away and spun back, end over end into the river. The plane violently veered sideways through the bridge before coming down hard on the water and somersaulting over. It lay upside down, then quickly began to sink.

"Go, go, go!" Jake hollered at the old man. In a minute they were over the crash site in the pontoon boat, but the plane was already submerged below the murky water. They circled around the area, but no one came to the surface. Jake walked around the boat, scanning the water for a sign of any kind, but none were forthcoming. This went on for fifteen minutes, by then police and rescue boats had arrived.

Jake sat down on the boat and the exhaustion of the chase hit him. For the first time in a long time, and for why he didn't know, he began to slowly weep. Was it because he had recognized the pilot he was shooting at? In a moment he stopped as he was able to collect himself. He stood up and moved over to the old man, now back at the helm of the boat. "You, sir, did one hell of a job." Then Jake grabbed him around the neck with his arm and squeezed him tight.

CHAPTER 32

The football game with Alabama was postponed. Tommy Prince was rushed to the UT Hospital where he hung to life for an hour as doctors frantically worked on him in the emergency room. That was as far as he got. Despite their best efforts, he did not make it, his wounds too grave.

The legions of fans who had gathered for what was to be a glorious day, hung around, waiting on word for what had actually happened. The stadium remained open and many just went on in and sat down in their seats. Tailgates, though subdued, continued throughout the afternoon. Rumors spread like wildfire. Thousands of fans lined the banks of the Tennessee River on both sides as divers went down to search for the plane.

The Knoxville police and the Tennessee state troopers had set up an operations center near the docks at the river, and that is where Jake waited for word on the bodies. The area was cordoned off. The FBI, the National Transportation Safety Board, the TBI, the state troopers, Knoxville police, and the University of Tennessee police swarmed all around. Jake had been questioned by all of them at some point in the last two hours. The national news media hung just outside the roped off area, hoping to talk with anyone that might shed some light on the story. News helicopters circled the sky. A drone, obviously with a camera, had buzzed back and forth around the bridge and over the operations center. The police, all branches, were beside themselves trying to figure out just who it belonged to. Jake even heard some talk about them possibly trying to shoot it down.

The governor and her detail had arrived. She ran up and hugged Jake when she saw him.

"Are you okay?" she asked.

"I'm fine," he replied. He tried to fill her in on what all had happened.

"I was a little late in getting there to meet you. Caught in traffic," she said, somewhat frazzled.

"That was a good thing this time," he said.

She brushed her fingers through his hair then kissed him.

"That will probably be in all the newspapers tomorrow," he said, an eye toward the media on the other side of the ropes.

"I don't really care," she said, hugging him.

"I'm not breaking anything up here, am I?" It was Sarah Workman who had approached them.

The governor shook her hand. "I guess you're here on official business?" she asked her.

"Well, since you asked, I have been working rather closely here with Jake on this investigation." She gave Susanne a look and a smile that gave Jake a feeling that he might like to be somewhere else.

Susanne gave Jake a look that said they would talk about this later. "I can only imagine," she then replied. She reached out and took Jake's hand and gave it a hard squeeze. "I think Jake has just gotten his five minutes of fame here today."

"Yeah," he replied. "Only problem is, that's not an ideal thing for a private eye."

Sarah was about to comment when a captain from the Knoxville Police Department came up to them. "Excuse me, but the boat is coming in off the river with the bodies from the plane. I thought you might want to look, Jake, and see if you can identify them."

"Sure," he replied.

"Follow me," the captain said.

"Susanne, you wait here. You don't want to see this." Jake proceeded down to the docks with the captain. Sarah followed a step behind. A police boat pulled up and tied off. A police diver pulled back a sheet and it revealed two bodies, lying in the bottom.

"Only two?" Jake asked.

"Yes, sir, that's it so far. The one on the left was the pilot. Looks like he was hit twice, once in the head and once in his shoulder. The head shot, I'd say it killed him and caused the crash."

Despite the head wound, Jake was able to recognize who it was.

"You know him?" the captain asked.

"Oh yeah, Virgil Smith is his name. Lives, or I guess I should say lived in Jonesborough."

"Well, he's carrying a German passport with a different name, a Rudolph Steiner," the diver replied. He handed over to the captain a wet passport.

"No, it's Virgil, I've known him all my life." Jake looked at the second man, but he did not recognize him.

Jake took out his gun and handed it to the captain. "I guess you'll be needing this to run some tests."

"I'll get it back to you as soon as I can," he replied.

"This other guy was in the front passenger seat, but not strapped in. I'd say the trauma to his body during the crash took him out. Most likely a broken neck, massive internal injuries," the diver explained.

"He got any ID?" the captain asked.

"Only thing on him was this German passport. Oscar Schmitt from Frankfurt."

"I'm pretty sure that's Bobby Wayne's old cell mate," Sarah interjected. "I'll go get my laptop and bring up his picture."

"Three people were in that plane," Jake said.

"These are the only bodies we have found so far, sir," the diver replied. "They were both still in the plane. The third one could be in the river somewhere. The door to the back of the plane was missing, he could have been thrown out. We'll be dragging the river. Sometimes it takes days to find a body, sir."

"Could someone have survived the crash?" Jake asked him.

"I don't know, I don't think it likely, sir."

"Nobody?"

"Well, sir, there might be one possibility I could think of."

"And what's that?"

"Someone that had been through one of the military's flight crash survival schools, sir. They might have been able to get out, that is if the crash didn't kill them. But surely they would have popped up near the plane."

"You don't say?" Jake said. "What if he didn't want to be caught?"

The diver shrugged. "I don't know, sir."

"He might float up," Jake said, not really believing it.

"I say he's in the river, sir. If he is, we'll find him."

Jake stood on the bank and looked about. "Yeah," he said. Then, to nobody in particular he said, "You have any idea how far it is from here to Dubai?"

"Sir?" The diver replied.

"Never mind," Jake said. He turned and walked back up off the dock and crossed the rope, pushing his way through the gathered media, ignoring their requests for comment. He reached the governor's Suburban, opened the back door, and climbed in. He laid back on the seat and let out a deep breath.

"What is it?" Susanne asked. "What did they find?"

"Two bodies recovered from the plane, neither one was Bobby Wayne."

"They'll drag the river and find the body."

"Virgil was flying the plane and my shot killed him."

"Oh, Jake, I'm so sorry." She grabbed his hand and squeezed it tight.

Jake stared down toward the river. Darkness was starting to approach, and lights were reflecting off the water. "They say Bobby Wayne's body will eventually turn up, but I don't know," he said, still staring at the river. "I got a hunch he somehow got away." He shook his head. "Don't ask me why, but I do."

CHAPTER 33

JONESBOROUGH
ONE MONTH LATER

Jake entered the golf shop on Saturday morning at 10:00 a.m. Things were rolling along as normal. Ralph was behind the counter working a crossword puzzle from Friday's *USA Today,* and Butch was laid out on the floor at his feet, halfway in and out of sleep as dogs are prone to do.

Roosevelt was back on the job, cleaning up. "Couldn't stay still Jake, thought I'd come in and do a little bit of work."

"I'm glad you're back," Jake said.

"Lord, this place has got to be quite the mess since I been gone. Don't look like nobody touched nothing," he replied, talking out loud to himself.

"Need some help there, Ralph?" Jake asked.

"I don't think so," he replied, never looking up.

"I thought you might be stumped."

"Never stumped, but sometimes it just takes me a while to figure everything out."

"How's business?" questioned Jake.

"Six foursomes out so far," Ralph replied, again not looking up.

"That's good," Jake responded. "Range is pretty busy, too."

"You heard anything yet?" Ralph asked.

"About what?"

"The body."

"The body?" Jake shook his head. "As of yesterday evening, nothing ever turned up. I think they have pretty much stopped any searching. They had been patrolling the banks down the river, thinkin' he might wash up somewhere. The guy I talked to said that they stopped that yesterday. He said a month was two weeks longer than they would normally look. Only reason they've gone this long is because it is such a big case."

"Well, if he does swell up and start floating, somebody will find him," Ralph said.

"Let's hope." Jake went to the cooler and got a Diet Coke.

"What do you think, Jake?" Ralph asked, finally pulling himself away from the crossword long enough to look up.

"Having witnessed it, I think he could have never survived the crash, but, then again, I don't know. I just don't know. I mean, if he did somehow get out alive, how did he manage to come up somewhere and not be spotted by someone with all the people that were around there?" He looked at Ralph with a feeling of hopelessness on this one.

"My God, how many people got killed over this deal?" Ralph said.

"Going all the way back to the Super Bowl? I'll try to count." He paused, then said, "Let's see, there was the aunt and the fiancée, Rockett's sister, Moore's grandmother, Moore, Rockett, the FBI agent, his uncle, Coach Prince, Virgil, the cellmate, and maybe Bobby Wayne himself." He stopped for a moment, then finished his thoughts, "I'm probably leaving somebody out."

"Not to mention those of us that got beat up," Ralph, still not feeling fully recovered from what happened to him, replied.

A group of four came into the golf shop and they dropped the subject. Ralph collected their money and sent them on their way. After they were out the door, he looked at Jake and said, "Tennessee is playing today, right?"

"I believe so, a three thirty kickoff against Kentucky."

"They ever get a coach?" Ralph asked.

"One of the assistants is the interim coach to finish out the season."

"They ever figure out a way to play the Alabama game?" Ralph inquired. Baseball was pretty much the only sport he kept up with on a regular basis. He might be the only man in Tennessee to not know the answer to these questions.

"No, it's cancelled for this season."

"I guess that's for the best."

"Yeah, I guess so," Jake responded.

The conversation stopped for a minute then started again.

"I thought you were going to Nashville for a few days?" Ralph asked.

"Still am, I'm leaving here in a couple of hours and coming back sometime Monday. I told you all that yesterday morning. You were so engrossed in the crossword, you weren't listening."

"Yeah, okay."

"I'm staying at the Governor's Mansion," Jake said, looking at Ralph. "I'm just telling you that because I know that's the next thing you're gonna ask me."

"Never crossed my mind," he replied.

"Yeah, right."

"She still mad over that FBI dame?" Ralph asked.

"I guess I'll find out more about that when I get there," Jake said.

"Well, she did invite you down,"

"That's true. I think she needs me on her arm for some big shindig on Sunday night."

"Black tie affair?"

"I'm sure."

"And you've got a tux?"

"She's got me one to wear, keeps it there in the Governor's Mansion for special occasions."

"You wearing your black cowboy boots?"

"Wouldn't go without them."

"She's okay with that?"

"It's perfectly acceptable in high society in Nashville."

The mailman came through the door. "What's up boys?" he greeted.

"Not much," Jake replied.

He handed him a stack of mail. "You still working on the crime of the century, Jake?" he asked.

"Well, I'm hoping that's pretty well done for."

"You got a letter there from the FBI," he responded.

"Aren't you just supposed to deliver the mail and not read it?" Jake said, looking at him and shaking his head.

"Sorry, it just happened to be on top, couldn't help but notice it," he said. "It's not every day that someone on my route gets a letter from the FBI," and with that he was heading out the door. "See you boys Monday!" he shouted as he left, the screen door slamming behind him.

"Nothing like living in a small town," Jake said, sorting through the mail. The letter from the FBI was a check for services rendered. There was one there for Ralph as well. Jake flipped it to him. "You might want this," he said.

"I believe I do," Ralph replied, examining the envelope. "Never gotten anything from the FBI before."

Jake kept sorting. It was the usual stuff; bills, golf magazines, junk mail. On the bottom, the last thing, was a post card. He read it, examined both sides of it, then read it again. Then he handed it to Ralph. "I think this will answer your earlier question."

What he gave him was a post card from Dubai. On the front was a picture of the city rising out from the desert. On the back, the right-hand side was addressed to Jake and on the other side it simply said:

BACK HOME –B.W.

Jake looked at Ralph and shook his head, then said, "I don't know how, but obviously, he survived and managed to get away." He stared off into the distance. "Unbelievable," he said.

He took out his phone. "I don't want to do this, but I guess I better call my favorite FBI agent and give her the news."

"Might give her an excuse to come back out here and confiscate the postcard and interview you again, if you know what I mean." Ralph said with a grin on his face.

"I know what you mean, and no, that's not happening," Jake replied. Ralph just looked at him and laughed.

CHAPTER 34
DUBAI
SIX MONTHS LATER

Bobby Wayne had survived the plane crash, thanks to some training he had gotten in the service, and a lot of luck. Knowing that he would be making a somewhat risky flight away from the stadium, he had carried with him a twelve inch long piece of flexible plastic tubing. Immediately, he had strapped himself firmly into his seat when he got into the plane. He had made his way out of the plane's open cargo door once it had settled at the bottom of the river, then made his way downstream by coming to the top and breathing through the tubing, letting the current of the river carry him downstream without him being exposed. When he thought he was far enough away, he came to the bank, took out his cellphone that he had secured in a plastic bag to keep dry, and called for his associates – whom he had on standby in case there was a disruption of his original plans – to come and pick him up. A chip in his phone gave them his exact location. The next day, on a forged passport, he took a flight from Charlotte to Paris, and from there he moved on to Dubai where he planned to settle in and live the rest of his life. Everyone on his list had been taken care of.

He now stood out on the veranda of his condo on the fifty-seventh floor of one of the many high rise buildings that shot out of the desert floor and watched the sun come up. He looked out on a golden sky that burned and shined brightly off of the glass of the surrounding skyscrapers, blinding him for a moment. In his hand he held a glass of vodka that he slowly sipped from. He wore nothing but a pair of khaki shorts and a white t-shirt. When the drink was gone, he stepped back inside, made his way to the kitchen and poured another, the glass maybe one third full. He went into his office, took out a cigar box from his desk and counted out eleven one hundred dollar bills, then made his way back into the kitchen. On the counter he laid out ten of the hundreds in a row. In a minute, a beautiful young Arabian woman with dark hair and dark eyes made her way out of the bedroom.

"Your money, my dear," he said.

She raked it off and stuck it in her purse.

"Same time next week," he then said, more of a statement than a question.

"Of course," she said, then kissed him on the cheek.

"A little something extra," he added, handing her the eleventh bill.

"You are so generous to me," she replied with a smile.

He cared little for the small talk and was anxious for her to leave.

She took it and put it down in her purse. But then she came out with a handgun that had a silencer on the end of the barrel. He was momentarily stunned, for once in his life caught off guard, and before he could react, she pulled the trigger twice, aimed in the middle of his chest, right into his heart. She was not a novice at this. He tumbled down to the floor, his head making a sickening thud as it hit the stone and seemed to bounce. She stepped over him, put another bullet in his temple, then leaned down and placed her first two fingers on his neck to make sure he was dead. She stepped off, took out a handkerchief from her purse, wiped down the gun, and left it on the kitchen table, then pulled out a cell phone, dialed a number, and waited for a response.

"It is done," she said and hung up. She wiped down the phone and left it on the table as well, then went over and unlocked the front door. In a moment, three dark-haired men, appearing to be either Italians or

Americans, came in, two in front and one trailing behind. The last one in locked the door behind them. All wore dark suits, white shirts, and dark ties. The front two pulled out their weapons upon entering, then split up and made a quick search of the place. They came back and nodded to the third man, who was standing in the kitchen with the girl, the body of Bobby Wayne laying off to the side on the tile floor.

He pulled out an envelope and handed it to her. "It is all there, fifty grand in American money as we discussed, but feel free to count it if you so wish. I would understand," he said, smiling. He looked at her and wondered how such a beautiful young woman had gotten into her line of work.

"There is no need for that," she responded. "Maybe someday I can do some more work for you." Her smile captivated him, but he knew who he was dealing with.

"I would like that very much," he said.

She looked him over, liking what she saw. Not everything had to be about business, she thought.

"From here, we will take care of the body, the gun, and the phone," he said.

She slid the envelope in her purse, looked at him once more, and said, "I can see myself out."

He watched her leave, admiring her all the way, then locked the door once more behind her. Taking out his cell phone, he dialed a number. "We are ready," was all he said, then he hung up and waited behind the door.

Three men in white coveralls arrived in a matter of minutes. A fourth man, in traditional Arabian robes and headwear soon followed them in. The body was placed in a body bag, along with the gun and the phone. The three men then cleaned up all around the kitchen, destroying any evidence that anything had ever happened there. They placed the body bag on a gurney and rolled it out.

"You tell the Prince that I am very grateful for him allowing me to take care of this problem," the man said to the Arab.

"The Prince is very grateful to you and your family for all you have meant to Dubai over the years," he said. "The body, phone, and gun will all be destroyed before the hour is out. I assure you of that, and as you know, my word is my bond," he said, looking at the man and smiling. "It is the least we can do to help you, Mr. Scarpino."

"An agent of the FBI, one that I know and trust, she came to see me and told me that they had proof that Foster had killed my father in his New York City hospital room. My brothers and I could not let this go unpunished."

"I guess the poor fool had no way to know that our government is very indebted to the Scarpino family for all your family has invested in our real estate, banking, and casinos over the years," the Arab replied.

"Yes, I know, my friend. He was supposedly a very deliberate and careful man when it came to making plans," he said. He looked hard at the Arabian man. "Those plans should not have included my father."

At just about the same time, the nurse, who was so fond of smoking, was shot dead outside a corner store in Brooklyn where he had just bought cigarettes on his way home, after getting off his shift at the hospital.

When Frank Scarpino was sent to Federal prison, his three sons met and decided that one of them would have to step up and handle any of the family business that their father had been taking care of. At that point, their father had kept them out of any illegal activities. The middle son, Christopher, was divorced and had no children. The other two brothers were married and had eight children between them, so Chris was selected to handle any issues in that area. When their father died in the New York City hospital, no autopsy was performed as was his request, and they all assumed he died from old age. FBI agent Sarah Workman let Chris Scarpino know that in their investigation of Bobby Wayne Foster, they were sure he had killed their father to settle an old score. That put into motion the events that led to Bobby Wayne's death. The FBI, unable to stop him at home, planted the story with the Scarpino family, knowing that they would go to Dubai and take care of him. Chris Scarpino was not bothered by this in the least. His younger brother had gotten a surveillance tape from the bank across from a side entrance to the hospital. He served on their board. On it, it showed a man that very much resembled Bobby Wayne going in and coming out of that door in a twenty minute interval around the time of their father's death. The brothers met and it was decided that Chris was to go to Dubai and take care of Bobby Wayne with the help and blessing of the local authorities.

He shook hands and thanked the Arab for his help. "We must go," he said. "Our plane is on the tarmac and awaits us."

Thirty minutes later they were in the sky, on their way back to New York City. The body of Bobby Wayne Foster was burning in an incinerator.

Over seven thousand miles away, in Jonesborough, Jake Bender sat up in bed, something having startled him awake. He looked at his clock and it was a little after midnight. His body was in a sweat, his breathing hard. A dream he was having, where he knew it was hot and someone was screaming at him, was what he remembered. The rest was vague, bits and pieces floating around in his brain. His sudden awakening sent most of that away. He lay back down on the sheets damp with his sweat, turned his pillow over to the cool side, and in a few moments drifted back asleep. And sleep he did, better than he had in a long, long time.

Author Acknowledgements

I would like to thank the following for their help in getting this book completed. To my good friend Philip Blevins and his staff at Sabre Printers for their help in getting everything done in the layout, and also helping me get the books ordered and printed. To Bill May and his staff at Stellar Studios for their help in doing my book covers and maintaining my website. A special thanks to Justin Doak, who has done all my book covers.

To my family; my wife Debra and daughters Mary, Laura, and her husband Justin. They read the original drafts before anyone else and offer valuable insight and opinions. Debra takes care of all things business related to my writing, no small task. Laura does all my editing.

Mary has become a very accomplished photographer and I used one of her photos on the cover of my second book, ALL FOR A SONG.

A special thanks to my good friends Steve Love and Roger Catlett who send my books to our troops overseas.

Last, I want to thank everyone who has purchased and read my books. One of the neat things about writing is meeting or hearing from people who go out of their way to tell you they have read one of your books and they enjoyed it.

I hope you enjoy reading them as much as I enjoy writing them.